THE LIGHTNING WARRIOR

THE LIGHTNING WARRIOR

MAX BRAND®

SAGEBRUSH
Large Print Westerns

First published in Great Britain by Gunsmoke
First published in the United States by Five Star

Published in Large Print 2013 by ISIS Publishing Ltd.,
7 Centremead, Osney Mead, Oxford OX2 0ES
by arrangement with
Golden West Literary Agency

British Library Cataloguing in Publication Data
Brand, Max, 1892–1944.
The lightning warrior.
1. Western stories.
2. Large type books.
I. Title
813.5'2–dc23

ISBN 978–0–7531–9008–1 (pb)

Printed and bound in Great Britain by
T. J. International Ltd., Padstow, Cornwall

CHAPTER
ONE

The Miracle Man

From Dawson to the Bering Sea, Cobalt had no other name. The flame of his hair never won him the nickname of "Red" or "Brick." He was only Cobalt from the beginning to the end, and this name, no doubt, was given to him by his eyes, which varied according to his temper from a dull-steel gray to an intense blue with fire behind it. Everyone knew Cobalt. He had come over the pass three years before, and for every step that he took, rumor took ten more. Lightning splashed from the feet of the running gods, and startling reports had spread like lightning from the steps of Cobalt. Many of the things which were said of him never could have been true, but he gathered mystery and an air of enchantment about him. Even what men could not believe, they wanted to believe. There is no human being who has not reveled in fairy tales, and Cobalt was a fairy tale.

He was not beautiful, but he was glorious. When one saw him, one believed, or hypnotized oneself into believing the tales that were told of him. Cobalt never verified or confirmed any of these stories. He never repeated a syllable of them, but of course he must have known about them. All of these tales were remarkable, and some of them were sheer impossibilities, but it is as well to note some of them at the beginning. Men are not what they are, but what other people think them to be. So it was with Cobalt and, in order to know him, one must know of the opinions of his peers.

They told of Cobalt that he once ate eleven pounds of beef, slept twenty hours, and then did a full man's work in hauling for eight days without any sustenance except the bits of snow which he picked up and ate to quench his thirst. Four men attested to the truth of this tale. They said that the thing was the result of a bet, but I never have heard that they actually weighed the meat. Also I have seen eleven pounds of beef and, when cut as steaks, it makes an imposing heap. That tale of Cobalt was typical in that it showed a superhuman quality and also a half-mad, half-gay willingness to tackle anything for a bet, a jest, or a serious purpose.

It was said that once he jumped from a fifty-foot bridge and spoiled a fifty-dollar suit in order to win a one-dollar bet. This tale is among the ridiculous and impossible stories which are told of Cobalt, so that one would say that the man must have been absolutely mad to inspire such talk. However, it just happens that I was present and saw him take the dive.

It was said of Cobalt that in a traveling circus he saw a strong man lift a platform on which there was a piano, a woman playing the piano, and a small dog. The man was labeled the strongest in the world as a matter of course. Cobalt, on another bet, added to the platform another woman, another dog, and the strong

2

man himself and lifted the entire enormous load. Of this story I have nothing to say, and I shall make very little comment upon the others. The items illustrating his strength were innumerable. It was said that he had taken a good-size steel bar and bent it into a horseshoe. This twisted bar was kept on the wall of a saloon in Circle City. Men used to look at it, shake their heads over it, and try their own petty strength in a vain effort to change its shape. They always failed and finally that bar became a rather silly legend at which men laughed.

Then one day Cobalt came back. Someone asked him to unbend the steel bar, and it was handed to him. I myself was there, and I saw the purple vein lift and swell in a straight, diagonal line in his forehead, as he bent the bar into a straight line once more. He threw it to the man who had asked him to attempt the feat, and thereafter the bar was reinstalled upon the wall. Long after, it still remained there and must have been worth a fortune to the saloon keeper, so many people went in to look at the famous bar where the metal had failed to straighten correctly. Nearly everyone handled it and tried it between his hands, or even across his knee, but no one could alter the thing.

It was said that once he hit a man and killed him with a blow to the body. That has been done before, and actually the blow of a gloved hand has killed a man in the ring, a trained heavyweight who was struck over the heart. The miraculous feature of Cobalt's punch was that it had landed not on the left but upon the right side of the body. The blow was said to have broken three ribs. This always seemed to me one of the most

3

incredible tales about Cobalt, but I have talked with Gene Pelham, now of Portland, Maine, and he declares that he was the physician who examined the body. He makes this report: that the man was a big Canuck with the build of a heavyweight wrestling champion and the bones to go with it. Upon the right side of the man, where the ribs spring out most boldly, there was a great purple welt and under this welt there actually were three broken ribs.

I asked the doctor if the breaking of the ribs upon the right side could have killed the man, big and strong as he was. He told me that it could hardly have been breaking of the ribs, but the effects of shock operate strangely. There was a bruise at the base of the Canuck's skull, and the doctor felt sure that his death had been due to concussion of the brain, owing to the manner in which his head struck the floor in falling.

Another exhibit for Cobalt was a row of four whiskey bottles in the Circle City saloon. Three were empty and one was about a third full. It was solemnly declared that he had drunk all of that whiskey during a single long session in the saloon. This would have been about two-thirds of a gallon of strong whiskey. The exhibit was kept on show partly as a curiosity and partly to demonstrate the excellent quality of the red-eye which was sold in the saloon. I leave those to judge of this feat who know what a strong head is needed to resist the punishment contained in a single bottle of whiskey.

In Eagle Falls I saw a large axe blade whose head was completely buried in hardwood and the handle shattered. This had been accomplished, it was said, at a single stroke by Cobalt. I examined the head of the axe carefully, and it seemed to me that I could detect the evidences of hammering to force the axe deeper into the wood.

These anecdotes may help to prepare the reader for the state of mind through which the men of the arctic looked at Cobalt. In person he was not a giant. I never heard his exact height or weight, but he looked not an inch over six feet, and his shoulders were by no means as massive as many I have seen. In fact, there was nothing remarkable about him except when he got in action. To see him sitting, Cobalt was nothing unusual. When he spoke, there was an odd quality about his voice that made men turn their heads and women also. When he walked, his step had the quality of one about to leap away at full speed.

He came in during the early days, well before the Dawson rush. He was twenty-two when he reached Circle City, and he mined there for two years before the Bairds arrived. That was the turning point in Cobalt's life. Most of the men who have been in Circle City can remember Henry Baird, his rosy face, his lack of eyebrows, and his wonderful luck at the mines. And even those who never saw her know all about his daughter, Sylvia.

I suppose she was what a scientist would have called a biological "sport," a freak, a sudden throw forward from her ancestry. Certainly there appeared to be nothing of her father about her. Her hair was glistening black and fine as a spider's web. She had black eyebrows, beautifully arched, and under the brows were blue eyes — not gray blue, not sky blue, but the lustrous and unfathomable blue of the sea. She was rather small; I don't think that a big woman could have been made so exquisitely. It was enough for me to sit at Henry Baird's table and look at her hand alone, at the luster of the pink nails and the white glow of the skin. She was a radiant creature.

Nearly everyone in Circle City went mad about her, but I don't think that even the most audacious thought of making love to her. She was too beautiful. Her beauty set her apart. We looked up to her as to a being of another world. We talked to her with an odd respect, as if to some famous sage or reverend divine. Then young Cobalt came in and saw her.

Some people said that he did not need to go mad, because he had always been mad. Nobody but a madman would have done the things he had accomplished or tried to accomplish. Nobody, for instance, would have driven a team of six timber wolves and treated them like dogs. So it followed, as a matter of course, when Cobalt saw the girl, he tried to scale heaven and get at her. He saw her once and went right down to see Henry Baird. Baird was new to the country, but naturally he had heard a great deal about Cobalt.

He was rather frightened when the famous young man came in, took his hand in that terrible grasp of his, and looked him in the face with those steel-gray eyes which turned to pale-blue flame when he spoke of Sylvia. However, Baird was a sensible man. He said that he had not the slightest objection to Cobalt. For his

6

own part he hoped that his daughter would not marry a man with less than a hundred thousand and a home to offer her. Of course, a hundred thousand meant a great deal more in those days than it does now. But everything really depended upon Sylvia herself. Had Cobalt spoken to her before on the subject? Did she care for him?

Cobalt said that he hadn't, but that he would make her care. That was how the trouble started. He went to Sylvia and spoke to her. And Sylvia laughed!

"Are you doing this on a bet, Cobalt?" she asked.

CHAPTER
TWO

Modern Gal

I can see Sylvia as she must have been that day, muffled in that fine suit of brown furs, with her lovely mouth, and her shining eyes glowing like heaven's light through a cloud. Cobalt stared at her as no human being ever had stared at her before.

"Do that ag'in," he said.

"What?" asked Sylvia.

"Laugh at me!"

She looked him up and down. No one ever had looked at him in such a manner before that moment — no one at least in his right mind. A man did not have to know about Cobalt beforehand. His strength advertised itself, as fire is advertised by its flame. Sylvia was not afraid. Why should she be? Men were merely — men! Cobalt might bend steel bars, but Sylvia had bent and molded whole brigades of young fellows and oldish fellows, too. Millions had been offered to her. She had stepped through rivers of gold and diamonds and never allowed the stuff to stick to her. She looked at Cobalt with the double strength of the proud and the good, with a spice of malice thrown in. How could she help being spiteful, when this fellow came along and dared

8

to look at her as though she were merely a desirable girl?

"Will you slap me if I laugh?" asked Sylvia, and with that she let her laughter peal.

She had a way of putting up her chin a little and lowering her eyes when she laughed. Cobalt stood there and watched her.

"It's good," said Cobalt. "It's dog-gone good. It's like medicine to me."

"Is it?" she inquired.

She must have widened her eyes a trifle when she heard him speak like this. If she had any wit at all, she knew that he was out of the common run of men.

"Yes," he said, "it does me good to hear you laugh. You're pert, aren't you?"

"Pert?" asked Sylvia, her spirit beginning to rise toward anger.

"You know," said Cobalt. "You're a little sassy, but I don't mind it. It's spice in you."

"Thank you."

"You're proud, too," said Cobalt. "You're proud as Lucifer. I can see that."

"Do you always talk to people like this?" asked the girl.

"Yes. Of course, I do. How else should I talk to them?" stated Cobalt.

He meant that. He always said what he thought, straight out. Often it was a shocking thing to hear him, a brutal thing. That was why so many people savored respect for Cobalt with a good dash, not of envy, but of hate. Only a few of us endured and loved him in spite of the way he trod on our toes.

"Almost any other way," said the girl. "Almost any other way, I should think."

"You tell me how."

"Why, make them happy, of course. That's what most people try to do when they're talking to others."

"No," said Cobalt, "that's not right."

"Don't you think so?" questioned Sylvia, beginning to smile and freeze.

"No," said Cobalt, "because mostly people are lying, and the ones they talk to know they're lying."

"Ah, and you always tell the truth?"

"Nobody could always tell the truth," he replied, "but I try my best to do it."

"I must have read that somewhere," said Sylvia. "Where did you get it, Cobalt?"

"Out of my heart," he said, as grave as you please, and pointed at his breast, as though she could look through bones and flesh if she chose. "You'll find a lot more in there."

"I only see a parka," said Sylvia.

"There you go again," said Cobalt, "but, when you're sassy like this, you ought always to laugh."

"Ought I?" she asked, lifting her brows to freeze him again.

But Cobalt didn't freeze. No, no, you might as well have tried to frost the equator.

"You ought to laugh and show that you're joking," Cobalt told her, "because, if you're serious, you simply need a spanking."

"You make me feel very young," said Sylvia, letting the temperature drop another hundred degrees toward absolute zero.

"Oh, don't stick up your nose and look down at me. It doesn't amuse me when I see you acting like that. You've learned that attitude out of your mirror, I suppose, but don't use it on me. Don't talk down to me because, after all, you're only a woman."

"I'm *only a what?*"

"You're so mad now that you can hardly hear me," went on Cobalt. "Get the cobwebs out of your mind and listen to the truth. I said that you're only a woman and, therefore, you've no right to look down your nose at anybody."

Sylvia must have nearly fainted. I know how other men were in front of her — like lambs, like poor willing slaves, cluttering up the heavenly ground on which she deigned to put her feet.

"I see that you're a profound fellow," Sylvia said to him. "You can see at a glance that I'm only a woman. What did you expect to find me?"

"I expected to find you a good deal better than you are," he said. "I saw only the shine of you from a distance. Now that I get up close. I see that the wick needs a lot of trimming."

"You men," Sylvia said as sardonic as you please, "are such masters. Of course, women always look up to such wonderful . . ."

"Don't do that," urged Cobalt. "If you talk like that, I'll begin to despise you so much that I'll never look at

11

you again. There's not much to women, you know. There's almost nothing . . . except loving 'em."

"True," said Sylvia, beginning to shake a little in the fury that was gripping her. "Of course, we're just mirrors, and nothing else. Mirrors for the parents, then for the great husband, then for the children. Is that it?"

"You mighty well know it's true," said Cobalt, "though, just now, I see that you're ready to scratch my eyes out."

"Not at all. I was only about to remark that my time is not entirely my own."

"No," said Cobalt, "that's true. A good part of it is mine."

"Ah?" said Sylvia, blinking a little, beginning to think him mad.

"Of course it is. One of these days, Sylvia, if you turn out to be half what I think of you, I'm going to marry you."

"I'm astonished and delighted," she said, forcing herself to smile at him again in such a way that any other man would have backed up as if from a tiger's claws. "Are you really going to marry me, Cobalt . . . I don't know any other name to give you, you know."

He merely grinned at her. "You handle a whip pretty well, but you can't cut me through the skin with your little turns and flips of the tongue. It won't do any good to flog me with ironies, Sylvia."

"As if I would attempt such a thing! Of course, I don't know what you mean, Cobalt, but then a woman never understands more than a part of what a man says. She only sees the feet of the god, I dare say."

12

"You've got a lot of stuff in you, but you need to be taken apart and put together again."

"Poor Dad. He'll be terribly upset when he hears that I have to be brought up all over again."

"I like you better and better." Cobalt was grinning again.

"Oh, how can you!" exclaimed Sylvia, putting her two little hands together in admiration.

"Dog-gone you're a feast for me. I could spend my life eating you, sauce and all, and spite, and malice, and thorny ironies, and all of that. Now let's get down to brass tacks."

"You mean, to name the wedding day?"

"That's the main idea. Your father says that your husband ought to have a home for you and a hundred thousand dollars. Now, what do you want?"

"I only want a great, big, wonderful, masterful man."

"You're going to be mastered, all right," said Cobalt. "Is that all you want?"

"Oh, yes. Just somebody I can look up to."

"You can look up to me, Sylvia. You can stand on your tiptoes, and still you'll have to look up."

She teetered up on her toes. "My gracious, you're right. I dare say that you're always right!"

"I'll have a hundred per cent average with you."

"Then I suppose that we'll have to be married at once. I can hardly wait and, of course, you have the lovely home and the hundred thousand waiting for us?"

"You she-wolf!" replied Cobalt, his grin flashing down at her. "I have a dog team, some dried fish, and my two hands. I'm going to rip that hundred thousand out of the ground this year."

"Oh, Cobalt," she asked, "do we have to wait a whole year?"

She made sad eyes at him. Cobalt drank it all in.

"What kind of a house do you want?" he asked her.

"Oh, for myself, just anything would do, but I'd never be happy unless I knew that my husband had the right surroundings. I wouldn't set a diamond in base metal. There'd have to be a night park for him to walk in when he's in the garden in the evening with his own thoughts. A good library for his study. Or do you need to study any more, Cobalt?"

"Go on," said Cobalt. "You write down the items, and I'll add up."

"Then you'd want two or three good servants to look after you properly, and a maid to dress me because I'd have to appear as well as possible in the eyes of such a husband. We'd need rooms for those servants, of course, and a good dining room because a little dining room is so stuffy and lacks dignity."

"Go on."

"Well, you can fill out the rest a great deal better than I can. The stables, the horses and such things . . . you would know exactly what to have. You'd need more, but three or four good hunters are about all that I would have, unless you wished to be too generous. But for myself I wouldn't want jewels."

"No?"

"Oh, no, nothing to speak of. Just a few nice, big, simple stones. Not emeralds. Oh, no! They're too expensive. I like rubies better myself. Just a few to help me catch your eye when you're losing yourself in meditations, you know."

"Now I begin to see the picture."

"Of course you do," said Sylvia, giving him a smile of childish adoration. "I shouldn't have said a thing. You would have known from the first, ever so much better than I do."

"Well," said Cobalt, "what do you think?"

"Why, I wouldn't try. I'd just leave all of that to you, dear! I know it won't take you long to make enough."

"Not long at all. Good bye for a little while, Sylvia."

He held out his arms to her. And she? Why, she stepped right inside them and let him kiss her. Then she followed him to the door and told him that she could hardly wait. That's the sort of stuff of which she was made.

CHAPTER
THREE

The Lightning Warrior

Cobalt went down to the saloon and staked his dog team against six hundred dollars as a start. Before the next morning, he had won forty thousand dollars. He took a week spending that money. None of it went in dissipation. Everything was sunk in the preparation to get more gold out of the earth. Then he disappeared from Circle City and went to the diggings.

Everyone knew about that conversation he had had with Sylvia Baird. That talk was so typical of Cobalt that people could not help repeating the details of it and laughing heartily. They even asked Sylvia about it, and Sylvia would laugh in turn. But Circle City stopping laughing, and so did Sylvia Baird, when it was learned that Cobalt was organizing his expedition and hiring many hands. Circle City stopped smiling because it very well knew that, when Cobalt bent his energies in any direction, the time for foolish comment had ended. I think that Sylvia began to worry almost at once.

I saw her shortly after Cobalt went into the wilderness, and I chatted with her a little about Cobalt. Her way of putting the thing was characteristic.

"I hear that Cobalt is a great friend of yours," I said.

"Friend?" replied Sylvia. "Oh, not at all. I've only met him once, you know. Yet he means a good deal to me."

"Does he?" I asked.

"Yes. Because he's going to marry me it appears."

"Great Scott! That's exciting!"

"Isn't it?"

She joked about it so openly that everyone could speak of it freely, but all the while she was uneasy. I could see that because I had come to know her very well.

"Suppose," she said one day, "that Cobalt should come back from the mines with a fortune and hold me to my joke?"

"Then he would have a chance to do the laughing," I said.

"Are you serious?" she asked.

"Are you serious?" I replied.

"I'm frightened, a little. For once he gets a thing into his head . . ."

There was one comfort, and that lay in the reports that came back to us. Cobalt and his crew were tearing up the ground and getting hardly a taste of color. In the meantime Circle City had something that drowned out even Cobalt as a topic of interest, and that was the appearance of a white wolf the Indians were said to have named the Lightning Warrior for so swiftly did he attack and parry. Having seen him, I can give an authentic account of his looks. He was closer to a bear in bulk than to a wolf. Those who know wolves realize that it is a goodish-size beast that has a footprint four inches across. When it is a giant, it has a spread of five inches. There have been some half fabulous reports from time to time of wolves with paws of more than five inches' measurement; but the Lightning Warrior of Circle City marked out a six-inch circle as he put down his paw. This I know because I measured the thing myself, not once but twenty times.

A wolf which makes a four-inch track is big enough to cause plenty of trouble. Swell the beast to the dimensions of the Lightning Warrior and the dangerous possibilities are multiplied by ten. When I saw that fellow standing in front of a wall of brush, with the wind ruffling his mane, he looked to me like the god of wolves. His whiteness was the amazing thing, the incredible thing. He shone as snow shines. His eyes and his tongue were bloodstains in the fluffing radiance. One hears of white wolves very often, but usually they are the color of coffee and milk or simply a dirty yellow, but this lord of wolves was entirely and purely white.

He called himself forcibly to the attention of Circle City and, having stepped to the center of the stage, he remained there. He turned himself into a frightful plague through his appetite which was for dogs. He would eat anything with no more conscience than fire, but his regular diet was dogs. Even for wolves a diet of Eskimo Huskies seems rather tough, for Huskies are themselves nine-tenths wolf. In the dog teams working from Circle City, there were more than a few pure-blood wolves pulling at the lines. However, the Lightning Warrior did not spare them. Anything which had been tainted by the hand of man was especially delightful to him. He cared not so long as the animal was large enough to make him a few mouthfuls.

There were in Circle City some Mackenzie Huskies that were twice the size of the average wolf and that were twice as hardy as well, for they were kept in the pink of condition by hard labor and spare feeding. A Mackenzie Husky will hamstring a horse or a cow as neatly as ever a wolf could do the same job. A Mackenzie Husky fights like a wolf, fencing for an opening, cutting and slashing as with a saber. Nevertheless, Joe Frazer saw two Huskies of the biggest type, weighing well over a hundred and fifty pounds apiece, slaughtered by that white plague, the Lightning Warrior.

At the time, Joe carried no gun. He could merely shout and run toward the fight from a distance, but long before he arrived the throats of the two dogs were cut. Joe said that the wolf seemed twice the size of the dogs. We knew this could not be. I suppose it was action which magnified the apparent size of the monster, that and the results of his daring play. He fought right on until Joe Frazer was almost on the spot. Then the Lightning Warrior gave the *coup de grâce* to the second of the Huskies, standing with a forepaw on each of the dead bodies and defying Joe with a look to come on.

Joe was not a fool. When he saw the silent snarl of that brute, he started backing up, and the infernal creature at once came stalking after him, sliding along on its stomach. Joe had only a hunting knife. He drew this out, but he said he would just as soon have faced a lion, armed with a stiletto, as to face that white beast with a mere hunting knife in his hand. He began to shout. Every time he yelled, the wolf paused a little and looked off at Joe's house in the distance.

Finally, the shouts of Joe got to the ear of Jim Bridger, who was Joe's partner, and Bridger came running out with a rifle in his hands. When the Lightning Warrior saw the rifle, he turned and went for distance and more air. Joe Frazer said that the animal started so fast and worked so hard to get into the middle of the horizon that he left a moan of effort in the air behind him. Certainly he faded out so fast that Bridger could not even attempt to shoot. At any rate Bridger was a strange fellow, and he did not shoot on principle. I heard him talk the thing over with Joe Frazer.

"You might have winged him," Frazer insisted.

Bridger answered: "Nothing told me to shoot at him."

"Nothing told you?" shouted Frazer. "Wasn't I there howling my head off to make you shoot at that white lump of murder?"

"No voice inside of me told me to shoot," said Bridger. "There's no good in taking a crack at any wolf unless you've got guidance."

"You talk like a crazy man," said Frazer.

Perhaps Bridger was a little touched on the subject, but he remained as sober as you please and swore that nobody in Circle City would get a bullet into the Lightning Warrior until it pleased the beast to permit the shooting. People laughed at Bridger, and very rightly after he had said this. When Bridger saw people laugh, he grew hot with anger. He actually made a standing bet that nobody in Circle City would shoot or trap the Lightning Warrior. He bet a hundred ounces of gold dust on the proposition.

A hundred ounces, at seventeen dollars an ounce, made pretty good pay for a small job. When people heard that Bridger was in earnest and actually had put up the sack at the saloon, they started to work their heads off to get that wolf. For a few days they burned up ammunition, but none of the bullets grazed the Lightning Warrior. Bridger used to hear the stories with a faint sneer.

"None of you will ever get him," he swore.

He began to grow complacent. I think that the wolf had been half a joke to him at the first, but now it more than justified all that he ever had claimed for it. So Bridger erected the thing into a mystery. He no longer smiled when the Lightning Warrior was mentioned, but he would put on a profound and understanding air and shake his head a few times, and he was apt to leave the room if people persisted in the subject. Then came the Morrissey affair, and after that the subject of the wolf was taboo with everyone.

CHAPTER
FOUR

Trailed by a Ghost

Morrissey, a big, powerful Irishman, had gone out from Circle City with a string of eight dogs, practically a double freight team. The Lightning Warrior went with him. He ate dogs one by one, killing them in the night. At last, Morrissey slept with the remaining in a huddle about him, the four wedging closely together. He did not need to tell them why he wanted them there. They seemed to know. The dread of the monster was in the air, and they had breathed it.

A dog was killed that very night. Poor Morrissey heard the crunching of its neck bones under the teeth of the beast as he awakened from a sound sleep and saw the Lightning Warrior go off, bearing the body of the Husky trailing from his jaws. After that Morrissey tried to keep awake all the way back to Circle City, but he was eight days out and, of course, he failed. He dropped all but one sled, and he put out at full speed with his remaining three dogs. Two days later, he dropped into a brief slumber after a halt. He was wakened by a wild outburst and saw his three dogs banded valiantly together, facing the white killer. They might as well have tried to escape from death itself. The

Lightning Warrior stopped playing when he saw the man waken. He broke the neck of the leader and, when the other dogs backed away, the wolf went off with its profits. This all had happened far too rapidly for Morrissey to intervene.

A day or two later, the Lightning Warrior no longer kept out of sight. He was always to the right and a little ahead of the sled team. He seemed to poor Morrissey as big as a lion, and a thousand times more diabolical. As Morrissey was staggering along, half dead for the lack of sleep, that infernal brute ran in and killed his seventh victim right under the eyes of the driver! Then Morrissey had only one dog, and he lightened the sled to skeleton proportions and made the burst of the last two days toward Circle City.

The first day the last remaining sled dog was struck down by the white lightning. On the final march which he made without a pack of any kind, with nothing to eat except a few tea leaves to crumble between his teeth, that fiend of a Lightning Warrior followed him closely, followed him with an increasing interest, until Morrissey felt sure that the diet list of the Lightning Warrior would be soon varied with flesh other than that of dogs. He managed to keep his eyes open but, when he pushed open the door of the saloon and staggered in among us, I can assure you that Morrissey was a very sick-looking man.

He was white and shaking, and he poured off three shots of that stifling whiskey, one after the other. Somebody asked Morrissey why he was so pale, and Morrissey asked the other how he would look if he had been jogging across country with a demon to dog his steps? Morrissey went quite out of his head when he talked about it. It was a month before he was sound mentally, and we used to have to sit and listen to him raving in the wildest way.

Poor Morrissey! He recovered his mental balance, finally, but he had been very hard hit. From being the most open-hearted, cheerful fellow imaginable, he became sullen and morose nor would he have anything to do with his oldest friends. After the Morrissey business, the hunting of the white plague became a passion with everyone. The town combined. Rifles, poison, traps of all kinds, lures and baits of all descriptions were employed. The townsmen worked together. I helped during the hunting on many a bitter day and night.

This whole episode made a terrific impression upon all of us in Circle City. Men had carried weapons before in the hope of getting a chance at the Lightning Warrior and the hundred ounces. Now, when we went armed, I think that none of us really wanted to encounter the brute, no matter how good the light for shooting. I won't go so far as to say that a single wolf had terrorized the entire community, but it was something very akin to a panic that gripped the men of the town. I can look back clearly to my own emotions of the moment and remember that the last thing I wanted was an opportunity to win the hundred ounces of the reward.

If it had not been for the Lightning Warrior, we would have talked about nothing but Cobalt and Sylvia

Baird until the following season, but the Lightning Warrior first divided our attention, and then he practically monopolized it. We had to rub our eyes when Cobalt suddenly turned up one day with five of his crew at his side. He had brought twelve hundred pounds of nuggets and dust from the diggings!

The few of us who were not at the mines at the moment went half mad when we heard of this bonanza. Cobalt gave up his claims now that he had his money. He said that three mule packs of gold dust were enough for any man, and I suppose that he was right. At any rate other people went out to work on the very spot where Cobalt had found his fortune, and they collected exactly nothing at all. It had been more luck than skill. He had struck some rich pockets. When they were emptied, there was little more than a trace of the right color remaining.

One can imagine the excitement in Circle City now. For here was Cobalt back among us, his pockets filled with gold. Yonder was lovely Sylvia Baird who had told him, in jest or in madness, that she would marry him when he could give her certain things. To be sure, he was not rich now, but he had enough assured him to make certain of a pleasant home.

I remember that we looked upon Cobalt with a gasp of new surprise. We talked the matter over among us, and we decided that, if the girl had asked for a crown of diamonds, Cobalt would have ripped open the earth with his bare hands until he found it. We had faith in him before. We had an infinite faith in him now.

25

He spent two days in resting, that is to say in drinking! The two terms were synonymous with Cobalt as with most of the other miners, but he had a head of well riveted armor-plate, and there was no addling him with alcohol. At the end of the two days he went to call on Sylvia Baird.

She was ready for him. At least she was as well prepared as a human being can be before meeting a giant like Cobalt. She told him how wonderful he was. When he named the weight of the dust he had brought in from the mines, she considered it and decided that the income from such a sum, well invested, would just about do to house her wonderful husband properly.

On this day snow was falling. The flakes whirled with a stifling thickness outside the window, and it seemed that the world had been clapped into a flour sack and well shaken with the dust. Sylvia kept poking at the window and scratching designs on it. Cobalt sat in the opposite corner of the room and watched her like a wolf. He knew perfectly well what she was thinking, and she knew that he knew. Their conversations were the oddest games in the world.

For instance, when her father came in, Sylvia said: "Look, look, Father! Here's Cobalt back from the mines and quite a rich man now. Have you met my father, Cobalt? Oh, yes, on the day you asked him if you could marry me. Sit down, Father, and talk to Cobalt a little and feast your eyes on him. He's looking a little thinner, don't you think, the poor dear! You've had some frostbite in that poor red nose of yours, Cobalt."

Henry Baird tried to break through the air of banter and mockery between that pair. "Look here, Sylvia," he said, "I want to know how seriously you are taking this whole affair?"

"Seriously?" cried Sylvia. "Good heavens, Father, of course I can't be anything but serious. Not considering the opportunity that's been cast in my path. Father, you don't suppose . . . oh, this will amuse Circle City. This will fairly dissolve Cobalt with laughter . . . to think that any woman could even dream for a single moment of refusing to marry him!"

Cobalt stuck out his jaw more than a trifle, but he did not answer this scoffer. Henry Baird looked sharply at the younger man.

"Cobalt," he said, "is this a game with you, too? Or are you really serious?"

"Mister Baird," Cobalt stated, "I'm going to play it the way she wants. If she wants to laugh at me, she can keep right on laughing up the steps to the altar because that's where I'll lead her one of these days."

"Of course you will," said that little imp of a Sylvia. "Of course, you'll lead me to the altar, if you want to. Oh, Cobalt, when I think of the number of girls whose hearts will break that day. When you think of it, Cobalt, how can you be so cruel to them all? Oh, the poor things! They can't help loving you, Cobalt. They can't help it any more than I can help it. You ought to know that."

"Go on. Go right on, Sylvia," said Cobalt. "I like the taste of you today better than ever. I like to sit down and close my eyes and just listen and pretend to myself that you're a man, after all, and big enough for me to put my hands on you."

"That's what I call real love, Father," commented the girl. "He cares for me so much that sometimes he thinks I'm as important as a man. Oh, Cobalt, what a delightful flatterer you are. Did you ever hear anything like it, Father?"

"I never heard anything like you, Sylvia," replied her father sternly.

"It's Cobalt who inspires me," said Sylvia. "You can't expect me to remain ordinary when such a man as Cobalt has noticed me. You can't expect that, can you?"

"Sylvia," returned her father, "you ought to be whipped and put to bed without supper. Cobalt, I don't know exactly your attitude, but I'm ashamed of the way Sylvia is acting."

"Yeah," agreed Cobalt, "she's acting, all right, but one of these days she'll find that I'm up there on the stage with her and signed for life in the same company. That's what I'm waiting for. Sylvia, what do you want for an engagement ring?"

She held out one of her lovely hands. "I never wear rings, my dear," she said, "but I'll tell you what I'd simply adore."

"Tell me then," said Cobalt.

"I'd be charmed to have the skin of the Lightning Warrior, Cobalt, without the marks of trap teeth, or knife, or bullet on any part of him," stated the girl.

CHAPTER
FIVE

Stalking

Some imp must have stolen into the mind of Sylvia. Otherwise, she never could have conceived such an idea. To capture the Lightning Warrior was almost fabulously difficult. The best hunters and trappers of Circle City, where all men could hunt and trap a little, had tried in vain, tempted by that offer of the two thousand dollar reward. But, to capture him without either traps or bullets or knives, this was preposterous!

Cobalt, as he listened to her, watched her deep blue eyes intently. He stood there like a stone, staring, while Baird was saying: "That's a foolish remark, Sylvia. As if a man could go out into the wilderness and capture the white beast bare-handed!"

"Oh, Father," said Sylvia, clasping her hands together in mock admiration of Cobalt, "you don't know what he can do. He himself hardly knows. No other man can match the things that he does. Do you think that he will shrink from a little thing like this?"

Cobalt asked: "Is that the price mark on the tag?"

She half closed her eyes. I imagine she was thinking fast and hard, and there was no doubting the direction of his last remark. Everything had been a jest. Even the ripping of that fortune out of the earth was a part of the joke. This was different. If he went out with his bare hands to do this marvel, their mutual jest would have drawn to an end. She did not answer the last remark directly, therefore, but merely said: "I've always wanted a big white fur."

So Cobalt said good bye and left her the second time and heard her father saying angrily that she should not press a jest as far as this. It was a joke, but Cobalt intended to turn it into earnest. That same day he went out from Circle City with his dog team, his half-wild string of savage brutes, and traveled up the Yukon slowly. His load was chiefly dried fish for his team, and the goal of his journey was the Lightning Warrior. The dogs were bait. The weapon and the trap consisted merely in a strong rope.

He was no expert with a lariat, so he practiced on the way, making a thousand casts a day to get the hang of the thing. Suppose that he managed to get the rope over the head of the brute, how would he proceed? His hands would have to be the clubs that beat it senseless. Or did he even think of what he would do when the crisis came? Perhaps not. His was a simple plan. To the execution of it, he would trust patience and his superhuman power of arm and body.

On the second day he saw the Lightning Warrior, the first time his eyes had rested on the beast. He had trusted that his team would be followed as Morrissey's was followed. He was right. When he saw the big silhouette of the monster, standing on a white hummock against the sky, the old superstition thrust into his mind that this might be a man-wolf, a *loup-garou.*

The brute seemed to know perfectly that the man carried no gun. He stood there on the top of the hummock and allowed the dog team to pass him at a distance of fifty feet. That savage team should have become wildly excited at the sight of the wolf. They should have tried with all their might to get at him. Instead, they hung their heads and seemed oppressed with fear. Cobalt stopped them and went out with his rope toward the brute that remained on the hummock. When he was six strides from him, he yawned at Cobalt like a cat, showing his red gullet and the teeth gleaming like pearls. Then he bounded to the side and was gone into a thicket.

Even Cobalt's heart beat fast, and he hesitated before entering the underbrush. But enter it he did. He walked cautiously. He was an excellent woodsman, and he knew how to step so that his feet made no noise that a human ear at least could hear. Before he had gone ten paces, he heard the terrified yelling of his team and rushed back to see what had happened. It was the Lightning Warrior that had happened. He had come out of the shrubbery and, giving his shoulder to the leader, had killed that dog with a single slash across its throat. Now the team cowered together. They did not seem to have offered the slightest resistance to the white thunderbolt which now sat at a little distance and licked the blood from his snowy breast and from his forelegs.

He went on about his toilet with the most perfect
care and indifference to the man approaching him. This
time Cobalt determined to try a long cast. When he
came within six steps, the beast yawned at him in the
same horrible manner. That instant Cobalt made his
cast. He flung with an underhand motion, which is the
Mexican way, and the swiftest of all. The coil went out
like a serpent striking, but it missed the Lightning
Warrior. He had not leaped back or to the side. He
simply jumped in, so that the rope flew over his head.
As the lariat fell, Cobalt found himself unarmed, empty
handed, with that massive killer crouching at his feet for
the spring. What other man would have done what he
did? He stepped straight forward, and the Lightning
Warrior bounded lightly to the side. He approached
again, and the snowy murderer fairly turned tail and
fled across the wastes. The dog team saw him go,
picked up heart, and sang a chorus of tardy defiance.

Then Cobalt went back and sat down on his sled for
a time. He was not feeling well. His hands were a trifle
uncertain, and there was a slight sense of numbness
about his knees. While he sat there, thinking of what he
was attempting, he told himself that he was a fool. He
thought back to Sylvia also.

It was not only her beauty that drove him. It was also
the memory of her dainty voice and her softly sneering
ironies. Perhaps she was back there in Circle City,
laughing at the idiot who had gone out into the
wilderness because she chose to make a joke of him!
But it was her wickedness which flavored her beauty.

There was no other person like her. She stood apart from all the rest.

After he had thought of her for a time, his strength and courage revived. He stood up, cut the dead leader from the harness, and drove on slowly. He knew that he was beginning a long duel. He was not prepared, however, for the full weight of the disaster which overtook him. His own relentless determination drove him on to court it.

Two days out from Circle City, he had already lost a dog. Ten days later, his last one was gone. He was mushing ahead alone, pulling the sled with patient strength. Still the Lightning Warrior was following him! Just as he had followed Morrissey and almost destroyed the man on the verge of Circle City, so now he followed Cobalt. When his face was toward him, the beast dared not attack Cobalt. On the first day he had established a moral superiority, and the balance never shifted against him. But the danger would not come from the front. He would attack him from either side or, most probably, from the rear. If Cobalt could defend his back, his face was safe.

Once, very tired, cold from a ripping wind, he built his fire and had it flaming when a sudden cramp of terror gripped the small of his back. He had heard, and he had seen, nothing of the Lightning Warrior all that day but, twitching around suddenly, he saw the monster in the act of leaping. Cobalt side-stepped. The big wolf twisted in the air and, striking the snow well beyond the fire, he was instantly gone among the brush again. That was a lesson for Cobalt.

From that moment he lived as though he were surrounded by hostile Indians. One instant of lack of precaution and the teeth would be in his throat, and the beast would be drinking his blood. He kept to the woods most of the time. They were tenfold more perilous, in that they offered a chance for stalking to that werewolf. At the same time they might give him more chances to use the rope. In fact, in six weeks he cast the rope three times, including the first failure. Once the edge of the coil struck the monster between the eyes. But that was the closest Cobalt came to success.

He decided that the rope was too light. It had to be heavier so that it could be thrown with speed, like a flexible metal cable. So he worked in strips of rawhide until the weight of the noose end of the rope was trebled. It was now like handling a mass of chain. The noose was stiffened, more likely to hold its form. As he practiced with the rope on stones and stumps, he told himself that he now had a half chance to succeed when next an opportunity came to him.

For that opportunity he waited on the bank of a small salmon stream. He was glad of the fishing. His own supply of provisions was getting very low, but he worked at the fishing patiently, cleaned the big salmon, then cured them on racks above a fire. He accumulated far more food than he needed, because of the pleasure which he took in being merely occupied. The surplus he cached as high as practicable in trees.

So the winter came, the river freezing to a stone. Still he waited there on the bank, and still the Lightning

Warrior never left him! Once, before the long winter night began, in the dusk of the year, he had a sight of the *loup-garou* hunting. The thing amazed him and filled his mind like a nightmare for weeks thereafter. He had heard the long, deep hunting cry of the Lightning Warrior not far off, flying through the woods. As the noise approached very near, he went to see what he could find.

There in a clearing he found the white monster, stalking in a swift circle around one of the biggest lynxes that Cobalt had ever seen. It did not seem possible that a wolf could undertake to make a stand against a full-grown lynx, with its equipment of needle fangs and knife-like claws. The wolf was attacking, but the manner of the attack was strange. There was no sudden rush in. The Lightning Warrior circled and circled, keeping just on the horizon of the cat's leaping distance. The lynx turned slowly, by jerks, to face the danger, always tensed, always ready for the bound whose striking speed must make up for its lack of weight. Still the wolf circled until the lynx, turning its head, seemed to look for an opportunity to escape. The Lightning Warrior, marking that movement, slid in closer. The lynx bristled with head close to the ground, ready to spring, but still the wolf was not ready.

For twenty minutes Cobalt, frozen with interest, watched the drama and gradually understood. The wild cat had the fighting power of an explosive, but its prodigious frenzy of strength could not endure with patience under any strain. Its moment for battle already was passing. Its nerves were crumbling. It was ready to flee. It dipped its head and licked at the snow. Its tufted ears flickered. Suddenly the Lightning Warrior struck. He had been going on his steady round for so long that even the cat who watched the scene was totally unprepared, and the big wild cat seemed hypnotized. It appeared to Cobalt that the lynx made not a single effort to save itself. The lobo simply caught it by the back of the neck and broke the spine.

Cobalt could remember, with a bitter spirit, how the great beast had stalked him and his dog team, day after day, and reaped a red harvest. The creature was made of blood lust. Now he stood above the prey for a moment, gazing about it, ready to scent any suspicious smells upon the wind. Failing in this, he prepared to eat, and this was the moment when Cobalt gathered his rope, prepared his noose, and began to slide out from his place of covert to make another effort.

CHAPTER
SIX

Man and Beast

Beasts of prey, if they are wise, eat with the nose upwind, so that the invisible telegraph of the senses will inform them of dangers approaching. Their trouble in so doing is that crafty enemies may then stalk upwind to approach them. Their rear guard must be simply an occasional glance behind them. Beyond this it is their sharp hearing and, beyond all else, the aura of nervous apprehension that puts out tentacles to a distance around the beasts of prey and the preyed upon.

Cobalt knew the manners of the wild well enough. He was amazed to see the Lightning Warrior reverse the procedure. He actually turned his back upwind, letting his nostrils gather their priceless tidings at a distinct disadvantage. It seemed that he despised the approach of any open foe. It was only the crafty approach from the rear that he wished to guard against.

The cunning of this procedure was instantly evident to Cobalt. If he came out of his covert and went down the wind, the Lightning Warrior was reasonably sure to smell him. If he came from the front, the beast was even more sure to see him. There was only one course which seemed at all feasible to him and that was to come out of covert, as he had done, and stalk toward the lobo. The slightest turn of the white brute's head would betray him, of course, but Cobalt could not overlook any opportunity, however small. He issued from the cover which had shielded him and went up on the quarter of the lobo.

How I wish that I could have been there to see that dead lynx stretched out on the snow, still warm and quivering as the wolf devoured the body half living and drank the blood, and the man coming from the dark of the trees, looking like a hunting animal, also, his eyes burning with the same red light. He went with his teeth set and, through them, he breathed out a prayer at every step until he found himself within throwing distance. He could not believe it. He doubted his luck with a passion of hope. Of what was to come, even should he settle the noose on the head of the monster, he did not even think, but on he went, a step, another, bringing himself closer to surety in the cast, gripping and re-gripping the strands of his rope, wondering if the cold would have stuck the noose and kept it from running. Then he saw the white killer stiffen suddenly, though its muzzle was still fastened in the kill.

The time had come. Like a flung stone that heavy rope shot straight from his hand. The Lightning Warrior, while the flying danger was still in the air, was already under way. He would have escaped at the first bound, his leap was so sudden and directed so far to the side, but the snow failed to hold under him. It had been moistened by the blood of the lynx at this spot. It was his own murdering ways that tripped him up, and so the lower rim of the noose struck him on the beautiful white fur of his shoulder and the upper rim of the noose flicked forward over his head.

The second bound followed before the man could pull up the rope; but luck was against the Lightning Warrior. His second jump merely served to whip the noose tight so that it bound his throat with a throttling force. Still in mid-air the lunge of his powerful body thrust him against the stiffened rope which held him like a rod, the hands of Cobalt holding that rod like iron. I wonder what Cobalt felt at that moment when for the first time he achieved, not his quest, but an actual contact with the prey for which he had been questing so long?

He shouted, still through his teeth, and the sound of his shout was like the whining snarl of the lobo as he tumbled in the snow, snapping at the elusive thinness of the rope. Cobalt gave the lariat a little play, enough to allow him to throw loops in rapid succession as he ran in, attempting to entangle the legs of the brute. But the Lightning Warrior was up in another moment and, instead of fleeing, he followed better tactics and drove straight at the throat of the man. Cobalt met it as he would have met a charge from another man under those circumstances — with a hard-driven fist. All that he had to aim at was a narrow frame around a vast expanse of red where the teeth glistened. He felt them already sinking into the throat at which they were aimed. Then he struck, a little to the side of the gaping mouth, a little beneath the glimmer of the evil eyes. By the grace of his cool brain and his accurate eye, his fist found lodgment at the base of the animal's jaw.

Even a bull must have gone down when that sledge-hammer stroke fairly met the mark. The bull would have gone down stunned. The Lightning Warrior was flung backward, head over heels, by the irresistible shock. He tumbled in the snow with his four legs, for the moment, thrusting upward.

Cobalt noosed two of those legs in a flying loop of the rope and, by a happy chance, one of them was a foreleg and one a hind leg. Then the Lightning Warrior went mad. The two legs which remained untethered were on opposite sides of the body and, therefore, the lobo was able at intervals to maintain his balance. He began to roll and leap in the snow. He came like an otter, wallowing on his stomach like a galloping seal, dashing himself toward Cobalt, but the strain of the noose began to choke him. In the wildness of the wolf's fury Cobalt heard clearly the snapping of a bone. An instant later the Lightning Warrior had partially brained himself against a tree trunk.

He lay still. A bit of wind got through the trees and fluttered the downy white fur, deep and rich, while Cobalt came up slowly and stared down at his quarry. He saw the fluff of snow near the nostrils of the brute stirring. By that he guessed that the animal still lived. He saw a foreleg crooked in the snow. By that he guessed that this was the broken bone. He leaned over and laid his hand on the shoulder of the wolf. Under the deep blanket of the fur he could feel the muscle, hard as iron and still tensed like strung cords.

Then Cobalt laughed silently. It is a horrible thing to think of that silent laughter under the dark of those trees. But he laughed, for in staring down at the Lightning Warrior, he had conceived another thought. He started to carry out the plan at once. In a sense, I suppose, that a more grotesque or brutal plan was never formed. Nevertheless, he went ahead with it. He muzzled the beast with a length of the rope. Then he made splints out of straight twigs and bound them firmly around the leg, first padding the joints with moss as he well knew how to do. The wolf roused up and made one more effort to get at Cobalt with his teeth, but found that it was hopeless. So he lay with a certain patience. He raised his great, wise head and looked the man in the face with an unflinching and deathless hatred and, the man, looking up from the splinting of the broken leg, answered that look with a sneer.

When he was ready, he lifted the bulk of the wolf in his arms. He could have carried a greater burden, but he was amazed by the bulk of this thing, for he knew the limits inside of which a wolf is supposed to range. Then the fact that the long-hunted prize was actually in his arms started him laughing again. As he laughed, he felt the wolf shuddering with hate against his breast, and Cobalt laughed still louder, until the icy corridors of that forest rang with his mirth.

He got the wolf to his camp by the river, and there he nursed him back to soundness. He nursed him with the devotion of a priest to a convert or a parent to a child. But in all the devotion of Cobalt there was no affection. He remembered the dead dogs of his team.

They were half-wild beasts, but they were his. He had chosen them, trained them. They were his pride, and every one of them had come to his hand willingly, without fear.

When he saw the red eyes of the Lightning Warrior fixed steadily upon him with the fire never dying down in them, he would sit for long minutes, concentrating his will upon the brute, until at last the animal's eyes could endure no longer against that human will, and the lobo would look away. From day to day the contest was waged with the same bitterness, until in the end the Lightning Warrior knew that he was totally defeated.

CHAPTER
SEVEN

The Return

To describe the hunting of the Lightning Warrior is a simple thing, but one has to remember that an entire year was cut out of the life of Cobalt. At the end of that time in the warmth of the year, when the sun was at its height and the mosquitoes were blackening the flats and the yellow Yukon was rolling unbarred by ice toward the sea, Cobalt came back. I had come in from the mines on some sort of business, I forget what, and there were enough others, what with newcomers and the rest, to fill the saloon when Cobalt opened the door and waved to us. He looked about the same, only a little blacker of skin from the long, bitter weathering that he had gone through. Of course, he was in rags that even an Indian might have scorned, but Cobalt often looked like that when he came in from a long trek. He had been in our minds for a year and, when he stepped back inside that door, he had not been forgotten. It showed the vast force in him that even an arctic year of starving, laboring, hoping, groaning had not shut him from our thoughts.

When he opened the door and stepped inside, with the flash of the sun behind him, a shout went up. Some people had said that he must be dead, that the wolf had got him before this. But to most of us he seemed a deathless thing, like a waterfall which may be frozen up for a time but which most of the year will be dashing and smashing at the rocks. I remember that there was a cheechako at that moment handling the bent iron bar that had been taken down from the wall for his curious eyes. In the midst of his futile efforts, he saw that ragged man in the door — not a very big man, certainly not a handsome man — yet the cheechako knew when he set eyes upon him.

"It's Cobalt!" whispered the cheechako, grinning like a happy child and straining at the bar.

Cobalt came with that light step of his, like the step of a man about to break into a run, and we surged toward him. But we stopped, like a wave that founders on a bar, recoiling suddenly. For behind Cobalt came the Lightning Warrior! Yes, striding in like a king, more glorious, more beautiful than ever, came the Lightning Warrior, holding his head high as a king ought to hold it and making himself blind to the poor, pitiful humans around him whom he despised. Mind you, there was no lead rope on him. There was no muzzle on him, either. All that he wore in token of being subdued was a pack fitted snugly upon his back. The Lightning Warrior was being used as a pack dog! How can I put down what I, for one, felt about this thing? It seemed that the entire universe had been reversed. For there was the primitive mind of the wilderness, the savage hunter, turned into a domestic servant.

After a moment we began to recover a little at the sight of Cobalt resting his heel on the footrail and calling for drinks. He set them up for the house, and we took the glasses in forgetful fingers and stared not at the red stain in the liquor but at the red stain in the eyes of the wolf. We could see him closely enough now to make out the color of the eyes. It was the whites of them which were red stained, but the eyes themselves were blue, a pale, clear blue, a strange color to find in the eyes of a wolf, almost as strange as the snowy purity of the coat itself.

"Come up," said Cobalt. "Come up closer, old-timer!"

He made a quick motion with his hand, and the wolf glided up under it. He did not shrink. Neither did he wag his tail nor snarl. Nor did a softer light appear in his eyes, but all at once every man in that room knew that the beast hated Cobalt with an entire and a deathless hatred. That made the miracle complete. There was no muzzle over those teeth which, at a stroke, could have cut half through the leg of a man or broken his neck at the nape. Yet Cobalt dared to walk freely forward with this menace behind him. Without a rope to control him, the Lightning Warrior followed at the heels of his master like a dog, though he could have turned and disappeared in a moment in the brush, to be free again forever.

No, it was not the body or the soul of the beast that Cobalt had mastered. It was only the brain. He left the body uncrippled and strong. He had not overwhelmed the hidden soul of the great animal and won his love.

He simply had subdued the brain until the monster felt helpless in the grip of his master's will.

How was all this finally accomplished? Cobalt would never say. He could be persuaded to say a little about the days when he used to sit and fix his eyes upon the wolf, and how they had stared at one another, but there he ended.

I remember how the bartender leaned across the bar, his eyes like two moons, and asked: "How did you do it, Cobalt?"

We all listened, as for the voice of a prophet, but Cobalt simply said: "Why, look here, boys, it's not the first time that a man has caught a wild wolf and tamed it. And he's tame, isn't he? Look at him. Gentle as a lamb."

Gentle as a chained demon, he should have said. Someone verged too close to the brute and got a silent snarl that made him jump ten feet. Yes, the Lightning Warrior was gentle to the hand and the will of his master, but in reality his very soul was plunged deeper in revolt and rage against all men. We thought that we could read one extra page in the story. Beside the right eye of Cobalt and running down his cheek, there was a thin red line. It was a scar such as a knife stroke might have left. It would whiten in time, but at this very moment it looked just like a little stream of fresh blood.

Yes, other men had caught wild wolves and taken them. They had caught the wolves with cunning traps, and they had taken them with a whip. But one glance at the face of Cobalt told us other things. We knew, in a flash, that his bare hands were the weapons with which he had schooled the beast.

For my part, as I looked at them, I realized another thing: that there was tragedy in the offing. It seemed that Cobalt felt my gaze for presently he said to me: "Chalmers, will you walk out with me? I want to talk to you a little."

I went out with him into the arctic sun, which is not like the sun of more southerly places. There is always some trace of a dream about it. It is a thing seen with the mind rather than something felt by the body, though in all conscience I have seen it hot enough even in that Far North.

We went out, with me stepping rather short and keeping half an eye or more upon that white monster. I think he was the most beautiful thing that I had ever seen. The whiteness of a polar bear was tawny compared with him, and the whiteness of the most brushed and bathed, combed and fluffed lap dog was dull compared with the pure brightness of the Lightning Warrior.

"Now, Chalmers, you're older than I am," said Cobalt, facing about and giving me his eye in that direct and almost intolerable fashion of his.

"I'm a good deal older, as years go, Cobalt," I said.

"What do you mean by that?" asked Cobalt, for he always hated the half answers which make up the talk of most of us. "What do you mean by older as years go?"

"I mean," I said, hunting through my mind, "that time is a thin effect with a lot of us, thin as arctic sunshine. I've seen men, Cobalt, who can age more in a year than others can in ten."

"Age how?" he asked.

"Ideas, thoughts, accomplishments."

"And trouble?" he finished off.

"Yes, trouble," I admitted, uncomfortably.

"Do you think that I've raised trouble now?" he asked me.

I hesitated.

"Oh, you know. Everybody knows about it," he said.

"Perhaps that's the chief trouble," I said.

"Why?" he demanded sharply.

"Well, you can see for yourself," I responded.

"Don't tell me what I can see for myself, man," said Cobalt. "Tell me what you see."

I saw that he was under a strain. He was at the breaking point and, if he broke, the explosion would shake Circle City.

"I'll tell you something," I parried. "Once when I was a youngster, there was a marriage advertised in a side show in a circus. The tallest man in the world was to marry the fattest lady in the world. They sold admissions for fifty cents. I was only a boy, and I went and saw the marriage."

"What has that got to do with me?" he asked. "What has that got to do with me and . . . well, with me and Sylvia Baird?"

He challenged me with his hard, bright eye, which was turning from gray to a pale, luminous blue. I think that the Scandinavian warriors of another age must have looked like that when they ran naked into the dance of the swords, the banquet of the blades as they used to call it.

"I mean," I said, "that it was a pretty public thing . . . the engagement, the marriage, and all in that circus tent."

He pointed a finger at me like a gun. "You really mean that I've dragged Sylvia too much out into the light of publicity."

I nodded.

"All right," he said. "All right! I see what you mean. And what do you think? That I'm going to back down?"

"Back down?" I echoed quite vaguely.

"You know, throw up the game, just because she's a little sensitive?" He tried to smile. It was only a grimace. Then he broke out: "You come along with me to the Baird house, will you? I want to talk some more to you."

I knew that he did not mean that. He wanted me there in the hope that my presence would help him to keep from doing some wild, absurd thing. I went, unwittingly and very much afraid, at his side up the street.

CHAPTER
EIGHT

Straight Talk

Before we quite came to the Baird house, we could hear Sylvia's violin singing and soaring over the voices of a couple of men. When she opened the door to us, flushed and happy and smiling, I saw Tom Benton and Jay von Acker there in the dimness of the room with her. It was one of her favorite amusements. There was mighty little music in Circle City, and Sylvia's fiddle accompanied anyone who had enough of a voice to attempt a song. She saw me first and gave me her usual smile, behind which I don't think there was any real design but which radiated in such a way that, wherever she looked, she seemed to have found something that peculiarly and particularly pleased her. I was a good deal older than most of the boys who flocked around Sylvia, and I should have known better, but now and again she pulled at the strings of my heart in such a way that a little pang of melancholy pleasure would be stirring within me all the rest of the day.

That was the smile she gave me and her hand asking me in. Then she saw two other things, Cobalt and the Lightning Warrior. She would have fallen, I think, or else she would have jumped back into the room. But

50

she got a good grip on the edge of the door and held herself in place. I saw the scream come into her eyes, swell in her throat, and die out again as she mastered herself. All in a moment she was herself again, and actually she went a step past the threshold and gave Cobalt her hand. She gave him her smile, too. I turned about and saw this. The smile was so perfect that no one except Cobalt would have noticed her pallor.

Then came two yells from inside the house. Benton and von Acker came tumbling out to see the great white brute and admire and exclaim over it. Cobalt gave them the smallest half of a smile and no answer at all. So they pulled in their heads and got themselves off down the street.

Sylvia gave me an inquiring look, and I saw that she wanted to be alone on the field of battle, but Cobalt said: "I asked him to come along because I wanted someone to see how you'd get along with the wolf."

"Why should I get along with the Lightning Warrior?" she asked him. "I only wanted his skin."

"There's his skin on him," said Cobalt, "without the mark of a knife or a bullet or the teeth of a trap."

"Goodness!" Sylvia gasped. "How did you manage to do it? But, of course, I knew that you would!"

"Did you?" answered Cobalt, with a little hard ring in his voice that sent tingles up my spine and a weakness down my legs. "Well, there's the skin exactly as you asked for it, Sylvia. Chalmers, she wanted the skin of the Lightning Warrior instead of an engagement ring . . . without a mark or a break on it. So you're a witness that she has what she asked for."

I hated this being used as a witness. He was going to drive her into a corner.

"Do come in, both of you," she said.

"You wouldn't leave the poor old-timer outside, would you?" asked Cobalt, patting the head of the wolf.

She looked at the Lightning Warrior very much as one might look at incarnate evil. "Well," she commented, "I suppose you think it's safe to have him in the house?"

"Why isn't it?" asked Cobalt. "Look at this!"

He spoke and, at his command, that white murderer sat down, lay down, gave his paw, fetched the hat which Cobalt threw on the snow, and finally stood up on his hind legs, put his forepaws on the shoulders of the man, and looked at him with eyes that were on a level. Their faces were not inches apart. I saw the Lightning Warrior begin to shake and tremble all over, while his lips twitched and blood seemed to flow into his eyes. It was not fear, mind you, that made him quiver. It was a frightful desire to have the life blood of the man, and that impulse was mastered only by a deep-rooted awe.

For my own part, I never saw a picture that chilled me more thoroughly. Poor Sylvia looked on with a sick face. Cobalt would not say a word about the year he had spent in the wilderness, working to get this animal and to subdue it so perfectly. Rather he chose this way of giving one an insight into what he had accomplished. I stared at the face of the wolf and the face of the man, and upon my honor I found them strongly similar, even to the sneering expression. The scar stood out on the face of Cobalt like a thin line of blood. Sylvia saw all these things with eyes at least as sharp as mine.

"If he's so gentle as that," she said, "of course he's welcome in the house. What a beauty he is!"

The Lightning Warrior dropped to the ground and followed his master into the house. There he backed into a corner of the room where the shadow was deepest but through which we still could see the red glint of his eye and the strange blue of its iris, like the blue of Cobalt's own eye. We sat down, and she offered us tea.

"I never drink tea when I'm not on the march," said Cobalt.

We were all silent for a moment. I suppose it was Sylvia's duty to carry on the conversation in some way, but she had to pause and gather her strength for the trial. Just then Sylvia's father came in. He had already heard about the coming of Cobalt, and he was puffing from his rapid walking, returning to his home. He gave us both an eager, worried, half-frightened look before he shook hands and sat down with us.

"A marvelous thing, Cobalt," he said. "Extraordinary! I don't see how you've accomplished it, and I . . ." His voice trailed away. His eyes had found the red mark on the face of Cobalt.

"Nothing at all," said Cobalt. "Sylvia didn't want an engagement ring. She wanted the skin of the Lightning Warrior. There it is, you see."

Baird tried to laugh, but his voice shook a bit. "You have a sense of humor, Cobalt," he said.

"I hope that I have," said Cobalt, "and a memory, too. I try to laugh when my turn comes. Did you say there was a joke somewhere in this, Mister Baird?"

"Why, Cobalt," said Baird, "of course you understand, man . . . you know that a girl . . . on one meeting . . . you know that a girl couldn't possibly . . . ?" He got altogether stuck.

Sylvia, leaning a bit forward in her chair, watched the two of them with an eager white face. Her hands were clasped hard together in her lap.

"I see what you mean," said Cobalt, appearing very easy in his manner. "Naturally at a first meeting a girl wouldn't send a man off to do a job like that unless she was dead serious. No right-minded girl would let him take his life in his hands and throw away the best dog team that ever hauled sleds out of Circle City and chuck a year of his life into the bargain. Why, Mister Baird, you don't suppose that I think Sylvia would take me as lightly as that? Or you either, for that matter?"

Baird got out a handkerchief and mopped his face. "Not lightly, Cobalt," he said with eagerness. "No one would take you lightly. Only, you understand that a casual remark in a casual conversation . . . you understand that a girl might casually say something to which she wouldn't actually wish to commit herself."

"Why, then I'll find out," said Cobalt, cool as could be. "Tell me, Sylvia, did you say the thing casually? Did you expect that I would try to do what you suggested, or did you not?"

I never saw grief and ghostly fear more vividly drawn than in the face and the staring eyes of poor Sylvia. My heart ached for her, and I wanted to break in with a few words, but I could find none. One can't jest with the owner about the architecture of his burning house, and one could not be light with Cobalt about his year of labor. He had given himself to the utmost. Something in the drawn lines of his face showed that. Now what would be his reward?

Perhaps a sheer spirit of perversity had driven him onto the thing, but was there some justification, after all? Had he, on the day a year before, seen something in the face, heard something serious in the voice of Sylvia when she made the proposal about the wolf skin instead of an engagement ring?

"Sylvia!" broke out her father suddenly, "we're waiting for you to speak. Were you serious when you spoke to him? Will you answer?"

She seemed about to speak when her father cut in again: "But take your time. Think it over. Remember everything in that conversation. I've heard it from you before, but I never guessed that there was anything serious in what you and he had said to one another."

She took a breath, then she said: "You can't help me now, Father. I'm thinking back to that day. It was a pretty light conversation, Cobalt, wasn't it?"

"As light," said Cobalt, "as eagle feathers. As light as the feathers that they put on arrowheads. Isn't that about it?"

She stared at him. "You mean," she said, "that we both felt seriously about what we said?"

"I mean," he said, "that I asked you to marry me."

55

"No," she said, correcting him, "but you did tell me that you were going to marry me. There's a difference."

He nodded. "Did you think I was serious?"

She did not answer for a second or two. My heart counted ten in a roll of thunder during the interval.

Then she replied simply: "Yes, I thought you were serious."

CHAPTER NINE

The Love Court

Her father got out of his chair with a lurch and a jump, like a protesting lawyer at a trial. In a sense, this *was* a trial, with vital issues hanging upon the outcome. "Sylvia," he cried, "think what you're saying, will you? Think how you're putting yourself into his hands!"

Then Cobalt said an astounding thing. "No, no, Mister Baird. That's not the right angle and that's not the way to look at the thing at all. As a matter of fact I don't want to follow my own blind conviction. I want to do something with my eyes open and my head up. For my part I'm willing to take the opinion of you and Chalmers here to decide the case between me and Sylvia."

I thought Baird would choke, such was the violence of his conflicting emotions. He cleared his throat once or twice and then began to blink and nod, his colorless brows going up and down, his pink face reddening. "Of course, Cobalt," he conceded, "you're a gentleman. Tut, tut, my dear lad, the whole north country knows that. There is only one way in which a gentleman can act at such a time. Tut, tut, I know all of that beforehand."

"No, you don't," answered Cobalt, not violently but perfectly matter of fact. "You know what I'll do. Nobody else does, because I'm in the dark myself."

This was a considerable conversational snag, and no one could say a thing for a moment. It was Sylvia at last who remarked: "Let me try to understand, Cobalt. You want to convince yourself that you're right, and then you'll go ahead. You want to find out if, in the opinion of Dad and Mister Chalmers, I really committed myself. Then, no matter what my own opinion is, you'll go ahead?"

"You can put it that way," said Cobalt.

"I don't want to put it that way," she responded. "I want to hear you put it in your own words."

"Words are not what count from my side of the fence. Now then, Chalmers, what have you to say about the thing?"

"How can I say anything, Cobalt?" I asked him. "I don't know what passed between you and Sylvia. I only know that of course no man can hold a woman against her will to an engagement so . . . well, so extraordinary."

"Do you really think that?" he asked. "Then I've lost before the trial begins. Because I want a unanimous vote of yourself and Mister Baird on one side or the other as to whether or not you think Sylvia committed herself."

He was wonderfully calm as indeed he remained throughout the interview, except for a flush now and again. When I heard these last words of his, you may believe that I pricked up my ears again. I saw that this was even a more serious matter than it had seemed before — far more serious.

"What happened, exactly, from your own point of view?" asked Baird, mopping his face again. For that matter I was getting pretty moist myself.

"Do you mean," said Cobalt, "from the very first?"

"Yes, tell us that," said the father, nodding and setting his jaw.

"Well, then, I'll tell you ... from my viewpoint," replied Cobalt. "The moment I saw her, I wanted her."

"Say that more clearly," I suggested. "You loved her?"

"I wanted her," he insisted. "I wanted her the way a boy wants a knife that he sees in a window, or a horse in a circus, or an air rifle on a store rack. Love her? I don't know. I wanted her. I heard a yegg one day telling how he saw an emerald pendant at the throat of a woman. He couldn't get at it that night while she was wearing it, but he traced it to the bank vault in which it was kept. He blew the vault, sifted through the stuff it contained, and got his hands on the emerald. He turned around, and there were five cops with a dead bead on him. They sent him up for ten years or so. He got out, went back to the same bank, blew another vault, and was caught again. He went back to prison a second time for a longer spell. When I saw him, he was a gray-headed man. I asked him what had happened to the emerald. He took a piece of chamois out of his pocket and unwrapped it, and there was the emerald lying in the palm of his hand. He had a peaceful look in spite of his years in jail."

59

Sylvia, who had been listening with all her heart and soul, asked: "Tell me, did you know him well? Or did he just trust you?"

"He trusted me," said Cobalt. "All men trust me."

Well, it was rather a grand thing to hear. There was perfect truth in it, too. All men trusted Cobalt, even those who wronged him. He might kill them, but he never would slander them, try to trick them, or take them from behind. He stood up and let the fire shine in his eyes.

"I say that I saw Sylvia, and I wanted her. I tell you just how I wanted her. The way that yegg wanted the emerald. The prison meant nothing to him. Well, prison would mean nothing to me either, except that there's a slight difference. Emeralds don't grow old, women do. I want Sylvia now. I want her where I can look at her."

"When she's happy?" I suggested.

"Oh, I don't much care about that," said Cobalt. "Mad or glad or sulking or dancing or sorry or jolly, I'd be about equally glad to look at her. People spend millions for a picture. Well, there's the picture that I want."

I wondered that he could keep the emotion out of his voice, but he did. You might have thought that he was speaking for another person and not himself. You may be sure that Sylvia neither smiled nor looked self-conscious when she heard those remarks. Rather, she looked as though she were on trial for her life. In a sense she was.

"Then I went to you and told you that I wanted her. I went to her and told her I intended to have her,"

60

Cobalt went on. "That sounds eccentric. Well, it wasn't as eccentric as I may have seemed. I wanted to get her attention from the crowd for a minute. So I made a bit of noise and gesticulation . . . at least I caught her eye. I made her listen. Now, you tell me, Sylvia, when I informed you that I intended to marry you, you were angry, weren't you?"

"Yes, I was angry," she admitted.

"But you believed that I seriously intended doing what I said?"

"Yes," she agreed slowly, "I think that I felt that."

"You only thought so?" he repeated. "You didn't know it?"

"Yes," she said, rather faintly, "I suppose that I knew it."

"Be honest," he urged.

"I am honest," she said. She drew back in her chair, seeming to feel that the presence of his argument and his questions were hemming her in. Her eyes flashed toward her father then toward me.

"If you're honest," argued Cobalt, "you knew by the way my eyes handled your face that I wanted you as desperately as the thief wanted the emerald."

She actually raised her hand and touched her face with a startled and pained look. It was a very strange thing to see. "Yes," she said then, "I know that you wanted me. No man ever looked at me like that . . . as if I were not even a human being, not even a dog or a horse, just something to look at."

"Ah," said Cobalt, "that's it. Now we're getting along."

"But what's the direction of all this talk?" she asked.

"I don't know," he said. "I hope that I can give it a direction. Then we come to the time when I said good bye to you."

"You mean that I kissed you good bye?" she said. "That was only a part of the ironical game which we were playing. You know that, Cobalt. You wouldn't be unfair about that."

"That kiss? Rot!" he expostulated. "That was nothing. That made no difference to me. The touch of the wind would have been as much to me. But it gave me a chance to see what your hair was like, and I saw that it was spun finer than cobweb. I thought it would be like that, but I couldn't be sure until my eyes were close. That finished the picture. I'd seen your hand and watched it moving. So that kiss meant a good deal, but not because it was the touch of your lips."

She sighed with relief.

"Now, man," I said, breaking in because I couldn't stand the tenseness of the atmosphere, "tell me what you think, no matter what has gone before, can a girl honestly marry a man she doesn't care about? And you don't love him, Sylvia?"

She clasped her hands together and stiffened her arms a little. She closed her eyes. "I do not love him," she whispered.

CHAPTER
TEN

Cave Man Stuff

Even as the case stood perhaps Sylvia might have found a little less emphatic way of speaking, but I must say that Cobalt did not seem in the least shocked. He merely looked at her with greater interest, at the repulsion that showed in the faint curl of her lip, at the small hands, the loveliest that ever were seen. With an impersonal interest he examined and analyzed her.

"From my point of view, that ends it," I said abruptly.

"That isn't the point on which I want your view," said Cobalt. "That angle doesn't interest me in the least."

"Great Scott, man," I said, "are you back in the cave age when women were chased and captured? Do you mean to say that affection isn't what civilization has been built on and . . . ?"

"Civilization! Stuff and nonsense!" replied Cobalt. "I don't give a rap about all that rot. Besides, there's the contract marriage of the Greeks and Romans. Love had nothing to do with it. They were fairly civilized, I dare say. Don't talk rot about civilization to me. Keep to facts. I want her. That's the important thing, and I certainly think I have a right to her. I'm trying to prove it out of her mouth."

"Go ahead, then," I said, not at all proud of my last sally. The man baffled me. He shamed me a little, too. I had a dawning feeling that, perhaps, he might be right — a thousand years hence a more cultured race might consider women in just such a light.

"Sylvia," he said, "when I looked at you, you know that you felt no other man had looked at you in just the same manner."

"I don't know," she said. She was beginning to be frightened. It was touching to see her try to stick to the truth in spite of her fear of what some admission might do to her.

"Oh," he said, "other men have looked at you like starved wolves, or like sick calves, I dare say. But no man ever looked at you as I did that day."

She nodded, speechless, her eyes haunted. This was not the gay Sylvia, bright and impudent as a bird. She raised a hand and pressed a handkerchief against her lips. Over this she stared at Cobalt.

"You felt," he pressed quietly ahead, "that I was in your power?"

"You?" she exclaimed. "I felt that you were in my power?"

"Yes . . . that day," he insisted. Then he raised a finger to caution her. "Remember," he said, "the whole truth, and only that."

"I suppose, in a way . . . I suppose that I felt I had some power over you."

"You had a feeling that you could use that power. You thought of the Lightning Warrior . . ."

"Because of you!" cried the poor girl, and my heart bled for her. "I looked at you . . . and I don't want to be unkind . . . but looking at you made me think . . . I mean, something about your eyes and your face and the wildness of it . . . I don't want to say cruel things!" concluded poor Sylvia.

"Come, come," I said, half under my breath. "This is enough, Cobalt?"

"Enough?" he asked. He turned his head in that quick way of his, and I shrank deeper into my chair and wished myself far away. Cobalt then proceeded: "When you smiled at my offer of the engagement ring, then the thing flashed over you. The sense of your power. The cruel pleasure. You thought of the Lightning Warrior, and you asked for his skin."

"I wasn't thinking!" cried Sylvia.

"You *were* thinking," persisted Cobalt gravely. "You thought in this manner: this brute of a man with all the strength he seems to have, what would become of him, if he were matched with that dog killer, the Lightning Warrior? The two pictures jumped into your mind. The thing came out of your mouth almost without your thinking. You wanted the fight."

"No!" cried Sylvia.

She got up from her chair. So did the three of us.

"Well," said Cobalt, his voice as always even and quiet, "I can't force you to say anything, I can only suggest. When you said it, you had in mind storm,

65

wind, starvation, fighting in the wilderness, all that sort of thing. Am I wrong?"

Sylvia looked at her father, then she looked at me hopelessly. Tears began to run down her face.

"That isn't fair," insisted Cobalt. "You've no right to cry to soften their hearts. Their hearts are like putty so far as you're concerned."

"I'm trying not to cry," Sylvia protested. "I don't want to, and I'm trying not to." She bit her lip. She dabbed at her eyes. She drew in a breath.

"That's better," said Cobalt in his calm way. "That's more honest. There's honesty in you. I'm glad to see that. Now, don't cry any more but tell us the truth. When you asked for the skin of the Lightning Warrior, did you or did you not think of a long, fierce battle?"

"Yes," whispered Sylvia, "I did."

"Sylvia!" interrupted her father, "what are you talking about?"

"And you knew that I would go and do what I could about it?"

"I didn't know," she said and halted.

"Tell us honestly. Did you feel convinced that I would go out and do what I could about it?"

"I wasn't logical," Sylvia confessed with a shaking voice. "I didn't follow things to their ultimate conclusion. But . . . yes, I thought you would do something about it."

"That meant life or death?" he asked her remorselessly.

She only stared. He did not insist on the answer.

"I took it that way," he said. "I jumped into the lion's den, but I'm not going to throw the glove into your face now that I'm out again. I'm going to hold you to your promise."

Sylvia, gazing like one enchanted by horror, backed slowly up until her shoulders were against the wall.

"Don't do that, child," cried out Baird. He went over and put an arm around her. "I'm going to take care of you," he said. "I won't let anything happen to you. Sylvia, look at me. Don't you trust me? I'm not going to let anything happen to you!"

She put a hand up to fend him off. She kept looking in that terrified way at Cobalt. "Don't you see it's no good?" she said rapidly to her father. "You can't help me. Nobody can help me, only myself. I'm alone with him."

I tried to help by saying: "There was no *real* promise, Sylvia."

"Of course, there was no real promise," agreed Baird. "Bless you, Chalmers. You help to bring us back to *terra firma*."

Sylvia shook her head. "Think it over a moment, and then tell me honestly. Tell him, and tell me."

When she said that, I looked toward Cobalt. He did not assume a threatening or a blustering attitude. There was no need of that. He had folded his arms and leaned a shoulder against the wall. He had finished his case, and now he waited for the decision. Realizing that, I cursed the unlucky chance that had brought me into the house this day. I cursed Cobalt as well in the silence of my mind. Why could not

67

one turn to him and say: "Man, you're mad! This thing cannot be!" But there was no use making an appeal to him. Public opinion did not matter to Cobalt.

"I'll tell you," said Baird, breaking in. Then he paused, began to shake his head, and exclaimed at last: "I don't deny the existence of some obligation on your part, some *slight* obligation."

"What sort of an obligation?" inquired Sylvia. "That's what I see myself. But I'm no good to him in a shop window. Don't you see? He wants me in his pocket, as the thief wanted the emerald. Either he takes me as a wife, or else I'm no good to him at all. That's the point. If he has a call upon me, that's what the call amounts to. I can't be one percent wife or a quarter wife, even. I can't be a wife for one day or a week or a month. I've got to step over the threshold. That's what I've got to do." Her voice faltered.

Cobalt said: "You're a good girl, Sylvia. You're such an amazingly good girl that I've almost made up my mind to let you get out from the contract."

"There's no contract," cried Baird. "I don't understand what's happened! Chalmers, because my girl out of excess of spirits . . ."

He saw me shaking my head and stopped there. I answered: "Out of excess of spirits, or however you want to put it, she challenged Cobalt to do an impossible thing. Well, there's the impossible thing accomplished."

I pointed to the white monster in the corner shadow. Baird, with an exclamation, threw up his hands. He was in a state of great excitement. Sylvia went to him and put an arm about him and tried to quiet him. It was charming to see her forget about her own trouble in her sympathy with his.

"Such a thing would never hold in a court of law! Never in the world" insisted Baird. "Any judge or jury would simply laugh at such a claim."

"Well, Father," said Sylvia, "I suppose that a judge would laugh. But we're not judges and juries in a law court, are we?"

I turned to Cobalt. "Cobalt," I said, "there are a thousand appeals that I could make to you. You have some claim, some slight claim on Sylvia. Her exquisite sense of honor admits that claim, as you see. But I don't believe that you'll take the pound of flesh nearest the heart. I see that you were serious, and that you've spent a terrible year in executing your part of the bargain. But look at it the other way. If you insist upon the bargain being fulfilled, you're wrecking her life. I can't believe that you'll do it. I won't believe it. Surrender your claim, Cobalt. You'll have the reward of friendship. Out of that friendship something may come . . . marriage, perhaps, in the end. What would this chains-and-slavery idea of yours amount to compared with Sylvia as a wife who loved you and had chosen you?"

These were not the most eloquent words in the world, but I put a good deal of emotion into them because I felt them to the quick. I could see also that both Baird and Sylvia thought that this was the final appeal. Baird looked at Cobalt with a face of wretched pain and suspense. Sylvia, suddenly weakening, was close in her father's arms, her face against his breast.

How could Cobalt resist the appeal of such a picture? Well, he resisted it well enough. In that casual voice which I was beginning to hate he said: "Friendship ripening into love, and all that rot, eh? Mutual esteem, followed by affection. Is that the new way to sing the old song? Stuff, man, stuff! I'm ashamed to hear you say such things. Sylvia, can you turn around and look me in the eye?"

Turn she did and faced him. She rested against Baird for a support. Her hands clung to his hands. The unfortunate part of it was that he could not be a real help to her.

"Now you tell me," said Cobalt, "married or unmarried, friends or not friends, in a hundred years do you think that you could ever come to love me?"

She looked at him very earnestly. It was a pitiful thing to see her honesty and her fear of him fighting in her face. Then she shook her head. "No," she said, "I don't think that I could."

"Well said!" muttered Cobalt. "There's honesty for you. But you see what remains? She'd never take me for love, but she's made the bargain, and she'll stick to it. Sylvia, when does the wedding take place?"

I could not speak. I was struck dumb. So was poor Baird. From the rolling of his eyes, I thought he was going mad.

"When do you think?" Sylvia asked. "After we're out of Alaska, of course!"

"No," said Cobalt, "right now is the time! You have the Lightning Warrior, haven't you, as sure as cash in the hand?"

CHAPTER
ELEVEN

Wolf Tamer

I had intended to remain in the town for a few days longer, but I would not remain there to see Sylvia Baird led to the slaughter. I went off to the Birch Creek diggings and arrived there to find that Cobalt had arrived before me. When I asked him how the wedding ceremony had gone, he told me that he was not yet married to Sylvia. He was going to spend that season in the mines and try to make what he could. In the winter he would haul Sylvia out overland. That would give her time to adjust her mind to him.

"I hope you're right," I reflected, "and I hope she doesn't run away."

"No. She won't do that," said Cobalt. "I don't think that she'll do that. Do you?"

"Not if she thinks that it's dishonorable."

"And what do you think about it?" he asked me, curious.

It took courage to stand up to Cobalt, but I managed to get my nerve together and say: "I think that anything she does to get away is all right. You've trapped her, Cobalt. It's always fair for the trapped thing to try to get away."

He was not angry, only thoughtful. He went off hanging his head a little on one side, and I saw very little of him during that summer. However, the rumors about him were always afloat. He panned hardly a dollar the first four weeks, and then he got into good pay dirt and made it by the thousands. Yes, I mean by thousands a day. He had nine men working under him. He paid them a full ounce a day, every day, and a short working day at that. Then he gave them double that rate for overtime, and that gang fairly tore up the tundra for their boss. I don't know how much he made altogether, but it was enough, with what he had already saved, to make a tidy fortune back in the States. He would not be rich, but he would be mighty well off.

I asked him one day what had given him his leads and where he had learned prospecting.

He replied: "I never learned anything, Chalmers. I'm stupid about it. I just throw in where other fellows are digging and trust to luck. Well, just now I'm having some luck."

"You've got your luck, and you're turning it into gold, all right."

"I've got my luck," he agreed, "but I'll need the hard cash. What does a good hunter cost?"

"A hunter?" I asked, not following him.

"I mean, a horse, a good hunter. One of the best."

"Anywhere from five hundred to fifty thousand, I suppose. Well, fifteen hundred for a bang-up good horse."

He whistled. "She's going to be expensive," he said. "She wants to hunt. She wants three or four hunters

73

unless I really am generous. Great Scott, what would generous be translated into horseflesh?"

"Oh, some people keep a string of a dozen or more."

He groaned. "She's expensive, all right. But I don't mind that. I want to see her on a horse. She'd look pretty good in the saddle, wouldn't she?"

"She'd be wonderful on the back of a horse."

"She'd be something to look at . . . ," he observed and fell into a day dream about her, so that I forbore talking to him any longer on this occasion.

It was a hard summer for me. The labor was all that I could stand, and the bad food and the worse cooking gradually wore me down. I did not wait for the winter freeze to come with its full force. I packed up and lugged all the way to Circle City a few days before the rush back began.

I arrived in time to see the beginning of the Yukon freeze. One could hear the noise of the ice miles and miles away, like a great and irregular cannonade. When I came up, I found the big yellow flood scumming across with glass in the shallows, and white piles and ruined marble masonry came crashing and heaping upon the sand banks.

I was glad to see the winter beginning. I did not care how much white iron there was on it, for I was tired, very tired. I promised myself, after one more year I could get out of the white North and back to my own land. A whole winter's rest did not seem sufficient to get the ache out of the small of my back. Yet, as a matter of fact, one good sleep was enough to set me up. The very next day I ran into Baird. There was a fine, seasonable sharpness in the air and a whirl of snowflakes which melted out of sight as they touched the ground, but the winter was approaching.

"Coming up this way, all right," I said to Baird.

"Is he?" asked Baird, giving me a wild look. "When does he arrive?"

I examined the man. He was much changed. He had grown thinner during the summer, and his eyes had receded into his head. He had the appearance of one just risen from a sick bed, in fact.

"I meant the winter," I said, frowning at him.

He gasped, only gradually arriving at my meaning. "Yes, yes!" he nodded. "The winter, of course, the winter!"

Off in the distance the ice just then gave a grumble and a grating like a thousand carts unloading in a single instant. Baird jerked about and looked in the direction of the river. I remember how the snow whirled about his head in a sudden flurry just then. He looked as hopeless and desperate as a tame beast in a howling wilderness.

I said: "Look here, Baird, what's the matter with you?"

"What's the matter with me? Why, nothing's the matter with me," he answered.

He began to look away from me, but I tapped him on the shoulder.

"How's Sylvia?" I asked him.

"Well, she's alive," he answered. "Why do you ask about Sylvia? How do you expect her to be?"

I disregarded his testiness. He was sick either in body or mind, perhaps in both. Certainly he could not be worried about his business. He had ripped a big fortune out of the earth and was still ripping it. Sylvia must be his worry, and Sylvia alone.

At last I said: "Baird, don't talk like a sulky baby. Be a man."

"Ah!" he said, "you can talk. You have no children!"

"You're wrong," I said. "I have two of 'em back home."

This appeared to be a startling revelation to him. He caught me by the arm and looked searchingly at me. "You have two children back home, and yet you're up here? You've got a wife and a pair of youngsters, and yet you are up here?" He spoke in a most excited tone.

"In one more season I'll have enough piled up," I answered. "At least, that's what I'm betting. Then I go back."

He paid no attention to this last answer. He exclaimed merely: "If you have children, you can understand. You can understand how a man's heart can be broken, I mean."

"Is your heart breaking about Sylvia?" I asked him. Then: "Yes . . . I suppose it is."

"Come home with me. I want you to see her. You have to see her in order to understand."

"I don't want to see her," I answered. "I don't want to understand, either. I'll tell you what, Baird . . . I'm sorry, but I don't want to have anything to do with you and Sylvia and Cobalt. I don't want to think about it, even. It makes me too sick."

He looked somberly at me, half occupied with his own misery. "Well, you'll come home with me, all right," he persisted. "I want to ask you a question."

"Ask it here in the street. I'm ready."

"You can't answer it till you've seen Sylvia."

"I don't want to see Sylvia. Is she taking it hard? . . . don't answer that either! Good bye."

I tried to get away from him, but I could not. He held me as the ancient mariner held the wedding guest. He simply took me by the arm.

"Come along," he said. "We're just wasting time standing around here."

He must have seen the surrender in my face long before. Now I gave up, muttering and mumbling in vain protest, and walked beside him to the house. When we were near to the house, I heard Sylvia's violin.

"That's good," I said. "That shows that she's keeping her spirits up, all right."

"Does it?" asked Baird despondently.

He knocked at the door. There was a scratching of feet inside, then the horrible, throat-tearing snarl of a wolf inside.

"Who is it?" called Sylvia.

"Great Scott, man," I said, "don't tell me that Sylvia's in the same room with the Lightning Warrior, and the beast on the loose?"

He shrugged his shoulders. "You'll see," was all he said. Then: "It's I, Sylvia. I've got Chalmers here with me."

"Oh, that's good," she returned. "Wait till I get King by the scruff of his neck. Now it's all right. Come on in, Dad!"

He turned around and gave me a good, long look, then he pushed up on tiptoes, I stopped so short. There was the Lightning Warrior, do you see, looking bigger and fiercer than ever, and the only thing that kept him from jumping at my throat was the little, childish hand of Sylvia which held him by a bit of the mane. He snarled again.

"Idiot!" said Sylvia, and with her other hand she aimed to slap him lightly between the eyes, just where the brow of a lobo wrinkles with such deep wisdom. "Idiot," she repeated once she had struck that terrible head.

The Lightning Warrior stopped growling and licked her hand. He gave her a furtive, upward glance of deepest love and then once more turned the full weight of his hostile attention toward me.

"Come in," invited Sylvia. "Come right in and don't worry about him. Only, don't touch him. That's all."

"I won't touch him," I assured her. "I don't need the warning."

I squeezed against the wall, trying to keep my distance as I edged through the door. That wolf looked to me like naked lightning about to strike, and there was only the restraining touch of that young woman to keep him quiet.

"That's what I wanted you to see," said Baird. "That's why I wanted you to come home with me, old fellow."

CHAPTER
TWELVE

Getting in Deep

It was worth a long trip, of course, just to see the way that *loup-garou* had been tamed by the girl. It seemed to me that there was no trace of red about the eyes, and that the very iris of the eyes was a darker, deeper blue now. He had become the very shadow of Sylvia Baird, so moving that his head was always under her hand. Nevertheless, it was not to see the wolf that Baird had brought me. He had carried me home so that I could see Sylvia herself.

I've said that Baird was much changed, but his alteration was as nothing compared with the new look of his daughter. Poor Sylvia! The joy and the sting had gone out of her. She was as white and still as a cut flower, and sometimes in talking the blank expression accompanying a far-off vision crossed her eyes. Yet her courage kept her head high. As I looked at her, I cursed Cobalt, then Baird for persuading me to come to the house, then myself for having been such a gull as to be dragged along. I had known that there would be nothing but pain inside those walls, and I was right. There was only one pleasant subject apparently, and you may be sure that I jumped at that and clung to it.

"How in the world did you do it, Sylvia? It's a miracle. That white fiend! I still can't believe it. He's dangerous. He'll get you one day when your back is turned."

"No. He won't attack her," said Baird. "She's turned her back on him a thousand times."

"Tell me, Sylvia," I insisted. "Tell me exactly what happened."

"I don't know," she replied. "We had him there in the back yard for a week or so, held by a regular horse chain, and he spent half his time trying to tear out the staple that held the chain and the other half would be grinding away at it until you could hear the sound of his teeth on the steel links all through the house. It put my nerves on edge, and so I decided to stop it. I went out and took off his collar."

"Hold on," I said. "Then he must have had a chance to slash you."

"Well, he had a chance, but he didn't."

"Go on, Sylvia," urged her father. "You never told me just what you did. Go on and tell us exactly."

"Why, I did nothing. I just unbuckled the collar."

"Didn't he attempt to tear your throat?" I asked her.

"He looked as though he would, for a minute."

"And then?"

"When I got my hand on the collar, he seemed to realize in a way that I was there to help him and not to make him more miserable."

I did not need to close my eyes in order to see that picture of the girl leaning over the fighting head of the Lightning Warrior. I could hear the vibration of his snarling and see the demon in his eyes. What had made her do it? And what silken tissue of mental power had kept the big wolf in restraint during that instant? No one who loved life would have taken such a chance. In fact, she must have hardly cared whether she fell to Cobalt or to the teeth of the wolf. So, even by way of the pleasanter topic of the wolf, I was forced back again to the thought of Cobalt. He filled the whole mental horizon in that house.

We had some tea with brandy in it, Russian style, and Sylvia sat up as bold as you please and told me the town chatter — how many log rafts had come down the river in the last month, how the Pickering boys had brought down the biggest raft ever seen only to have it swept on a swift current past the city. It went to pieces, and their summer's work went out to sea to make driftwood another day for the fires of the Eskimos. That was the summer when Judge Colfax was killed by Sidney Rice, and she told about that, while I watched her in pain and admiration, hearing little of her words but seeing her effort, most of all when she forced herself to smile.

When she got up to bring more hot water for the tea, I turned to Baird and abused him to his face. "You couldn't keep it to yourself, could you?" I said. "You had to invite me in so that I can have bad dreams the rest of my life, too. Confound you, Baird, if you want to keep her out of the hands of Cobalt, it's your own business. Go ahead with it. But it's rotten to drag me in here. Poor Sylvia! What a brick she is!"

81

Baird sighed. "She's not a brick. She's an angel. She's all blue and gold as a cloud. I love her. You love her. Everybody loves her. But she goes to Cobalt!" He bowed his head. There was no doubt that his hair had turned quite a bit grayer during the summer. "There'll be children, too," he went on bitterly. "More of the wolf breed, the wolf strain. Chalmers, tell me what I'm to do about it?"

"That's enough. Another word, and I leave the house. Don't you try to drag me into the business!"

"Ah, man," said poor Baird, "don't talk to me like that. You know that you were in on it the day the hand was dealt all around. You were here. You helped to make the decision. Now, you can't dodge that. Dig down into your deepest pocket, and for Sylvia's sake tell me what I'm to do!"

I fell into a perspiration, but just then Sylvia came back, carrying the pot of steaming water and with the head of the great wolf just under her hand. After she'd refilled our cups, she sat down, with one arm around the shoulders of the huge fellow. When she was sitting beside him, his head was almost on a level with hers.

"He's crazy about you, Sylvia," I observed. "I can see that. You make a grand picture there, my dear, with that cannibal beside you."

"Do I?" queried Sylvia, scratching the wisdom wrinkle between his eyes until he turned his great head and looked fixedly in adoration at her.

"Was it this way from the start?" I asked. "From the minute that you leaned over him, like a suicide, and took his collar off?"

When I said that about suicide, I kept a straight eye on her and had my reward. For her head tipped up suddenly, and she gave me a frightened glance. I had been right in my guess. It was as if she had tried a revolver that day, and the gun had misfired. I grew a little sick. I thought of that delicate body lying still and the crimson welling at the throat. I had to shrug my shoulders and so bring myself back to common sense and the things of the day.

She went on to explain: "He kept slinking away and snarling when I came near. But every day I spent a long time in the yard. Perhaps he got used to me. Then there was a time when I came up behind him as he was snapping at a bone. He whirled about, snapped at me, and got my arm in his mouth. He seemed to remember while his teeth were in the air, as it were, and he didn't even break the skin. He just held onto my arm, and his eyes were on fire, let me tell you. He sort of dared me to budge, and you can bet that I didn't stir. I just talked to him until he got quieter. He let go my arm and licked my hand."

"I wish I had seen that," I said. "You're a brave girl, Sylvia."

"Look, look!" scoffed Sylvia. "He's admiring my self portrait. Now, don't you be so silly."

"You *are* a brave girl," I insisted, "and now, by heaven, something is going to be done!"

She just rubbed the head of the Lightning Warrior and looked thoughtfully at me. At last she began to shake her head. "What could be done?"

"We'll cut and run for it," I suggested.

"I've thought of the same thing," put in Baird.

"You bet you've thought of it," I told him bitterly. "You just wanted me to bolster up your courage a little. Well, I forgive you. Sylvia, we've got enough time. Cobalt won't be in from the creek for a week. We'll make tracks. There's going to be snow by tomorrow morning. Listen to that wind! You feel the fingertips of it beginning to poke under the door and through the cracks? Yes, there'll be plenty of snow in the morning, and we'll get out and travel. That's settled."

The girl only wagged her lovely head at me, without a smile, without a gleam. "You know what would happen?" she asked.

"Well, what would happen?"

"He'd catch us. He might not hurt Dad very much, but he'd kill you, Tom Chalmers. He'd kill you as sure as sin. You know it, too."

I didn't need to have her say so. Of course, he would kill me, but I said: "Oh, don't you be so sure. After all, guns are guns and bullets don't pick and choose."

"I'm not so sure," she said. "I don't think that a bullet would choose Cobalt."

"Why not?" I asked her. I was curious to hear her explanation for such a belief.

"I'll tell you why. I think that a bullet won't stop him until he's done some other things that he's meant to do," she said.

"Oh," I responded, "you're feeling fatalistic about him, are you?"

"Yes, I am. Aren't you?" she queried.

"If I hear his name again, I won't sleep all night," said her father.

"You bet you won't," I said. "You're going to sit up all night anyway, while we plan things and get our outfit together. It won't be the easiest thing in the world to get out tomorrow morning, making as late a start as this."

"Do you mean that you'd go through with it?" asked Baird.

"Wait, wait!" cried the girl. "It won't do. You're both quite mad. He'd overtake us so easily, and then what would we do? Even if you're mad enough to try the thing, I wouldn't go along. Not I! I wouldn't let Tom Chalmers be thrown away. Father, what in the world are you thinking of? I'm going to get us some more brandy. You wild people really need another drink."

When she was out of the room, the white ghost stalking beside her, I leaned a bit toward her father and the thing I did not want to say but had to finally came out: "She won't go peaceably, so we'll kidnap her, man. We'll take her along by force!"

CHAPTER
THIRTEEN

A Screecher

Like some animal that hears the clang of the trap and the bite of its teeth at the same instant, I realized that I was caught in the thing for good and all. Baird would hold me to it. I could see that by the joy in his face, but we could not talk any longer as Sylvia came back at that instant. We pretended to have dropped the matter, persuaded by her, but afterward, when I left the house, Baird found an excuse for going along with me. He was frightened and excited, and the moment we were outside, bending our heads against the wind, he shouted to know whether or not I had been in earnest. I told him that I was, so we went down to the saloon and found a quiet corner for talking.

It was a dreary day and a dreary place. The bartender kept shrugging his shoulders to work his coat collar higher up around his neck. He kept glancing up too, as though he feared that the storm would slice off the room — all the beams were groaning with the weight of the wind. In fact, winter was on top of us in a stride, and the windows were plastered white with frost and snow. And winter meant the beginning of the long, cold silence in Circle City. The howl of the wind and the thunder of the ice jamming in the river simply were the last guns of the summer.

Sitting there in the corner, we made our plans. We were like two helpless, hopeless children trying to act in a lost cause. Baird was white and did not get his color back. I felt a hollowness in the pit of my stomach and could guess that I was as white as my companion. He began on an unexpected key, asking me how big a pile I wanted to make before I went back home. I told him that I aimed at eighty thousand. It was not a great fortune, but in those days it meant a good deal. A man could sit back pretty comfortably. He wanted to know how much of it I had stacked up, and I told him that I had raked in nearly fifty-five thousand dollars altogether.

"If you leave now, you cut yourself short," he said.

"I'll come back in for another season," I told him. "I'll be glad to get back to see the family. The kids are growing up. I'm hungry to have a look at them."

Baird was a good fellow. He grinned a little at me and shook his head. "Look here, Chalmers, this thing you're going to do for me . . . why, money wouldn't pay for it. I know that. But you'll let me make up the difference between what you have and what you want to have? I'll be glad to give you that twenty-five thousand at the end of the trail out."

I couldn't take his money. He insisted that it was not hire. "Compensation" was what he called it. Otherwise, he couldn't let me go along. We had quite an argument, but in the end I had it my way. I really felt that money did not much matter. To me it appeared that I had about one chance in five of getting through alive. As a matter of fact, as it turned out my chances were a good deal less than that, and frankly I would never have undertaken the job if I had dreamed of what lay before me.

When the money matter was put aside, we got down to our actual plans. Jack Silver had five good dogs for sale, and I would pick up three more. Eight made a long string, and we would load three sleds with nothing but food and the lightest sort of camp equipment. The girl was a good hand on snowshoes, he told me, but it probably would be necessary to let her ride a part of every day if we wanted to stretch some long marches behind us. I made a list of everything. There would be no trouble in getting what we wanted, though the prices would be high now that the last steamer had come up the river for the season.

Then Baird stood up, ready to go home, and shook hands with me with tears in his eyes. "We'll carry our rifles, at least," he said.

I looked back at him and understood what he meant.

"We'll carry one rifle, at least."

"You'll come at midnight?"

"I'll come before that a little, if I can. Can you handle Sylvia?"

"I can handle her. I'll simply pick her up in my arms and carry her out, if I have to."

"Suppose that she squeals?"

"She won't squeal. Well, she might. I'll keep a hand over her mouth. Don't worry about Sylvia. She's only a child. I can handle her all right."

We had both left out one detail. It wasn't a small thing either, but it must appear in its due place. He went home, and I started to collect the outfit.

I shall never forget how my heart failed me when I saw the things gathered into a heap on the floor of the store. It was the sight of the snowshoes that upset me more than anything else, for I could not look at the infernal things without thinking of the hundreds of miles of slogging we would have to cover with those clumsy instruments of torture lashed onto our wet, freezing feet.

When everything had been gathered, I left the outfit of eight dogs with Jack Silver. It was a good lot of animals. I've seen plenty of Huskies that looked heavier and more fit to lug burdens, but these fellows were rangy and looked fit for speed dragging a light load. Jack Silver swore that his lot were all flyers; and I had selected the other three to suit.

Then I went to get supper, and I laid in a good meal. It seemed that I could never get enough, when I looked forward to the long monotony of bacon grease and the flour and tea that lay ahead of us. The wind was still howling like an evil spirit, nudging the building with a solid shoulder and seeming to shake the ground. I sat in a corner chair, smoked a pipe, and then slept soundly in the chair for about an hour.

When I awoke, it was close to half past eleven. The saloon was empty, and the bartender was sitting beside the stove, biting his lips while he read in a time-yellowed newspaper the description of a prize fight. He only grunted at me when I got up and went out. I looked over his shoulder and saw a picture of the two fighters, looking white and naked under the glare of electric lights, with the shadowy ropes fencing them into the pen.

That was the picture that I had in mind as I passed outside, and it seemed to me that the thing was appropriate. I was going into a ring against Cobalt. I was stepping out of my class. The one comfort was the size of the arena. Outside in the dark, I hung onto the wall for a moment and practiced breathing. There was so much edge to that wind, and the snow kept flying so thick and fast along it that I was half choked, but I got my bearings.

It's an odd thing that a man will go through almost anything if he's ever experienced it before. If I had not marched on worse nights than that one, I would have said, offhand, that no human being could face such a wind. Now I plowed ahead through snow and wind and got to the loaded sleds and the dog team, with Jack Silver sitting on the forward sled, asleep.

I woke him up. He cursed me for being late, but I gave him a little money extra above our agreement, and he counted it and stopped grunting. He helped me break out the sleds, one by one. It was a tough job, not that the runners had frozen in very solidly, or that the sleds were heavily loaded, but the team did not pull together. Even Jack's five dogs did not seem to know what it was all about.

We got them going at last, and I steered for the house of Baird. When I drew up in front of it, I whistled twice. Then I waited. I began to hope that the screeching of the wind would drown the noise of the signal. I began to tell myself that if Baird did not hear that first signal, I would not whistle again. Then, like something on the stage, the door of the house opened with a bang and out came Baird with the girl in his arms. He had promised to stifle her with one hand if she cried out. He had promised to handle her easily, because she was still a child to him. Well, she was young enough and slender enough but, when I saw her at that moment, she was all arms and legs, kicking in every direction and screeching like a Scotch bagpipe with never a stop for breathing.

It shocked me. I thought she must be out of her mind and ran to help Baird. He was cursing and groaning, trying to handle her, but she was fighting like an eel. So I took a big bandanna out of my pocket and put it around her head and over her mouth and gave it a good screw at the back of her head. I was rougher than necessary, but I was pretty angry. I had begun to think of myself as quite the hero, quite the dauntless and self-sacrificing fellow. To have Sylvia spoil my little act with this squealing upset me.

I said at her ear: "Now quit it, Sylvia. Don't be a little fool. Quit it, and I'll stop choking you. Nod your head if you'll promise to come along peaceably and stop the yipping."

She nodded. I took the handkerchief away from her mouth. She turned about and caught me by the elbows. "Tom!" she said, "if you force the thing through, there'll be a frightful tragedy. You don't think about it now, but I can see what will happen. I dreamed it this

91

night. I dreamed that we were on the march and out of the white behind us a speck loomed, and we tried to go faster, but we couldn't. We ran, but it did no good, and the speck got bigger and bigger, and it was Cobalt. We knew him in the distance by the way that he was running. He came up to you, Tom. Do you hear? He took you with his hands. He seemed to break you."

The storm blew the last words far away and thin.

"If he kills you, Dad and I will be the murderers!" she shouted through the wind.

"Dreams go by opposites," was all I could think of, like a fool. Then I asked her: "Will you go quietly?"

"I've told you that I will, if you insist, Tom. Dad, it's only fair that we should leave Tom out of it. We can leave together, but don't drag poor Tom into it."

"You come back into the house if you're over your screeching fit," said her father, "and tie on the snowshoes."

CHAPTER
FOURTEEN

Ruling Wolfish Passion

How easily a man grows irritated! I loved the girl for wanting to leave me out of the dangerous business. I almost hated poor Baird for overruling her so abruptly. Together they went back into the house but returned after some moments. Baird now carried a considerable bundle of additional clothing and odds and ends for Sylvia's comfort. She came along without resistance as she had promised to come but, when she came near to me, I saw that she was crying. Tears, however, don't mean a great deal at such a time. They're only an extra depressant.

I got the team started after some trouble, and I ran ahead to break trail for them through the fluff of the newly fallen snow, while Baird took the gee pole. I led straight out from Circle City through a white fog in which no one could see us and in which we would have looked like phantoms more than realities if we had been seen. So we headed up the country paralleling the river at a short distance inland.

No matter whether a fellow is undertaking a possibility or an impossibility, it makes the heart rise to stop struggling with the mind and to begin working with the muscles. So I felt a great deal better as we went striding along, and I told myself no matter what he might be, Cobalt was not a bird. He could not skim the ground. He would have to walk over it, just as we were doing.

I comforted myself in other ways as well, recalling that the greatest horse in the world is only a half second faster in the mile perhaps than twenty others. The winner of any race, as a rule, is not a great distance ahead of the last trailer. We now had a good advantage. It would probably not be until after this storm that the miners came in from the creek. Their progress would be slow. It would not be until Circle City was reached that Cobalt would learn that the three of us were no longer in town. If he could overtake us after that, more power to him. Gritting my teeth, I vowed that that would never be.

Progress through the soft snow was not easy. Sometimes we hit bare rocks. Sometimes we skittered through feathery drifts. We got on. I remembered, for the thousandth time, what an iron-hard, half-breed 'puncher once said to me: "The man who makes the long march is the man who keeps his legs moving a long time every day." I believe it is true. On the trail across the White Horse and up through the lakes, I've seen the splendid athlete beaten and exhausted because every day he was aware of his own speed and tried to make the most of it, while little, skinny, narrow-chested clerks kept on with the uncaptained host because they were accustomed to mental pain, mental plodding — and this is easily translated into snowshoe work.

We went on for two hours. I continued to break trail when we had an odd interruption. I heard a wolf's howl behind us. It was repeated nearer at hand. It came again, close upon us, and suddenly I looked back and saw the Lightning Warrior coming through the dimness. When he reached the girl, he bounded around her like a playful puppy — multiplied by a hundred! — and then he started forward for the dogs. Sylvia stopped him, just as the whole string of the dogs turned about and went for the big brute. They intended to mob him, but he had not the slightest intention of budging in spite of their numbers.

He stood with his head high, ready to strike and jump this way and that. I never saw anything more splendidly fit and ready for trouble. Then the running dogs reached the limit of the traces and the lines and tumbled into a twisted, confused mass. They began to fight with one another, and it was half an hour before I could get them straightened out, Baird helping. We both were bitten once or twice during the mix-up, but luckily the wounds were only surface scratches.

The Lightning Warrior — or King, as Sylvia now preferred to call him — had been left behind and a note to a neighbor asked him to feed the brute. Some instinct must have told King that his mistress was leaving, and in a desperate manner he had managed to scale the lofty fence of the yard and get away, a thing he had never succeeded in doing when he was first captured, even after he had been unchained. He complicated our task. There would be his big mouth to feed from the food reserved for the dogs. There would be his saber teeth to keep from the throats of the team also. But now that we had started, it was impossible to go clear back with him. Sylvia took charge. He walked along at her side the rest of that march. When she was fagged and had to ride, he went close beside her, snarling at the sled which carried her and sniffing at the load on which she was lying.

Taking turns in breaking trail, an exhausting business on account of the snow, Baird and I kept on until we were done in, and the dogs wavered against their collars. Then we made camp in the brush, and I was delighted to see Sylvia make herself useful. Baird and I put up the tent, which had a small partition in it so that he and I could occupy one section and Sylvia the other. We unharnessed the dogs. Sylvia in the meantime took the hand axe and cut down wood in the most business-like manner and then took the cooking in hand. She filled the kettle with snow which would melt into water for the tea, and at the same time on top of the little, flimsy stove she started bacon frying in the skillet. When it was fried, she took the grease and poured it into a hole made in the top of a sack of flour. In the same hole salt and baking powder already had been mixed with the flour, and now the mass of grease dough was kneaded and divided into three flapjacks. That's what the Northerners called them, but there is no real name for their indigestibility and toughness. She made two of a size and a smaller one for herself. The flapjacks, bacon, and tea made up our meal and, now that the frozen fish had been thawed, the dogs ate and watched as they turned about in the snow to make themselves beds.

We consumed every crumb of the food, making an odd picture, crouched there like beasts over our provisions. Behind us, right in the entrance to Sylvia's section of the tent, was the Lightning Warrior, watching. The fish I had thrown to him he left untouched with a regal indifference, but he quickly accepted it in one gulp from the hand of the girl.

And Sylvia herself? She was always a surprise to me. She never ceased being a surprise. She looked half child and half angel, but she was always turning out a real woman, with tough muscles and plenty of common sense. Now that she had been dragged into this flight, she bent every energy toward making a success of it. She kept her spirits high. She had a special smile for each of us. When at last we turned into our sleeping bags, my mind was full of thoughts of her.

Another thing that occupied my attention was the strangeness of the entire business and the singular linking of the parts together until the final picture of danger was complete. These parts were Cobalt, first of all, and then Sylvia, elements totally without danger if other things had not been added. Then came the Lightning Warrior and, by accident or through perverse inspiration, this was drawn into the chosen circle. From the Lightning Warrior came the real danger, the real climax. Finally, nothing would have been done about it except that Baird and I at last tried to change the course of probable events — and that's why we were upon the march and Cobalt, like an invisible thunderstorm, was off there in the far distance.

Somehow it seemed to me that even Cobalt was not the most significant part of the picture. It was upon the Lightning Warrior that my mind rested most as the pivotal point of the adventure. Nothing could exceed the unreality of having him lying there in the entrance of the little tent on guard. The only way to parallel it was to go back to the *Arabian Nights* in which the power of a ring induces an evil spirit to become the slave of a mere weak human. But there was magic in the power of Sylvia also. It was in her courage, her gentle voice, and the greatness of her love.

I fell asleep literally — I fell, that is to say, into a region of abysmal turmoil, strange images, unrest — only to find Baird tapping my shoulder in the morning and telling me that it was time to get under way. We cooked breakfast and started to harness up after eating. Then we found the first real touch of tragedy. One of the dogs was missing.

We kicked around in the snow until Baird uncovered the body. The beast was dead. Its throat was cleanly cut, as if by a pair of knives. We turned back. King was watching us with an air of splendid detachment, but we well knew what had happened. The sight of the dogs had been too much for him, and he had tried his old handicraft. Baird, without a word, got the rifle, loaded it, and took a bead, but Sylvia knocked up his hand.

"He's only started," warned Baird. "He'll never rest until he's butchered them all. We can get on with one dog the less. But, with two gone, we're handicapped, with three gone, we're fairly hamstrung. Stand away, Sylvia. You go forward and we'll catch up with you. It's a dirty business, but there's one thing certain, that it has to be done for the sake of our hides!"

She stood squarely in front of him. She called and King came close up beside her, so that her hand rested on his head. "You can't do it," said the girl. "You don't understand, Father. I don't know how to explain. He gave him to me without a mark on him, no wound from a knife, or a bullet, or a trap's teeth. You can't touch him. Nobody has a right to touch him, except Cobalt."

"Sylvia," said her father, "I don't like to hear you talk like this. It sounds as if you've lost your wits. What sort of a mystery is in your head?"

"Mind you," she said, "there's nothing but the most terrible sort of harm would come of it. It's wrong. It's a sin to hurt him. He doesn't know right from wrong, except as a wolf. To kill dogs is good in a wolf's consciousness. A man conquered him and dragged him back among men. Then he found me and got to love me. Now, Dad, you see how it is. Or don't you?"

"You're talking sentimental rot, Sylvia," said Baird.

I thought so, too, but she was entirely serious.

"Let me try to tell you," she went on. "It's a ghostly feeling that I have about it. Right or wrong, we all want to get away from Cobalt. It's life or death. Well, I have a feeling that King is a sort of talisman for us. Cobalt conquered him in one way. We've conquered him in another way. Don't you see that? If we can keep King what he's been made, I think somehow that Cobalt will never catch us!"

CHAPTER
FIFTEEN

The Ice Trail

Now having put down the words just as she spoke them, I am rather confused. They seem ridiculous but, as she spoke them with a troubled eye and a great deal of conviction, I know that they gave pause to both Baird and me. One can't help superstitions in the great Northland. The fear of space cuts at one's soul like a wind of ice. God is in the light and Satan is in the shadow that walks at one's heels. That's the way one is likely to feel up there. Baird and I were helpless the moment she told us that she felt the Lightning Warrior was the talisman through which we might beat Cobalt in the end. Besides, we could not help feeling some essential mystery in that big white killer.

"He might be some good if he could step into the traces of the dog we've lost. Do you realize that he's killed our very best leader?" asked Baird.

"Then I'll take him up there and try him in the harness," replied Sylvia.

She did it. We started off that morning with me breaking trail, Sylvia behind me, stepping in my tracks and improving the trail, too. Behind her came the Lightning Warrior. He hated the dog harness that was on him with a shuddering hatred. He had even bared his fangs at Sylvia when she put it on him, but he made no violent resistance. Once in the harness, he was worth any two dogs I have ever seen. There was no fatigue in him. His muscles were built up from ranging a hundred miles a day through the snows. His spirit was stronger than spring steel and, when Sylvia got a bit ahead of him now and then, he seemed to pull all the three sleds with his unaided might in order to get to her. I've heard of a dog pulling a thousand pounds. If that is possible, then King could have done more, much more. For whatever a dog could do, he could do it just that much better.

We felt the difference when Sylvia was tired out and could not shuffle a step forward on her snowshoes. Then King had to be taken from the harness and put back with Sylvia on the rear sled, while the second leader took the place of the wolf. What a change in our way of going! It seemed as though half of our motive power had been snatched away. With that white monster out there in front, we were a part of the landscape. When he was gone, we were simply lost in it in the most amazingly sudden way. Our team seemed to limp uncertainly along. The joy was snatched from our progress.

Later on, when Sylvia was sufficiently rested, we put King again in the lead. I watched the team, and I could see the change. They moved differently. Each straightened out head and tail and pulled as though trying to get its teeth into the animal just ahead. They seemed to know King. They feared him. They acted as though they would have liked to sink their teeth in him while his back was turned.

It was not my idea alone. Baird noticed it also, when he was behind and I was breaking trail, and he could not help muttering to me that there seemed to be something in what Sylvia said — our chances of escape were linked with King. "As if," concluded Baird, "he knows that Cobalt is behind us, and he doesn't want that human wolf to overtake us."

This was going a bit far. I could not reduce the thing to words as exact as these, but I know that from this day we all shared Sylvia's conviction that our luck was wrapped up in the wolf. He was our charm, and a dangerous charm at that.

Winter never closed in more rapidly or with a more iron hand. The temperature dropped, day and dark, and the snow seemed always falling. That was because the wind picked up the dry flakes and whirled them. Then came cold so intense that the wind was shut away behind an invisible wall of ice. In my beard and in Baird's the moisture of our breathing turned to ice. We became like men with faces of stone with our heads always oddly nodding as we trudged along. When at last the wind was still, we found ourselves in a white world. The trees were piled with it, the branches sagging. The brush along the river banks was rimmed with crystal frost until it looked like an imitation in glass.

We were on the river now. It made the better road. Later on the ice would be smoother perhaps, but still it was an easier, a more graded way, even though we occasionally found the ice blocks scattered in heaps, like the ruins of a primitive fortress. We kept to the graded river way, and at night we pulled up a bank and camped where there was plenty of wood. Our spirits were so relieved in time that we could even talk about Cobalt.

My idea was that he was a good fellow with wild impulses which were stronger than he could handle. "I'll tell you what," I remember saying one evening as we drank the third or fourth cup of tea, "Cobalt is like the fellows in the circus who span four horses with their spread legs and ride them around the race course. All right on a circus race track. All right with circus horses on a circus track, but it wouldn't do for pitching broncos. Not a bit! The rider would get a tumble, and the mustangs would eat him likely, instead of grass. They'd prefer him, probably . . . some of the mustangs I've seen on the range. Cobalt is like that. I mean, he's straddling emotions which the rest of us don't feel. You feel kindness and anger and hatred and joy, and all that. So do I. But we're not like Cobalt. Everything is multiplied in him."

"You're wrong," said Baird. "He's simply not a man. He's a wolf. That's what he is. When I see a wolf, I think of him. This white *loup-garou* . . . I get chills simply looking at him because he reminds me of Cobalt."

I turned to Sylvia. She was sipping her tea with a mild, thoughtful look.

"Tell me your idea, my dear," I said.

She seemed a bit startled to be drawn into the conversation. As though she had heard us only dimly, she recollected for a moment, and then she answered: "Well, I don't know exactly. You can't put a whole man into just words, I suppose, but I'd say that Cobalt is different because he's natural. He doesn't care."

"What do you mean by natural?" asked her father. "And doesn't care?"

"The way animals are natural. Not even wild Indians are natural the way Cobalt is."

"Go on, explain!" we asked her. "Indians are pretty free."

We were both interested. She seemed to have the finger of her mind upon some real idea, and our curiosity was aroused.

"Well," she said, "Indians have taboos. Things they mustn't touch, mustn't do. Then again, there are a lot of ceremonials they submit to. Ceremonial dances, I mean, before they go to war, magic the medicine men preside over. In a way, the Indian's hands are tied almost as badly as a white man's, but there's nothing to tie Cobalt. He doesn't believe in anything. He's an absolutely free soul."

"It's true!" cried Baird, thumping his fist on his knee. "He believes in nothing. That's why he's strong. He has the strength of the evil one because he is a demon. He's free, just as Satan is free. That's your idea, isn't it, Sylvia? It's mine, too."

104

"Well," she said, "did you ever hear of Cobalt cheating, or taking advantage of a weaker man, or failing to do his share on a march? Aren't there twenty stories of how he's carried the other fellow's pack for days at a time?"

"To show off his strength?" countered Baird, rather weakly I thought.

"You can't just call it that," said Sylvia.

I agreed with her.

"Go on, then," urged her father. "Tell me more about it. I want all of your idea."

"It's simply that he's neither good nor bad. He's not between, either," she said, frowning as she dug further into her own thought. "He has nothing to do with good or bad. He does what pleases him. Most of us live almost entirely under the thumb of public opinion of one sort or another, but Cobalt doesn't. He lives inside his own conceptions. He goes for what he wants. He lets the chips fall where they may. Think of murder. It curdles the blood of most people but, if Cobalt found a man really in his way, he'd kill that man just as quickly as King would kill one of the sled dogs."

Suddenly she stopped talking and looked across at me. I knew what she was thinking, and my blood curdled because I was most certainly in the way of that terrible fellow. Our conversation ended for the evening abruptly at that point. And I had dreams again when I went to sleep.

The next day we were cheered again by a splendid march. The only depressing thing was the howling of wolves in the woods along the banks. Sometimes we had glimpses of them big, strapping lobos with high shoulders and bellies tucked up with famine, though I don't know why they should have been so hunger-ridden at this season of the year. However, there they were, following us, winding in and out through the shrubbery.

Baird was so annoyed by them that he got out the rifle and raised it, but the wolves had vanished before he could get in a shot. Five minutes later they were once more paralleling our course, and we could hear their melancholy howling. Poor Sylvia was in a panic and feared that they would rush our camp. We laughed at her for having such thoughts.

"How many ordinary wolves would King dispose of in five seconds?" I asked her.

We found a good camping place at the end of that march and ate an extra lot because the going had been rather rough. On the river ice, the cold was bitter beyond belief. The freezing trees kept popping just like cannon in the distant woods.

Then we turned in, and the sweet poison of sleep was getting into my brain when all at once I heard wolves yelling, and the next moment there was a hurricane of sound right about our ears. Our tent was knocked flat by heavy, leaping bodies, and we heard snarlings, yellings, and growlings.

When I managed to get clear of the tent canvas, the mischief was over. Baird, with the rifle, had scattered the wolves with a single shot, but the villains got off after doing their work. Every one of the dogs of our fine team was dead. In that single moment of attack the work was completed, and the only toll the wolves paid was right in front of our tent, where white King stood with a crimson front, disdaining the two limp forms in the snow before him. He had broken their necks for them.

CHAPTER
SIXTEEN

The New Team

The extent of that disaster was so great that no one of us spoke about it as a misfortune. Only to be mutely aware of it was enough. We merely ate our breakfast in silence and prepared for the day's march.

This was our position. We were half way from Circle City to Skagway, our destination. We had four hundred miles of bitter weather, ice, and snow before us, and we were stripped of our freight team which had hauled our food and shelter. Our provisions were laid in with the thought of completing the trip by dog team. The added length of time it would take to trudge it on foot, dragging the sleds by sheer, wretched man power, appalled us.

Yet, as I said before, none of us spoke about the calamity. We met the disaster by splitting the necessary load of equipment and food into two equal portions. These halves we put upon two of the sleds. The third sled we would abandon. When we had arranged the burdens, we then wondered how we should apportion the tractive power. The Lightning Warrior would have to be used, but he would only work under the hand and the voice of the girl. If he and she worked together at one sled, then it seemed right that Baird and I should take a considerably increased portion upon the sled to which we hitched ourselves.

We were about to remake the loads when the girl suddenly and firmly protested. She said that she and the wolf, she thought, could outpull us anyway in the course of a day's march and make trail as well! We smiled at one another, a little grimly because smiles came hard that day, but we agreed to let her try to execute her vain little flourish. Only Baird and I, of course, struck out ahead to make trail.

It was a melancholy day. Under the dim sky the wind was moaning, and it came at us aslant, like the line of a swooping hawk, a continual sleet, iron-hard when it struck and burning with cold. The dark of the storm clouds blackened still further the twilight of that winter sky. They seemed to brush just above the touch of our fingertips. We rarely looked up. Luckily the wind was not full in our faces and therefore, by putting down our heads and covering our faces as completely as possible, we could keep going. Even so, every moment there would be a numbness of ears or nose or cheek that warned us to rub the spot vigorously in order to prevent frostbite.

We went for a quarter of a mile, and I suggested that we had better tell the girl that she need not keep on with her share of the contract. We would remove a portion of the weightiest goods to our man-drawn sled. Baird told me that she was a stubborn minx, and that she had better receive a thorough lesson while we were about it. So we actually kept going for a full two miles, and still she was close up behind us.

We turned to survey this miracle. For the pulling had been hard, the ice gripping at the runners where there was no snow, and where the snow lay it meant difficult tramping to break the trail. However, there she was behind us, swaying a little at the end of the pull rope, so that it was easy to tell that she was giving her strength to the work. I was greatly touched by the sight of her laboring in this fashion. She looked like a child in that man's costume.

"Poor girl!" I said to Baird.

He snapped back at me: "We'll start out with no pity on this journey, or else we'll very shortly begin to pity ourselves, and that's ruin."

There was a deal of obvious truth in this, and I did not answer, for now the rear sled came up with us. I expected that poor Sylvia would drop down in her sled dead beat, after she had pulled so far, but to my amazement she turned out with King and circled around us, taking the lead. As she went by she called to us: "Catch me if you can!"

What a sight that was for us, that lovely face and that good cheer breaking through like a brilliant sunshine upon us. She seemed to me a very human and delightful little saint.

"Look," I said, astonished. "The girl's not even panting."

"The wolf, the wolf!" cried Baird hastily. "Look at that beast and the way he pulls. He's got the tractive power of a horse."

110

He actually seemed to have — three feet pressing ice or snow and thrusting back, while the fourth foot, before or behind, shifted quickly forward for a fresh grip. A casual glance at him seemed to show him simply leaning forward. A dog that can pull in this fashion is worth two of even bigger size and power. The steady lugger is what one wants for the wheel or sled dog. It appeared to me a miracle that the Lightning Warrior should have been willing to cast aside his freedom and toil like one who loves slavery. But some dogs love to work for work's sake, and it seemed that this wild-caught peregrine of the North had the same spirit — at least while his mistress was close to him, pulling at the same sled.

Sylvia took the lead from us, and all through that day's march she maintained her place with ease. The trail was broken, and the pace set by that child and the Lightning Warrior. The girl had been toughened by the first marches, and she had a dancer's talent in learning the proper step and cadence for the snowshoe work. It's hardly truthful, I suppose, to say that she danced along through the day, but that's the only explanation I can give of her power. Many a girl will dance an athlete off his feet. So it seemed that Sylvia could do with the snowshoes. I don't imagine that she was pulling a very great part of the weight, but she kept her line taut and was always contributing something to the total traction. So she set the pace for us, and we accomplished a good march, considering the conditions.

In the end we had our reward. For the wind fell, the air cleared, and in comparative brightness we made our camp in a cluster of good-size trees. I think that Sylvia was less exhausted than her father and I. At least she was able to smile and find some small thing to laugh about, and she taunted us too for not having overtaken her. King, she announced, was worth a whole team of ordinary dogs, and to this we were both inclined to agree.

One day after another we slogged along on the trail, and it was Sylvia's good spirits more than food that sustained us. She seemed made of iron actually. She was throwing herself into that competition against two men with all the will in the world. When we camped, her delightful voice scattered the blue demons that attend a camp of melancholy silence.

A storm caught us on the broad breast of Lake Labarge just as we were making good progress over the ice and promising ourselves that the end of the journey was not far off. The wind came in a hurricane, heavy with snow and sleet, and whipped us in a pelting run to find shelter at the margin of the ice sheet. Behind the first low promontory we crouched, with the force of the wind broken a little and a chance to breathe and rest. Through the brush we looked out at the milky exhalations of the snowstorm, whirling into great forms, dissolving, reforming again.

It was bitterly cold. Our feet were wet and threatening to freeze if we remained long inactive, and Baird suggested that we work farther back into the woods and make a fire in the first shelter so that we could dry out our things. A low cry from Sylvia stopped him. She was pointing out into the heart of the open storm and, as she pointed, she crouched lower.

We stared in the direction indicated and, as we stared, we saw a rift in the flying sleet and snow and through the rift four dogs hauling head down in front of a sled, and at the gee pole of the sled strode the driver. How could we recognize a man at a distance and in that dim light? It was a very simple matter. People on snowshoes move most variously. I've said that Sylvia seemed to be dancing along on them, there was such grace and rhythm in her step. This fellow strode like a machine of inexhaustible power. No one whoever had seen him on the march could have forgotten that step and that carriage. Besides, his whole silhouette differed. Just as one can tell by outline whether it is a fox, a coyote, or a wolf that is standing on the rim of the distant hill, so we could tell, of all the world of men, this could be no other than Cobalt! What other man, in fact, would have been able to make dogs face such a wind? What other man would have been willing to put his face against such a storm? It was Cobalt, yonder, passing us as if in the dimness of a dream.

We shrank down to the ice and lay still. Only after a long moment did we breathe freely again and, when I saw the face of the girl, she looked as though she had just awakened from a nightmare. So felt we all, I know, by consulting my own heart.

"By right," said Sylvia slowly, "I should have gone out to him."

"By right," answered her father savagely, "you shouldn't be a fool, my dear."

Nevertheless, this remark of hers gave him something to think about. He talked it over with me later on at the end of that day's work when, the storm having cleared, we camped. We agreed that Sylvia, if her chance was fair, would still feel herself impelled by a sense of duty to go to Cobalt and take the consequences. There was only one thing to do, and that was to push ahead and trust to the blind luck which had helped us so far on the march. It might be that Cobalt had gone for the Chilkoot, to cross down to Dyea. It might be that he was to take our way over the longer White Horse. However, both of these places were close together. A canoe would fetch him around the point that separated them, and he could make inquiries on both sides. Then he would wait for us, but where?

Perhaps he would guess Dyea. Then he might be there as we slipped down into Skagway and, getting into Skagway, we might find a ship ready to sail and so leave him behind us. But only for the time. We could not really trust that such a man as Cobalt would be thrown off the trail so easily. He would be certain to follow in the next steamer any ship we departed in, then he would pick up our trail from the first port and follow us on land. Well, that horror was postponed at least and, once back in the true realm of law and order, we could hope that a power even greater than his own would take him in hand.

CHAPTER
SEVENTEEN

Shelter at Last

When we came through the pass down to Skagway and the gray ocean lay level before us, we fell to laughing and shouting and flopping about on our snowshoes in a ridiculous way. The very feeling of the air was different, and the wind that blew into us from over the inlet and the great Pacific beyond was warm to us, so warm in comparison with the freezing weather of the great inland plateau that we wanted to get into lighter clothing at once. You may believe that we came down the last slopes with a will. When we got into the little town, we stared at the buildings as though each were the face of a friend. They seemed like flesh and spirit and kindliness, though as a matter of fact kindliness was rather at a premium in Skagway as we were soon to learn.

At that time of year it was a fair day in Skagway. The wind had blown warm for some time, the snow had grown soft, and the street we went down was a bog of mud. We had to abandon the sleds and take what little we needed from the loads upon our backs in hastily made packs. But we minded neither the burden on our shoulders nor the mud through which we were sloshing. We were near the end of the journey, and our spirits were so high that we hardly cared whether we met with Cobalt or not. We had pushed through to a decision — that only was important.

We got to a hotel. You might rather call it a caravansary, or one-night tavern. At any rate there was shelter over our heads, food to be had, food cooked by hands other than our own, and no more of the piercing cold blasts of the wind. Only a few chill drafts slid under badly fitted doors or through cracks in walls and touched us in the feet or the small of the back. I verily believe that such drafts cause a thousandfold more deaths than the fierce, open attack of the storms upon the vast, frozen tundra. At that moment we saw nothing evil. Everything was indeed good to us.

Our first inquiry was about Cobalt.

"Has Cobalt come in?" I asked.

The proprietor of the hotel was one of those men who always seem to be dressed in the clothes of five years before, so that they are swelling out of the old pattern. He had a double chin, a dark look, and a half-smoked cigar stuck in a corner of his mouth. That part of the mouth never stirred when he spoke. But he did not need to use it. There was plenty of lip yardage remaining. The cigar looked to me as though it might be a relic from the party of the night before.

"Has Cobalt come in?" I said to this red-eyed hulk in his bulging coat and collarless shirt.

He was looking at Sylvia as I spoke. No man could help looking at Sylvia and, with the wolf alongside, she was something to stop the heart. The monster had no eye for anything but her apparently, and yet no one was deceived. Every man in the room knew dogs, I suppose, in a big or a little way, and every man was intent on the points of this giant, yet no one came near.

Instead of answering me, the proprietor said: "Is that an all-white Newfoundland?"

"I guess that's what it is," I said. "Has Cobalt come in?"

"Come where?" he said without looking at me.

"To town . . . to Skagway," I said. "This is Skagway, I take it?" For he irritated me, the fat-faced beast, slowly getting a new lip hold on the foul-smelling cigar butt.

"Yeah!" he said, hardly hearing me. "And Cobalt. Who's Cobalt, buddy?"

I was staggered, not at all by his insolence, since men grow accustomed to the most brutal discourtesy in the wilderness of the North, but because I saw that he was not affecting this ignorance. He really did not know the name of Cobalt. He never had heard of the man before this moment! I was properly shocked, for in the Northern camps Cobalt was such a familiar name in the most casual conversation that one could hardly get through the evening without some reference to him. Dogs and weather and even gold hardly got more attention than Cobalt. But here I had returned to a part of the world where Cobalt was not known.

Not entirely unknown, of course, but Skagway had grown. People were coming in from the outside in numbers, and there is nothing like a cheechako for

117

ignorance in all things wherein he should be the most concerned. I went back to Baird with my information.

"He never heard of Cobalt," I said.

Baird shook his head. "He's lying. Nobody this far north can grow up without knowing something about Cobalt. He's lying. He looks like a liar."

"He looks like anything you want to call him," I returned, "but he doesn't know Cobalt. He was telling the truth. We'll have to ask somebody else. In the meantime get some rooms. You get the rooms, and I'll go out and circulate a little."

Baird looked me up and down critically. "Are you packing a gun, Tom?"

"I don't want a gun," I told him, and I meant it. For, if I met with Cobalt, no skill of mine could save me. He was far too fast and accurate with shooting irons.

We got a room for Sylvia and another for her father and me. While he arranged the packs and had the luxury of a bath and a shave, I went out with my trail beard still on my face and tried to hunt up information about Cobalt. I went into the first saloon. It was a big affair and worked up a good deal — for that far north. It had some long mirrors behind the bar and gilded lamps, and there were gaming tables covered with green felt. I gave that felt a good long look until I saw how the nap was worn and knew that a lot of money was trotted out on those green lawns from time to time. It excited me a deal. Wherever there is heavy gambling, there is likely to be danger in the air, and the look of that saloon already was hostile enough, though only a few fellows were sitting in at a poker game in a corner of the gaming room.

The bartender had a decent look, from a distance, and I decided that I would try to pump him. When I got closer to him, however, I saw that my first flash had been all wrong. He was blond and slender and small, with a retreating chin and a buck-toothed grin that flashed like a silver dollar in the sun. As I approached him, I could see why they trusted that bar to his keeping even in Skagway. He kept right on smiling, but his eye was as cold as a gray January morning.

I ordered a drink and offered him one himself. He thanked me and poured half a thimbleful of liquor into the bottom of his glass. I had not opened the door of his confidence by buying that drink. I could have bought a barrel full of whiskey without buying his confidence because there was no confidence in him.

"Is Cobalt in town?" I asked him.

"Cobalt who?" said the bartender. "Or what Cobalt?"

I looked hard at him, but I saw that he meant what he said. They didn't know Cobalt in Skagway.

"If he comes in," I could not help saying, "you'll learn a lot about Cobalt on the jump. That's all!"

I was ready to turn away when the barkeep reached over the bar and touched me on the arm. "What's all this play about Cobalt, brother?" he said.

"I asked you about the toughest man in Alaska," I said, "and you ask me right back for his front name. I tell you, there's no other name for him. What's the matter with you? You look normal, but to hear you talk

119

a fellow would think that you never knew anything but newspapers."

He listened to this little denunciation with quite an air of interest. He glanced me over in a casual way, very much as though he were saying: *Shall I rap this loon over the head or not?*

"This Cobalt," he said, "must be quite a card."

"He's not a card. He's a whole deck," I said.

"What's his specialty?" asked the barkeep.

"Bending iron bars into hairpins," I said.

"Oh, one of these strong men, is he?" That tough youth yawned at me.

"Yes, he's one of these strong men," I said. "With a slap of his open hand he breaks your jaw, and he smashes the wrist of the gunman just with his grip."

"Tut, tut," said the bartender, "does his mamma know about these things?"

"You're hard-boiled, my boy," I said, "but, when Cobalt arrives, you'll be able to tell what's in the can by the label on it."

"Pineapple," guessed the barkeep.

He amused me. He was as calm and as cool as iced tea. He kept that buck-toothed smile flashing at me all the time until I was afraid that he would cut the corners of his mouth. "Well," I said, "I'm not his press agent."

"I was just wondering," said the barkeep.

At this I laughed openly and loudly. This bartender, boy though he was, was so entirely and perfectly tough from rind to core that he tickled something in me.

"What's the matter?" he asked.

"Hay fever," I said. "It just comes on me now and then."

His eye grew more friendly. For the first time a wrinkle or two came beside it. He seemed to be almost amused.

"Tell me one thing," I said.

"Mostly they don't ask for it like you do," he replied.

"What I want is information."

"Lay out your goods, brother. I gotta take something home for little Minnie."

"I guessed by your kind eye that you had children at home."

"You guessed wrong. Minnie's a cross-eyed cat that I'm trying to get straight."

I laughed in my turn. "Here's my question. What's Skagway? I've been here before. But what's Skagway now?"

CHAPTER
EIGHTEEN

Tommy's Age

The barkeep ran a finger inside the collar of his shirt and looked me up and down. He seemed so little interested that I should not have been surprised to see him turn away from me, but he did not turn away. He decided that he would answer. Without a movement of the head, without a gesture, he fixed his fishy eyes on me and said: "Over there at the table, that's Skagway."

I looked them over. It was the table of poker players of which I have spoken. There was a bearded man just off the trail apparently, sitting deeply in his chair with a gloomy, bulldog look. There was a tall man, thin as a knife blade, with hands that moved so fast they blurred the eye. There was a chap with angling eyebrows. He kept his head down most of the time, and he had a way of looking up from under the brows like a Mephistopheles. The fourth man looked like a pig, not the domestic kind, but a wild boar whose fat was ninety percent muscle. The fifth had a bald head, a black beard, and a white face. He might have been a minister, he kept his head so high and his eyes so low.

"You mean the preacher yonder?" I asked.

"What makes you think so?"

"Because he's ten years younger than he looks."

"Well, that's Soapy Jones. That's Skagway, too, as you can take for granted."

"I've been inside for a long time," I answered. "Perhaps I'm out of date."

My friend drummed on the edge of the bar with light, rapid fingers. "Have a drink on me and tell me how you learned to keep your face."

"I mean it," I said earnestly. "I haven't seen many newspapers."

"You're asking me for a lot of faith, brother, but I'll tell you something. When they go out walking in Skagway, they leave their pokes at home."

"Thanks," I said. "I begin to understand. He's not alone . . . Soapy?"

"No, he's got a full deck."

I went back to the hotel and found the Lightning Warrior and Baird in Sylvia's room. I sat down and talked things over with them.

"Skagway is wide open," I told them, "and the chief thing inside is a fellow named Soapy Jones. He works with a big gang, and he runs the town. He's the big boy here. I can't get any information about Cobalt. It may be that he is here now, lying low and waiting for us. It may be that he's at Dyea. It may be that he's already gone on to Vancouver or San Francisco to meet us at the dock. Any of those things may have happened. In the meantime we'd better lie low in our turn and wait for the boat. This ought to keep us amused."

I pointed toward the wolf. My move was a little too sudden, and he flashed from his corner half way across the room to meet my gesture. He made not a sound, but the silent beast was ready to leap at my throat. Sylvia spoke one word, and he sank at her feet, but he still kept those wicked blue eyes fixed on me.

I went downstairs, got some hot water in a kettle, and a big laundry tub. Then I went back to my room, shaved, stripped, and gave myself a bath. It had to be a scrub, I can tell you. When I finished scrubbing and rinsing, I felt lighter, and I looked lighter. I stared at myself in a small, cracked mirror that hung on the wall, and I saw that I wore a mask of tan that covered my forehead, eyes, nose, and cheekbones. But all the lower part of my face was white as could be. That was the effect of the beard which had grown out upon the long trail. That mask of tan had a strange effect. It really gave me the look of a robber, and this amused me so much that I laughed a little out loud. I was neither very big, very strong, nor very bold, but the white and the tan made me seem a fairly dangerous fellow.

When I joined Sylvia and Baird for a meal a little later, they both laughed at me. The Lightning Warrior merely snarled. Sylvia put down her hand and slapped him until he was silent, but he kept on watching me. I never had manhandled him or even given him bad language, but he had built up a growing hatred for me during the outward march. The beast was human in his sympathies and antipathies.

124

What a meal we had! Not that Skagway offered much beyond meat and coffee, but the coffee was a change from tea. It tasted like nectar to us all, and we finished off with plum jam in quantities on fresh baker's bread. Afterward we sat around for a while, Baird and I smoking. Sylvia came out of her dreams to talk a bit. She began to put questions to me.

"Tell me, Tom, why you never talk about yourself?"

"Oh, I talk enough," I said.

"I mean about your past life."

"Well, on the inside, a man's a bore if he begins to talk about his home."

"I used to talk about mine," she said.

"You're different, Sylvia. You could talk about anything," I assured her.

She shook her head at the compliment. "I used to talk about everything, from the pet canaries to my poor old pinto, Jerry, and the story of Champ Allison at the rodeo and everything."

"You could tell them all over again, and I'd sit as still as a mouse eating bread and butter and listen. Start now, and I'll prove it."

"Tom, do you think that I'm such a baby?"

"You're not a baby, Sylvia. You're a great big grown-up woman. That's what you are."

Baird laughed a little. Then he got behind a newspaper he had bought and began to grunt and cluck from time to time with surprise and interest as he read the items. It left Sylvia and me alone, and I stood up.

"If you'll excuse me, Sylvia," I said, "I'm going to go up and take a nap."

125

"You sit down again, Tom," she commanded. "You can't run away now. I've got you safely here. This isn't inside. This is outside. And you're not sleepy. You're only nervous. That's why you want to get away."

I sat down again gingerly. "Oh, what's the matter, Sylvia?" I queried. "I won't be able to tell you as much as the back page of that newspaper."

She looked at me. I began to feel worried and cornered.

"Everybody else used to talk to me," she said, "but you always dodged. Why do you dodge, Tom? Have you got a black spot?"

"You can call it that." I would have agreed to anything to avoid argument.

That girl had the most impish persistence. She looked over calmly. The assurance of a pretty girl is an amazing thing. "How old are you, Tom?"

"I'm middle-aged, my dear."

"Fortyish or fiftyish?"

"Oh, fortyish, around about."

"Mostly around, and not about. Why won't you tell me? I'll tell you my age."

"I know."

"What am I, then?"

"Eighteen, last summer."

"Humph. No wonder you talk to me like a baby. I'm twenty-two."

"Stuff!"

"Ask Dad if I'm not. Dad, how old am I?"

"How should I know?" responded Baird, involved in finding the continuation of a long article.

126

Sylvia frowned, then she smiled. "Well, I'm nearly twenty-one, anyway. Now you tell me how old you are, Tom."

"I'm going to get out of this."

"You sit where you are. If you get up and go, I'll tag along."

"Oh, leave Tommy alone," growled Baird. "Leave him alone, can't you? You're a torment, Sylvia."

"I'm not flirting with Mister Chalmers. He's forty-something. I don't flirt with middle-aged men."

"Hum!" said Baird, looking over the edge of his paper at her with a scowl. "You don't, don't you? Since when, please? You'd flirt with Father Time. You make me a little tired, Sylvia. Stop the nonsense and run along."

"Will you run with me, Tommy?" Sylvia suggested.

"Confound it, Sylvia," I said, "what's the matter with you? Can't you leave me alone?"

"Isn't it undignified . . . to call you Tommy? Is that why you're angry?"

"I'm not angry."

"Yes, you are. You said 'Confound it!' and you frowned at me."

"I'll say worse than that. Leave me alone, Sylvia. You're a young demon, and I won't let you make a fool out of me."

"I don't know what you're talking about. I only asked you how old you are."

"Well, I've told you."

"You haven't at all. Let me guess."

"I can't keep you from it."

"You're twenty-seven," she said, after thinking for a moment.

I pushed my chair back a little. "Great Scott, my dear, where's your sense of humor? Twenty-seven? With a growing family? Well, well!"

I grew rather hot, but Sylvia did not mind in the least.

"You may be a bit older than that. But not more than thirty, I know."

"The deuce you do. I'm not thirty, eh? And you're sure, are you?"

"I can always tell."

"Perfect rot. How could you tell?"

"Oh, by a certain sign . . . it never fails."

"What sign? I never heard of such nonsense!" I was getting still hotter at the way she sat back, assured and certain.

"By the wrinkles around the eyes. You haven't any, hardly. You're not more than twenty-eight . . . about."

I banged my fist on my knee. "I tell you what, you bright young thing. I'm thirty-two years and three months and four days old. There you are with your infallible signs!"

She leaned forward with a little gesture of interest and compassion. "Oh, Tommy, are you only thirty-two? Are you really only thirty-two, poor fellow?"

CHAPTER
NINETEEN

Sylvia at Work

When I saw how neatly she had trapped me, I grew hotter than ever in the face. Baird noticed the moment of silence and glanced at me.

"What's the matter now?" he asked. "Are you two fighting?"

"She's got a long way past that," I answered. "She's started pitying me."

"Look out for her," said Baird, yawning, and went back to his paper.

"I'm not pitying you," protested Sylvia. "I mean I'm only being sorry that you've had so much pain."

"I really wish you'd stop, Sylvia. I'm a little tired of it."

"I know. People don't like to talk about sorrow and all that. I didn't mean to intrude on you, Tommy. I do humbly beg your pardon. Tell me that you're not offended?"

"I'm not offended, and you don't have to be so starry eyed about it. Do your rehearsing with somebody else, will you? I'm too old to enjoy the sport."

"Don't you know, Tommy, that a girl much prefers an older man, somebody that's stable, with greater experience and knowledge of life? Don't you really know that, you strange fellow?"

"You treacherous little cat. You mouse eater, you! Take your claws away from me."

Sylvia leaned back in her chair, sighed, and shook her head. "Oh, Tommy," she murmured, "you don't understand me a bit!"

"Only a few footnotes," I admitted. "The text is in a foreign language. I'm not a scholar in your sense of the word, Sylvia. Not a bit."

Baird stood up. "I'm going out to have a look around," he said.

"I'll go with you," I proposed.

"I don't want to be left here all alone," said Sylvia.

"Then you come along," said Baird.

"I'm too tired. I'm worn out. Are you going to leave me Tommy? Please!"

"Oh, plague take it. I suppose I'll stay."

Baird grinned down at her with a wise and understanding twinkle in his eyes. "You watch her, Tom," he warned. "She's poison, slow but sure."

"What a way to talk!" said Sylvia.

Baird went out the door, turning up the collar of his coat, and tucking the newspaper under his arm.

"The thing to do," I said, "is not to march aboard the boat when it comes in. He might be watching. We can take a canoe and go on board after it's started south and then . . ."

She broke in on me dreamily. "How old are your two children, Tommy?"

130

"Oh, let me see. Seven and five. Why? I was saying about the boat that . . . ," I started off again.

"Seven and five! That's a charming time. It's the boy who's seven?"

"No, it's the girl."

"That's a pity. Girls need older brothers."

"She's an independent youngster."

"What's her name?"

"Celia."

"That's a charming name. And the little boy?"

"Bill."

"I'll bet he's a man!"

"He's kind of cross-eyed."

"Which is their mother's favorite?"

I looked at her for a moment before I answered, gathering myself a little. "Their mother died when Bill was born," I told her at last.

Her face puckered up with pain. Then, suddenly realizing why I had wished to avoid this conversation, she caught her hands together with a faint cry.

"It's all right," I assured her. "I don't mind. I ought to talk about her. It does me good."

"Oh, Tommy, why should life have hurt you like that?"

"A harmless little fellow like me?"

"She meant a frightful lot to you? Her name was Celia also?"

"Yes. She was one of the best. She was about the best."

"Was she a lovely girl, Tommy?"

"No, not lovely. She could have done with a little more nose and a little less mouth. But her heart was right. She never yipped during the pinch of the hard times."

"That's why you're up here, Tommy . . . to try to get for the youngsters what their mother never had?"

"In a general way."

"But you've chucked that in order to help me. That's what you've done!"

"Don't be silly. I've got a pretty good stake now. Close to sixty thousand. I know some range land I want. Thirty thousand will get me the grazing land. I know where it's cheap. The rest goes into a shack and barns, horses and cows. You know? A small beginning and a lot of hard work but youngsters turn out well in a life like that."

"Is that your ambition?" she asked dreamily.

"Yes. To develop my own strain of tough ranch stock, horses and cows. To have my brand known. To spread the elbows of my outfit on the range. To make a garden. Improve the house. See the kids grow up, wild but straight. That's about my whole ambition. You see, I'm a simple fellow, Sylvia. I'm not one to set the world on fire or take it by the hair of the head."

I was amazed to see moisture in her eyes. "I'd better go upstairs and leave you. I'm going to be crying over you in another minute."

"Great Scott, Sylvia, what's the matter? Are you pitying a poor fellow who can be contented with a few acres of bare range land and a few cows bawling on them on a winter's day? Yes, you're pitying me. You're thinking of something else."

"You tell me what I'm thinking of." She put her head on one side, not archly but in grave thought, with her eyes almost closed, so that the blue of them was lost and there was only the black shadow of the lashes curving.

I said: "You're thinking of Fifth Avenue shops and houses that have Persian rugs on the floor, the real quill, and country houses with hunters in the pasture, and ocean liners to link you up with Nice and Seville and Oxford, and all that."

"Look, Tommy . . ." She pushed back the hair from her temple and let me see the beginning of a white scar. She raised her sleeves, and I saw another cut on her arm, the white sign of it.

"That top one is where a mustang's shoe grazed me. The one on the arm I got from a mesquite thorn, going lickety split . . . you know how!"

"I know how!" I agreed. "By jiminy, Sylvia, I never thought of you as a ranch girl, but you'd make something to fill the eye, all right. I'd like to see you ride over the rim of the world."

"Where's the rim of that old world?" she asked, smiling at me and wrinkling her eyes a little.

"Right on the land I'm going to buy. That's why I'm going to buy it, because it's the top rim of the world. You'd look grand riding over the eyebrow of Talking Mountain."

"Look, Tommy, you know what I can do?"

"Plenty, but go on. You tell me."

133

"I can ride. I can ride 'em straight up. And I can fan 'em, too."

"Aw, go on. You can land on your head, too."

"You bet I can, and you bet I have. I'm not bragging, but don't you go thinking that I'm so *crêpe de Chine*."

"I saw you on the march. You're tough enough, all right."

"Go on and laugh at me, but you said that I'd tie up with Nice and Seville and Oxford. What would I want to be doing in Oxford? Feeding the swans in the gardens? I'd rather be out daubing a rope on a yearling."

"Go on! You couldn't daub a rope."

"Couldn't I just?" She crowed with indignant protest. "I could go and daub a rope right with you, Tom Chalmers, I'll bet."

"I'm not much, but I've got a big brother that can do a day's work, all right."

All at once she leaned back in her chair and began to chuckle. It began away back in her throat, and it just bubbled and bubbled.

"Why, Tommy, you're not so serious after all. You're fun!"

"Don't stop laughing, Sylvia. You look great. I like to see you laugh with me or at me. When I get Talking Mountain, you come and we'll have that ride. You can daub that old rope, too. I'll bet you throw it underhand, like any Mexican."

"And overhand," she said with pride. Then she grew serious. "But don't you be sidetracked. You hold out for Talking Mountain. You keep heading that way."

"Do you think I may be sidetracked?"

She sat very still, her chin on her brown fist, and studied me. Her eyes were as blue as one of those little mountain lakes that drink up the whole sky in an acre of water. "Oh, I'm afraid you've been sidetracked a good many times."

"Yes," I admitted, "I've always been beaten. I've always been a bust."

"Because you've tied to the wrong people!"

"Except one."

"I wish I had known her. I would have loved her. It makes me pretty sick at heart when I think of you, Tommy, up here in the North and the two youngsters down there."

"I left them pretty well heeled."

"I don't mean that, but all they're missing, and all you're missing . . ."

Baird came in then and stood over us. "Has she been working on you all this time, Tom?" he asked.

"Yes," I said. "I'm a little dizzy, but I feel like a new man now. What have you seen?"

"I've seen him," said Baird.

CHAPTER
TWENTY

Prodding a Memory

I thought Baird was joking because of the casual way in which he had first spoken but, when I looked up to him, I saw the pupils of his eyes staring as though he had just come in out of pitchy darkness. He was thoroughly wrought up, and he showed it. Sylvia and I stood up.

We huddled off upstairs to the room which belonged to Baird and to me, and there we sat in a mute and wretched conference. Baird told how he had seen a crowd of a dozen men just landed from Dyea, and among them he recognized the head, the shoulders, and the springing step of Cobalt. He drew back into the mouth of a small alley and watched the group go by. It was Cobalt beyond a doubt. He had seen his face.

When we heard this story, we sat for another long moment in silence. I remember that the Lightning Warrior chose this instant to stand up, stretch, and yawn, and then couch himself again at the feet of the girl. He seemed to know something keenly affecting her was under consideration.

"Well," I said at last bitterly, "all that we can do is to lie low."

"He's sure to find us out," said Sylvia sensibly. "In a town of this size, every coming and going is pretty well noted."

This was plain.

"This end of the town will get to know Cobalt for the first time," I reflected. "The next time I ask about him, they'll recognize the name at least. I suppose that's only a pale consolation, but I'd like to see him in action against some of the thugs of Soapy Jones. He'll break up a few of them like kindling wood."

"Soapy Jones? Soapy Jones?" murmured Baird. He fell into deep meditation. "I've heard of him before."

"Of course you have. Tom told us about him when he came in this morning," Sylvia put in.

"I've heard of him before that," said Baird. "I heard of him in Spokane one winter, if I'm not mistaken. I'm curious to find out . . . I'm going to find out now!" He got out of his chair.

"What are you going to find out?" we asked him.

"Well, you'll see. Maybe there's a way out for us after all."

He seemed excited and very keen. We let him go without further protest and since what he did that day was important — so important that all that followed hinged upon it — it will be best to follow his steps to discover, as we discovered later, what he did.

He went straight down to the saloon in which I had seen Soapy and the four men who were playing poker. The place was nearly empty now. Soapy and the rest of the poker players were out of sight. Only two lumbermen were off at an end of the bar, bending over their drinks and talking mournfully of the good days in the great logging camps and lamenting this miserable North country.

Baird beckoned the bartender down to the place where he stood, and he looked into the pale-gray eyes of the little man. "I want to see Soapy Jones."

"Do you?" replied the barkeep. "Wait a minute." He felt in one pocket and then in another. "I don't seem to have him about me. I must have left him at home on the shelf."

I can imagine how he would have said all that, and the sneering, steady way in which he would look into the eyes of poor Baird. The latter was stumped.

"Hold on a minute," he said. "Could you send a message to him for me?"

"I dunno," said the barkeep, beginning to polish the bar with a soiled towel. "We don't keep many messenger boys around here. What sort of a message?"

"Five words."

"What are the words?"

"These: 'Do you remember Digger Merchant?' "

The barkeep considered for a moment. "I don't know you," he said then.

"He does, I think," assured Baird.

The little man made up his mind. He called to one of the lumbermen: "Buck!"

"Well?" answered Buck.

"Go find Soapy and tell him that there's a man here asking: 'Do you remember Digger Merchant?' "

"What's a digger merchant?" asked Buck, looking for the point of the joke with a scowl.

"Never mind about that," insisted the barkeep. "You hop and find Soapy and tell him what I've told you. If anybody starts following you when you're on the way, come right back here." He looked darkly at Baird as he said this.

The other lumberman showed signs of wishing to be friendly, but Baird retired to a corner to wait. He sat there for a full hour. The time of good business arrived. Another barman joined him of the buck teeth. A crowd began to seep in. New lamps were lighted. All at once there was the reek of cheap whiskey in the air. The floor and the ceiling were sweating with moisture. Around the big stove in the center of the room men were standing to dry themselves or for sheer need of warmth. Baird stuck in his cold, dim corner and waited. He stared continually through the wraiths of tobacco smoke expecting each minute to see the celebrated Soapy.

Someone stood suddenly beside his chair. "Who are you?" asked a voice.

Baird looked up at a long black beard and a bald head, curiously pale and polished. He rose. "My name is Baird. Are you Soapy Jones?"

"I'm Soapy Jones," said the ministerial presence. "What is this about Digger Merchant?"

"You wouldn't remember me. I don't remember your face, either. You weren't wearing that beard when I last saw you."

"Where was I?"

"You were lying in the middle of the road with four bullet holes in you. You were sopping with blood. That was four miles from Spokane."

Soapy Jones looked at the other intently. He wound his long white fingers into the black of his curling beard and hung the weight of his arm upon it.

"Come along with me. We'll talk," Soapy said.

He led Baird into the rear of the saloon. There he unlocked a door and admitted him into a small room, a mere closet, for there was only one window, very small and close to the ceiling. A screen hanging in front of this aperture prevented any eye from looking in from the outside. In the closet there were two chairs and nothing else by way of furniture.

"Now we can talk," said Soapy. "Sit down."

He took one chair. Baird accepted the other. Both of their faces were in shadow from the light of the lantern which was bracketed against one wall. Only a high light gleamed steadily upon the bald head of Soapy.

How many other men had sat in this room with the gangster? — wondered Baird. He began to grow a little nervous for the eye of Soapy would never let him go.

"When you saw me lying there in the road, as you say," Soapy took up the conversation, "what did you do?"

"I got you into the back of the buckboard I was driving and headed for town as fast as I could drive. You were bleeding to death."

"Go on." The eyes of Soapy were eyes unchanging as he listened.

"After I'd gone half a mile," continued Baird, "I decided that the blood was running out of you too fast. You wouldn't last until we reached a doctor. So I stopped and got off your clothes. I cut them away for the sake of speed. I used your clothes to tie up the wounds."

"Where were they?"

"Two through the body. One looked as though it went straight through your lungs. But you were not choking with blood. Two more were through the right thigh, and the thigh bone was broken. I put a tourniquet above the wound in the leg. That stopped the bleeding. Then I covered you with the buggy rug and went on. I got you to a doctor on the edge of town."

"Go on," Soapy urged again.

"That's all. I left you there and went on. I had important business ahead of me."

"You could have heard of all this," said Soapy.

"Yes. Perhaps I could."

"What you say is not worth anything. You could have heard it all."

"I'll give you proof. One bullet had cut through your wallet. Cut through it at the lower edge. The wallet was sopping with blood."

"You could have heard about that, too."

"Yes, I could have heard about that, I suppose, but I didn't. I saw it."

"Were there any initials on that wallet?"

"There were."

"What were they?"

141

"I don't remember."

"The first question I ask you, and you don't know the answer."

"No, I don't remember the initials. One of them had been clipped off by a bullet."

"You remember that, do you?"

"Yes. It was the middle initial."

Soapy Jones turned his eyes up to the ceiling in thought. "I think you're straight," he said at last. "Now what do you want out of me?"

Not a word of gratitude, mind you. The man was as practical as a banker.

"I want help," answered Baird.

Soapy waved his hand. "Of course you do. What kind of help?"

"A kind that will cost a lot of trouble."

"Partner," said Soapy Jones, without the slightest warmth in his voice, "I've never had a chum, but I've never let a friend down, and I've never let an enemy off. I'm logical, and I'm logical now. You can have anything that belongs to me, from my gun to my wallet. You have the cards. Deal any sort of a hand that you think fit . . . and you can pick them off the bottom."

CHAPTER
TWENTY-ONE

This is Friendship

The unmoved, the indifferent manner of Soapy Jones when he made these large proffers was what convinced my friend, Baird, that there was something in him that might be trusted. He thanked Soapy. The latter merely shrugged his shoulders, as though all he offered should really be taken for granted in the normal course of events.

Baird said: "What I'm going to ask you to do is probably harder than anything you've ever undertaken before."

Soapy merely smiled. He never appeared weary, and he never appeared excited. Except that his eyes were dark, they were something like Cobalt's, bright and steady.

"There's a man in this town named Cobalt."

"I've heard of him," Soapy said. "He's usually inside. He's a hard nut. I've heard something about him. He breaks men up when he gets into a fight. Is that the one?"

"That's the one."

"Well, he won't break me up."

"I would like to have Cobalt kept in hand for two days until the next steamer sails south. Do you think you could manage that?"

"I'll manage it so that he'll lose all interest in sailings south or north."

"I don't want him harmed. Rather than that, I'll ask you not to bother about him."

"I see what you are. You're one of the kind that wants to sell a horse and ride him, too." Soapy said this without a sneer. He was merely and calmly placing Baird in a category.

"No matter what you think about me," responded Baird, "I wouldn't have a hair of his head harmed."

"He might lose a little hide. What about that?"

"He can't be handled easily. I know that. Only, there must be no real physical damage done to him. Otherwise the thing's not to be considered."

Soapy raised a hand, dismissing the subject at once. "He'll be handled. What's the look of this fellow, Cobalt?"

"You can spot him in any crowd. He looks bigger than he is, and yet he's bigger than his looks. He has pale-blue eyes. There are muscles around the base of his jaw. You'll know Cobalt the instant you see him. He's quiet. He never makes trouble but, if it starts around him, he'll do the finishing."

"Not in this town." Soapy Jones smiled again. He had an ugly smile. I've seen it myself, and I know.

Then Baird said: "This affair will be a good deal of trouble to you. You name your own figure for it."

Soapy stared at him. "Partner," he answered, "this is friendship. You can't pay me money for this sort of work."

"I'm grateful."

"I guess you are. This fellow Cobalt has thrown a chill into you, but you don't need to worry about him now. He's in my hands."

"I've warned you about him before. I warn you again. He's a hard man. He's the hardest man we ever saw inside."

"They don't have any hard men inside. I have the hard men here. I have all the hard men. They have some fellows inside with strong hands, but I have man-breakers here that ride the tough boys to death. Let me tell you something. I won't send two men to tackle your friend, Cobalt. I'll only send one."

Baird sat still and stared, agape. "Do you mean it?"

"I'll send one man. As small as this. Hardly more than a boy. And he'll ride your tough friend to death. He'll tame him." He leaned back a little in his chair and laughed. "That's the kind I have around me," he went on. "Man-breakers. Experts. I train them myself. I have the best-trained man-breakers in the world. That's all, now. Go home and stop worrying. This fellow Cobalt is already out of your way. I've taken him out of your way."

Baird certainly knew a great deal about what Cobalt could do and had done, but he could not help believing what Soapy told him. He thanked the crook again and came straight back to me. Sylvia had gone to bed, tired out, and I asked Baird what he had done. He was afraid

145

that I would not approve, and therefore he merely said that he had seen Soapy and discovered that he had known the man before in Spokane. He said that Soapy seemed to be a human devil, and that was all. But Baird told me not a word of the real subject of his conversation with Soapy Jones. If he had, it might have saved something in the end.

We did not go to bed. We were too excited. Besides, there was a rising tide of noise through the muddy streets of Skagway, so we went down to find out what was in the air. We got no farther than the downstairs entrance hall, where the desk was located before we had a chance to learn everything that was going on. There were twenty men gathered around one speaker. The speaker was a rough-looking fellow with a brown, weathered face, a resolute expression, and a deep, harsh voice. He talked rapidly and with emotion, but he did not shout. He seemed rather like a man expressing his fury in the bosom of his family.

He said: "Gentlemen, we've stood quite a pile from Soapy Jones. I don't hanker to stand no more. If there's anybody here that has any backbone, he'll stand by me. I mean to fight Soapy Jones. I'm wearing a gun, and I intend to use it on him the first time I see him. You all may think that's boasting, but it ain't. I come here from the inside with a partner. We'd worked like dogs for three years. You know what it means to work three years on the inside of Alaska. Well, we'd done that.

"We go to the first saloon that we sight to get a drink. My partner pulls out his poke to pay and lets the poke drop with a thud that shakes the bar. There's

146

thirty pounds of good red dust in that poke. What's more, there's three years in it. Three years of hard slogging. Maybe that's not much. I don't say that it is. But thirty pounds is around ten thousand dollars. That was his half of the work we'd done. I had the same amount. Well, the bartender in that saloon is a little fellow with buck teeth and a sort of a foolish, smiling look, except around the mouth . . ."

Someone broke in to say that they knew the man. So did I. The description was unmistakable. "Jess Fair," someone named him.

"This bartender ups and tells my partner he'd better leave that money with him for safe keeping, seeing it's so heavy to tote around. My partner only laughs and says that he knows how to take care of his own money.

" 'Do you?' says the barkeep, this fellow you call Fair. And he reaches over the bar with a big Colt in his hand and slams my partner over the head with the barrel of the gun. While my pal drops, Jess Fair takes the poke and shoves it under the bar!

"I didn't have no gun, but I jumped for that thug. He just jammed the muzzle of his gun into the hollow of my throat and told me that I was stupid to associate with such a fool, and he told his bouncers to throw the pair of us out into the street. They did it, too. They threw us out, and I got my partner to a room and found a doctor. Maybe his skull is fractured. Anyway, he's still got a fever, and he's out of his head.

"I left him flat on his back, moaning and muttering. I hired a kid to look after him for a while. Then I bought me a gun. And I went and looked up a fellow

147

who they said was a deputy sheriff. He said the matter would be looked into. I waited two days. I asked him what he'd done about it, and he had forgotten who I was. I had to remind him, and he said he'd had his hands full and that he would look into it the first chance he got, but I knew when that will be . . . just never.

"Well, that's why I'm here. You've averaged about a dead man a day for a long spell here in Skagway. Why? Because you've got Soapy here with his gang. That's why! Every kind of dirty work in the world is done by him and his gang. Now, gentlemen, I'm gonna tell you that in half an hour there's gonna be a meeting where the best men in the town are gonna be present and try to work out some way of handling Soapy and cleaning up Skagway. I'm gonna be present. So will a lot of Soapy's agents. But we want the decent people to come along with us. Why, every man here oughta follow me!"

He finished with this and, turning on his heel, walked out of the room and into the street. Just as he suggested, every man followed him. For my part it seemed impossible that such things as the brutal robbery he described could be tolerated by the adherents of law and order even in a wild frontier town like Skagway.

I went along with Baird at the heels of this group. Looking back, I saw that the proprietor remained at his desk, smiling sourly after us.

"I'll bet he's one of the gang," I said to Baird.

"Of course he is," agreed Baird. "Every crook in town is with Soapy, or else he's not in the town long.

148

Soapy won't allow any rivalry, they tell me. He's a monopolist, pure and simple."

On the way to the meeting place, we fell in with a decent sort of fellow who had the look of a gambler, if I ever saw one. His fine long hands were a treat to see, and I could imagine him doing real magic with a pack of cards.

"What do you think of all of this?" I asked him. "I'm a newcomer. I'm an old hand in Alaska, but I'm a cheechako in Skagway."

"I'll tell you," replied the stranger. "Soapy's about half a curse and half a blessing to Alaska. He weeds out the crooks. He keeps some, but he knocks others over the head. Besides, Soapy's not such a bad fellow in a way. He knows his friends."

"Does he rob people in open daylight in his saloon?" asked Baird, growing hot.

"Of course he does, and the poor fools still flock there," said our new friend. "The trouble with us Americans is that we don't particularly care about law and order. It takes time and trouble to organize an efficient legal system and protection for the people. We don't waste that much time and trouble. We leave it for the other fellow, and the other fellow is as likely as not to be a crook himself. He knows we won't watch him. Look at Canada . . . the difference just over the border. Six Northwest Mounted Police could clean up the whole of Skagway in a week if this were in Canada. They have the public and the public interest behind them."

We could not help agreeing. There's no finer body of men in the world than the Northwest Mounted.

"What's your line here?" I asked the stranger because he interested me.

"Oh, I'm one of Soapy's dealers," he said with a grin and drifted away from us in the crowd.

CHAPTER
TWENTY-TWO

Soapy and the Crowd

As we wedged with the entering crowd into the big room that housed the meeting, Baird said to me: "That's pretty cool. I wonder how many more of the same kind are down here spotting for Soapy?"

"Plenty," I suggested. "Keep your voice down. Let others do the talking. Soapy has Skagway in his pocket, it seems to me."

It was true, too. Soapy's reign of terror has become famous since that day. I saw the town when his reign was in its prime, and still I look back to those days as to a bad dream.

The room was packed. We remained rather near the door because it was impossible to get in much farther. Then somebody stood up on a chair in the middle of the room and began to harangue us. He was a fat man with a big, round, bald, red head and a thick-lipped mouth. He looked like a white Negro. He was quite a talker, and he painted the picture of Soapy Jones with all the colors of the rainbow. He told us that Skagway could be the key to Alaska. He told us what Soapy was making of it. He gave us a list of crimes that made my blood run cold.

I whispered to Baird: "There's going to be a riot at the end of this meeting. White men won't stand for the sort of things that Soapy's doing here."

"I don't know. It may be that Soapy has this meeting already salted," said Baird. "Look yonder. There's Jess Fair, the barkeep. Look at him applauding. He's not afraid."

"He's a young demon," I said, and added: "Keep your voice down. You don't know who's listening in on what we say." It was my second warning to Baird, and I thought it was very good advice.

In the meantime the people in the crowd were getting hot under the collar. When the first speaker ended, others jumped up on chairs, sometimes four or five at a time, all ready and bursting to tell about the evil things Soapy Jones had done. Finally a man of dignified presence stood up and raised his hand until he silenced the others. He then asked them what was to be done. He wanted to know the sentiment of the meeting — whether they considered Soapy a public menace or not?

There was a hoarse, deep-throated roar from that crowd. It sounded like the barking of the sea lions on the Cliff House rocks at San Francisco. When the roar died down, the tall fellow raised his hand, and the crowd was silent again. Then he said: "My friends, I propose we march in a mass to Soapy's saloon, smash the place, and search it from top to bottom. We may discover some interesting things there. I'd particularly like to examine the inside of his roulette wheel!"

There was a sour burst of laughter at this.

"After we've smashed the saloon, we'll close up the place tight. To the thugs we catch in it, we'll give a fair trial and a quick ending. There's plenty of rope lengths in Skagway, I take it!"

Another roar went up from the crowd. I was once the unwilling witness of a lynching. The faces I saw around me looked like the faces I remembered having seen in that other crowd long before.

Just then a voice spoke from the doorway, a loud, ringing voice, that made every face jerk around to see who was speaking. "Gentlemen!" said the newcomer in a loud voice.

It was Soapy Jones standing in the doorway, with a high hat on his head and wearing a long-tailed coat. Over the bend of one arm he carried a riot gun.

"Gentlemen," said Soapy, "have I your attention?"

He hardly needed to ask that question. I could hear the breathing of the people about me, but I could hear nothing else.

He went on: "It seems to me, friends, that it's time for you to disperse."

He waited. No one stirred.

"A good pow-wow is an excellent thing at times," continued Soapy Jones, "but after a talk there's nothing better than a little walk. I advise you to start walking gentlemen!"

Still no one moved. The air was tense. Just before me was the fellow who'd made the talk in the hotel lobby. I saw his hand stealing inside his coat — probably for that gun he had advertised having, but I did not actually see the glint of the weapon.

153

Soapy was saying: "Mister Haven, no one seems willing to take the place of honor. Will you lead the way out?"

I heard a man near the door mutter an oath, but suddenly he slouched forward and went through the doorway past Soapy. The whole crowd lurched a little.

"Mister Jenkins," said Soapy, "suppose you go next. And you, Mister Cross, and you, Marrow!"

I got to know Marrow later. He was quite a humorist and now he said: "I'd like to stop and argue with you, Soapy, but some of your friends might help me along from behind!"

He laughed at his own joke. Others began to laugh. I felt the danger melting out of the air. I felt the crowd weakening.

"We're all salted down with his thugs," muttered somebody near me. "There's no chance to do anything today!"

Suddenly I knew that he was right. Nothing would be done on this day. Nothing would probably be done on other days for a long time. It was that remarkable man who stood there in the doorway that had quelled them. I never have seen such an exhibition of the force of will power, never in all my life, and I've seen some odd corners of the world and some hard breaks. Soapy Jones, smiling faintly there in the doorway, seemed to reach every face and every soul with his bright, moving eyes. He seemed to be writing things down in his memory. As the people brushed by him, going out — he occupied half of the entrance, so that we had to get out in single file — he made cheerful remarks here and there.

"The air's bad in here," he observed. "You know, I've studied to be a doctor, and I wouldn't keep even a dog in a crowd like this. You'll like everything a lot better once you're out in the open."

In a steady file the people went past him. Some of them looked at him with angry defiance. Others were plainly frightened to death, hanging their heads and hurrying by him as though they prayed that he might not file a picture of their faces in his cunning mind. Still others — and I think these were in the majority — smiled or laughed openly, as though they found the whole thing a joke and had looked on it as a joke from the first.

"Don't forget Soapy Jones's emporium, gentlemen," he was saying. "An asylum for the thirsty and a place where one can make the time pass quickly. A day is like an hour in the Soapy Jones saloon."

"It goes like an hour, and it costs like a year!" said some wag who was passing him.

"So it does," said Soapy, laughing in the most amiable manner. "I remember you, young fellow. You did very well at faro last night. Come and try your luck again."

"I've had my luck, and I'll keep it," said the other.

"That's not a bad idea, either," answered Soapy. "Now, who's for Soapy's place? You know how it got that name? Because it's scrubbed clean every day. Every floor, window, and every door."

"But some of the stains don't come out," said one.

"So they don't," agreed Soapy. "If you're ever bored in my place, you can look at the floor and find more there than you would in a book. Come along, boys. Who's for Soapy Jones's saloon?"

It was an amazing thing to see how he gathered them. They went in troops after him. They began to laugh and whoop and shout. A great many of them were wild young boys, such as always form the body and the forefront of every gold rush, but some of them were old enough to have known better.

I've always felt that it was the very nature of Soapy's place that intrigued people and got them in. Robbery, murder even, walked through the rooms of Soapy Jones and, therefore, every man prided himself on the number of times he had been there and his ability to call the bartenders and the dealers by name. To be recognized as an old patron in the saloon of Soapy Jones qualified a man, not so much as a fool as a desperado.

That was the ending of the first memorable meeting of protest against Soapy Jones. If there had been really efficient preparation and leadership, the power of the man might have been broken on that day. But the leadership was lacking and, therefore, the whole scheme fell through. Instead, the hand of Soapy Jones was strengthened for days to come. Many a man can remember that meeting. Many have described it. But I believe that it went almost exactly as I have remembered and written it down. To the end of my life one of the clearest of my memories must be Soapy at the door of the meeting, smiling and chatting with the people who filed past him, the very men who had just been discussing a necktie party at which he was to be the honored guest.

Baird, watching the people drift down the street, finally said to me: "I've a mind to go with them."

"Have you lost your head?" I was alarmed.

"It may be worthwhile, for one to know some of those fellows better."

"You'll be tapped over the head. And you have something in your poke, too!"

He smiled at me, a faint smile "No, you don't have to worry about me. You don't have to worry about yourself, so long as you're with me. I have what you might call a pass with Soapy Jones."

I rubbed my chin with my knuckles and shook my head at him. It was long after this before I understood the details of his interview with the thug and, therefore, I was thoroughly mystified. I knew Baird was a man of many experiences, and I was willing to let him keep his mystery a secret.

"If you're sure it's safe," I said, "of course there's no place where I'd rather see a show than in that tiger's den."

So we went down the street after the rest, and at their heels we pushed through the door and entered the rambling rooms that made up the establishment. There was already an air of mad gaiety, and people were thronging between the bar and the gaming tables. Then Baird gripped my arm. His fingers bit into my flesh like teeth.

"Cobalt. Let's get out," he whispered.

CHAPTER
TWENTY-THREE

The Wild Man Again

When one sees lightning, it is already too late to run. When we saw Cobalt, he was stepping straight toward us. How do you think he greeted us after the long absence and after all that had passed between us? He simply said: "Hello, fellows! What did you think of that meeting? There was a show for you!"

"Were you there, Cobalt?" I asked.

"Yes. I was there. I was standing a little behind you." A glint of amusement came into his eyes.

I understood at once. He'd been following us. He knew all about us. He had known, perhaps, ever since we came into town, but he did not gloat over us. Neither did he show the slightest feeling of any kind. He merely said: "It was a good show. That fellow, Soapy, he'd be worth knowing. He has something more than cloth up his sleeve."

I looked at Baird, and Baird looked at me.

"It's a wonder we ever left Circle City," I said, taking the conversational bull by the horns.

"Well, you might have waited," said Cobalt. "You were afraid of trouble with me, weren't you?"

"Of course we were," put in Baird.

"As long as we didn't meet on the trail," said Cobalt, "it was all right. That might have been bad. Did you ever notice the queer ideas that a fellow gets when he's on the trail?"

I listened to him and could not believe my ears. "Cobalt, you would have killed me on the trail?"

"Yes," he replied as calmly as you please. "Of course, I would have killed you . . . if I could."

Baird glared at us in a wild way. This sort of talk was too much for him. It was like having a bounding, roaring lion come up and lick your hand. "I've got to get back," he muttered. "I've got to get back to my girl."

"Oh, she's all right," said Cobalt.

"What?" exclaimed Baird.

Cobalt grinned at us in a friendly way. "Don't you worry," he said. "I only looked at her. I didn't steal her. She's asleep."

"You looked at her? Through the window?"

"No, not through the window. I opened the door."

"That door has a lock on it," exclaimed Baird, all in a sweat.

"I jimmied the lock and walked in."

"The mischief you did," said Baird.

"I wanted to see her. It had been ages, since the last look. So I spoiled the lock on that door. It doesn't amount to anything, and it'll save me some trouble the next time."

"Cobalt," I said, "why did you do it? Did you throw her into a fit? A thing like that's enough to kill her."

159

"Of course it is, only I didn't wake her up. I didn't want to talk to her. I just wanted to look. I would be there still looking, except that the wolf got a shade restless, and I was afraid he was growling loud enough to wake her up." He gestured toward a corner. "Let's go over and have a drink."

I was still more than half staggered. My brain reeled. Toward this encounter I had been looking as toward the end of the world, and yet here was the great enemy who'd haunted our very dreams as calm and as gentle as a lamb.

It was quite too much for Baird. He repeated hoarsely: "I'll see you later, Cobalt. I'd better get back to my girl . . . broken lock on the door . . . all alone."

Cobalt laughed, answering: "Do you think another man is likely to walk into that room? If he does, he'll walk out again with his throat cut. The wolf is fond of the girl, it seems."

He took us each by an arm and determinedly carried us into the corner where he set us down at a table and ordered three drinks. While he was getting the drinks, Baird said to me: "Tom, he's lost his wits. He's completely mad!"

It showed me how excited he was. "What makes you think so?"

"I know it. I can tell by the look of his eye. His mind's on fire, but he's choking off the flames."

When Cobalt came back, Baird said: "You're sure she doesn't know you were there?"

"She won't know it till she wakes up. She was sleeping soundly with one arm curled under her head.

160

She was talking in her sleep and laughing a little. It was a pretty sight to see." He smiled as he thought of it then went on: "She was murmuring something about Tommy being fun. Does she call you Tommy now, Chalmers?"

I gave him something like two looks in one. He did not seem angry or jealous as his remarks implied that he might be. He looked at me with a new interest, only I could not tell what was in his mind. A watchdog looks as he did then — when its head is raised and its eyes are shining. It may be ready to jump forward and lick your hand. Again, it may be ready to jump forward and slit your throat. That was the way Cobalt looked. Anything might have been stirring within him.

"She calls me Tommy. That's her way of talking down to me."

I was all in sweat, but Cobalt simply smiled.

"I'm glad I didn't meet you on the trail, Chalmers. You're all right. You won't burn through steel, but you might rust it."

It was not very hard to see there was an insult in this speech, but I was not the man to take up the challenge in any haste. I let it fall flat, in fact. I would as soon have picked up and held in hand a nitroglycerin bomb as to trouble Cobalt on this day. Besides, we had something coming in our direction, after the way we had run out on him at Circle City.

"I'm glad you didn't meet me on the trail," I admitted. "In other words, I'm glad to be here!" I smiled at Cobalt, and he smiled back.

"You talk against yourself a lot," he said. "As a matter of fact, you're about the only man in Skagway with the nerve to walk the streets and not pack a gun."

"How do you know that I don't pack a gun?"

He sipped his drink. It was poison so rank that one could almost see the fumes from it rise. But Cobalt tasted that liquid fire and ran it casually over the back of his tongue, though it would have removed the membrane of an ordinary person.

"I know," said Cobalt, "because you're afraid you might get scared into using it. But you're all right, Tom. You'll fight when you're cornered, and you might be hard on the eyes of the fellow who cornered you."

I suppose there was an insult in all of this too, particularly in the suggestion I might scratch like a woman but, again I repeat, I was not looking for insults in the speeches of Cobalt. I was sedulously avoiding them.

"Well, Cobalt, I'm glad that you're not doing the cornering."

"Of course, I'm not doing it. I'm only glad to have met you all again. You made good time coming in with only the three of you and two sleds."

"Sylvia and the wolf pulled one," said Baird.

Cobalt half rose and suddenly slumped back into his chair. After the real or the affected calm of his meeting with us, it was a shock to see him hit hard by what seemed to me a thing of no very great consequence.

"You mean she made the Lightning Warrior get out and pull on a line?" he asked.

162

"That's what she did," I said. "I never saw a wolf pull so hard or a dog, either. He was like a horse, and I remember once when . . ."

Cobalt waved this remark to one side. "Tell me how she did it?" he said, leaning forward and looking eagerly at me.

"How she tamed the wolf?" I asked. "Yes, I'll tell you how she tamed him."

"Start in. I'm interested."

"She went out into the yard, back there in Circle City, and let him off the chain he'd been chewing on." As I explained, I kept looking him in the eye. "You know what that means. The wolf was ravening, but she simply went out, leaned over him, and took off his collar."

Cobalt looked blank. "She sort of hypnotized him, you mean?"

"No, but she didn't care. She didn't much care what happened. That was the way of it. And the unexpected happened. The wolf loved her because she wasn't afraid of him."

Cobalt took his face between his hands and rested his elbows on the edge of the table. How he stared at me. "The wolf never loved me," he said then.

"You know how it is with dumb beasts," I said. "They're apt to give you back exactly what they get from you."

He nodded at me, a mere jerk of the head. "I guess you score off me there. But she made the beast love her, eh? That's what I wanted to talk to you about. He stood between me and her bed. The longer I stayed, the

163

worse he got. He would have jumped me in another moment. He seemed to have forgotten everything."

What had he forgotten? Why, the manhandling that Cobalt had given the brute when they fought it out there in the wilderness. The mystery of the girl's accomplishment seemed to interest him more than the actual meeting with Sylvia herself.

Then he repeated: "You don't know what her methods are?"

"Just fearlessness," I said.

Cobalt laughed in a very odd way. "Maybe she'll tame me one of these days."

"Well, maybe she will," I said.

He gave me an ugly look, his upper lip lifting at one corner in a way I shall never forget. One doesn't expect to see such an expression, not in the face of a man.

"Let it go at that!" said Cobalt, leaning back in his chair suddenly. He glanced about then remarked: "I know that there are some people watching me here in Skagway." He turned to Baird. "Have you put somebody on my trail?"

I did not know at that time what had passed between Soapy Jones and Baird. Therefore I was surprised when Baird changed color.

"Would that be out of the way?" Baird spoke, frankly enough.

"No," replied Cobalt, "but I'll have a look at that lad over there." He got up from the table and turned his back on us.

CHAPTER
TWENTY-FOUR

The Rawhide Kid

He went straight toward a young fellow who was seated in a chair tilted back against the wall, quite close to us. In one glance I read him to be one of the Soapy Jones's men. I cannot tell exactly why I was sure of this. It may have been because Cobalt already had mentioned that he was being followed. It may have been simply the look of the boy, for he was hardly more than that, nineteen or twenty, lean as a greyhound, strong as rawhide. He seemed very slender, but the size of his neck showed his real strength. When Cobalt came before him, we could hear perfectly what they said to each other. Cobalt spoke first.

"I didn't get your name, friend."

The other looked up at him as fresh as salt. "I never seen you before," he said.

"Is that so? Then it was your ghost that's been following me around Skagway."

"I never follow anybody. I show the way, old-timer, and don't you forget it."

"I'm not going to forget you easily, but I'm going to try to put you out of my mind."

"How will you go about the putting?" asked the lad.

165

"I'll show you."

Cobalt reached for him. At this gesture the boy moved as light moves when it twinkles on the face of a mirror. All in a flash he was on his feet and in the same instant a gun winked in his hand, a gun which was polished with use and good care so that it shone like something translucent. You could tell that the lad did his thinking, not pen in hand, but gun in hand, so quick was that draw. But as the gun came out, Cobalt reached the wrist of the gun arm and his grip froze on it. The boy smashed the other fist into Cobalt's face and tried to hit him again, but Cobalt picked the second drive out of the air and held the fist fast. It looked as though the boy had struck a wall of iron. There they stood, the lad cursing, his face contorted with pain, and Cobalt smiling at him gently. Their faces were only inches apart.

"Skagway is getting introduced to Cobalt," I told Baird.

He looked very grave. "Cobalt will be a dead man inside twenty-four hours!" he predicted.

I paid little attention to that remark at the time. It seemed to me to come rather out of Baird's wish than any possibility. Cobalt stepped back to the table, bringing the boy with him. He held the gun hand of the lad over the top of the table and squeezed the heavy Colt revolver out of his grasp. It was not surprising that the gun fell. Blood fell with it. With my own eyes I saw a thin spurt spring out from under a fingernail of the youngster. His white, writing face was too much for me.

166

I sprang up and clapped Cobalt on the shoulder. "Cobalt, hadn't you better let him go? He's done no harm!"

Cobalt turned his head slowly until he could look at me and there, for the first time, I saw the thing that had frozen so many hearts. I saw the mask of Cobalt fighting, a mask of ice and fire, and it sickened me. I slumped back into my chair as though he had struck me. All he said was: "That gun was meant for me. Murder was all this lad meant. Isn't that enough?" It was enough. In the meantime we had the eye of the crowd. All heads were turned our way. I saw Jess Fair, behind the bar, watching with a curious detachment.

"Keep a good hold on the Rawhide Kid," said one of the men nearest to us. "When you let go of him, he'll sting you sure."

"This Rawhide Kid will never sting again," said Cobalt gently. "His nettles are all gone."

I thought the Rawhide Kid was about to faint. Cobalt had shifted his grip so that he held him by both hands. I could judge of the pressure that was being exerted by the tremor of Cobalt's forearms. He backed the boy into a corner. The big lad laid his shoulders against the wall and endured the punishment. He set his teeth in his lip. His eyes bulged a little.

"I just wanted to say a few words to you," Cobalt told him.

"I'm going to kill you!" said the boy.

"There'll be time for that later on, but you're going to begin by talking to me a little."

"I'll have the heart out of you before long!"

"Not until you get a new pair of hands!"

The Rawhide Kid gasped. His head jerked back and rapped against the wall as he felt the pressure increase. There is little else so painful as having the hand gripped so hard that the knucklebones grate together. The Rawhide Kid was enduring his share of the torment and something more. No one moved to interfere with the procedure. The men looked on with keen interest, but they kept at a distance. It was simply known that the Rawhide Kid had pulled a gun. It was not the first time that he had flashed a weapon in Skagway, it developed. Being a killer, he got only that sympathy which a killer may expect. No one could hear what Cobalt was saying to the boy except Baird and me.

"Now," said Cobalt, "I want the name of the man who set you trailing me."

"Nobody. I ain't trailing you."

"I want the name of the man who started you on my trail," insisted Cobalt.

Suddenly there was a dull, cracking sound. I knew that one of the boy's metacarpal bones must have snapped. His head jerked over on his shoulder, pulled by the twinge of agony, but he did not cry out. He had his share of manhood and more than his share.

"The name!"

The twisting lips of the boy whispered: "Soapy!"

Cobalt released him instantly, picked the gun off the top of the table, and offered it to him, but the hands of the lad were stiff and white from the frightful pressure they had endured. There was only the ugly stain of red about the fingertips. He could not take the weapon. So

Cobalt dropped it into the pocket of his coat, and Rawhide stumbled blindly away and was lost behind the shoulders of the crowd.

Cobalt came back and sat down with us. His calm outwardly was entirely restored. He lifted his half-finished drink of whiskey with a hand which did not tremble and drank it off slowly, as before.

"It's Soapy Jones," he said softly, as he replaced the glass upon the table.

The crowd was already busied about its former occupations. Only now and again some head turned and a glance went to Cobalt, but he did not seem to notice these looks. I could not help saying: "If it's Soapy Jones, you'd better get out of Skagway, Cobalt."

He grinned at me. "That's good sympathetic advice, brother, but I'm not getting out of Skagway."

I said: "You ought to know the power Soapy has here. The man owns the town. You've just seen today what he can do with it."

"Yes, I saw. I saw plenty of what he can do, but I'm not leaving Skagway."

"You think," I said, aroused by a real concern for him, "that it's only a question of one man. He may be a hardcase, but no doubt you could handle him alone. It isn't that. He has a mob behind him. Half these fellows would kill you for the sake of getting one smile from Soapy. That's the fact. I've heard the talk."

Cobalt shook his head. "D'you think that I'd leave town before I've finished my business here? You wouldn't think that of me, Tom, would you?"

169

I had to shake my head. As well think of a bulldog loosing its grip at a word of good advice. "No," I said, "I don't suppose you will."

"I'd like to know just what your business is," prompted Baird.

"Why, it's Sylvia, of course," Cobalt replied. "Sylvia alone. That is to say, it was Sylvia before Soapy Jones mixed into the affair. Now I'll have to have an interview with Soapy. There doesn't seem to be any doubt about that." Suddenly he made a gesture with both hands, palms up. "It looks to me as if I'm going to have a real party in Skagway, as if I'm going to be able to fill both hands in this town."

I understood, with a chilly touch of insight, just what he meant. He would have his fill of fighting, and battle was what he lived for. His lips were compressing in hardly visible twitches.

"Tell me, Cobalt," I said, "did you never have both hands full before?"

He half closed his eyes in thought. "No," he conceded finally. "I never had both of them full." He looked down. You would have thought he was pitying the bad luck of those hands. "When I was ripping away on Birch Creek last summer, I just about filled them . . . thinking of Sylvia, I mean, and working for her."

He had worked twenty hours out of the twenty-four, men said, and one hour of his labor was worth five hours of another man. He worked in a frenzy, as a dog pulls at a sled when it has hydrophobia of the peculiar variety which appears in arctic sled teams. I remember thinking how foolish we'd been — Baird and I — to

170

dream we could escape from this man when his heart was really set on finding the girl. He had worked hard enough to show that he would never give her up. It hardly needed his frantic rush from Circle City to the coast to prove that to us. We had argued like children, and like children we had obeyed a blind impulse.

I stared at Baird helplessly, and he likewise stared back at me. What could the solution be? Nothing except the will of this giant of mind and body.

"What's the next step, Cobalt?" I asked him, expressing our despair in the foolish question.

"Soapy Jones is the next step," he answered.

I saw Baird change color.

CHAPTER
TWENTY-FIVE

An Incident

I think Cobalt would have gone straight to find Soapy at that moment if an odd event hadn't intervened and filled our attention for a little. Otherwise, it would hardly deserve a place in this narrative, but the thing was so diabolical, and it has been repeated so often by old-timers who only heard of it, that I've deemed it fitting to set the thing down in black and white exactly as it happened.

This was the way of it. A man with a wide, good-natured looking face came into the saloon and asked in a loud voice: "Where's Jess Fair?"

It seemed a strange question, seeing that Fair was actually standing there behind the bar. At the moment he was polishing up the bar and giving some directions over his shoulder to an assistant. He was wearing a white coat and a blue bow tie with a fancy figure in it. He was always dressed just like a dandy.

When the stranger asked for him, he continued to polish the bar and to speak to his assistant without turning his head. No one answered the man's question, but I heard Cobalt murmur: "There's going to be trouble."

172

Well, I could feel it too. The air became suddenly electric. Danger will prickle like a current through the skin of a man.

"Where's Jess Fair?" repeated the stranger.

There was still no answer. People looked at him, some of them smiling a little and expectant. So he addressed a man standing close to our table.

"I've got a warrant for a man named Jess Fair who works for Soapy Jones," he said. "Can you tell me where I can find him?"

"I can't tell you," said the other. "What's the warrant for?"

"Oh, just a little thing. Just a couple or three murders and some little things like that down in the States."

"Well, you look around for Jess," said the man he'd addressed. "I don't recollect having heard the name before."

He turned and winked at us as the stranger went away. Then we heard him say to a companion, "That's the new deputy sheriff. The fool don't know what he's about, coming in this place to make an arrest."

"He's drunk," suggested the other.

"No, he's just a fool," said the first man.

Perhaps he was right. At any rate we now heard Jess Fair saying from behind the bar: "Step over here, Sheriff, will you?"

The deputy sheriff walked over to the bar. "Well?" he said.

"You're looking for Jess Fair?"

"Yes. I want him, and I want him quick."

173

"Jess is a friend of mine," said the bartender.

"Is he?" answered the man of the law. "Then I dunno that you keep very good company, brother. Where's this friend of yours hang out?"

"Why, he's right here, most of the time."

Broad grins appeared on the faces of all the men except those nearest. They continued to wear masks of iron self-control.

"Is he?" asked the deputy, looking suddenly around him. "But he ain't here now?"

"I don't know. I'll ask." He actually called to the men and asked them: "Have any of you seen Jess Fair today?"

"Why," said one man, "I've been looking right at him, here in the barroom."

There was a chuckle from one man, instantly suppressed, for fear that the game might be spoiled. The deputy sheriff had turned to the last speaker.

"What does Fair look like?" he asked.

"Why, ain't you ever seen him?"

"No. They just told me that pretty nearly everybody would be able to spot Jess Fair to me. He works here in this place. He works for Soapy Jones, whoever he is."

"You don't know Soapy, either?"

"No, I've barely heard of him. I've only been in town for three days."

Three days in town and already a deputy sheriff! Well, the law moved in mysterious ways and with strange agents in Skagway. This fellow had the look of a professional bouncer or thug. He had simply gone looking for trouble in asking for the job of law enforcement, and trouble was what he found, the poor boob.

"Soapy's quite a fellow," said one of the bystanders to the sheriff.

"I guess he is. But I'm only looking for Jess Fair," said the deputy.

"Well, I'd talk to that bartender," was the suggestion he got.

He turned back to Fair. "This fellow, Fair, what's the look of him?"

"Why," said the barkeep after a moment of pretended reflection, "he looks a great deal like me."

"Now, how do you mean that?" asked the deputy in an irritated tone. "Is he your height, your complexion, got a mouth like yours?"

The bartender looked calmly upon him. "Kind of like me in all those ways. But I think that he's a good deal better looking than most people do."

"Do you?" said the deputy. "I ain't asking what you think of him. I'm only asking where I can find him."

"Hunting for him would be the best way, I suppose."

"Hullo!" exclaimed the man of the law. "Are you handing me some lip?"

"No, I've hardly got enough lip to cover my own teeth. I couldn't spare any."

The deputy swelled like a toad with anger. He strode up to the bar and dropped his fist on the edge of it.

"I wouldn't be doing that," cautioned Fair. "You look pretty good natured already."

Someone in the crowd broke into a roar of laughter. This was the end of self-restraint, and the whole room exploded and rocked with mirth. The deputy was so angry that he glared about him, as though looking for the first man he could strike in the face. There were too many and all equal offenders. He decided to concentrate on the barkeep whose remark had excited all the mirth.

"That last crack of yours was too fresh," he said.

"It got a laugh, though. That's what I'm hired for. It ain't the booze we peddle that keeps the boys contented at this bar. It's the jokes that their bartender is always cracking."

This caused another burst of laughter, and the deputy turned purple. "Come here to me!"

Jess actually leaned closer across the bar. "Yes, sir?" His appearance of humility tickled the bystanders still more.

"Somebody ought to warn that fool," said Cobalt. "I'm afraid that something will happen."

"Not here. Not before all this crowd," said Baird.

I agreed with him, but Cobalt merely shook his head gloomily.

"You been shooting off your face a lot," said the deputy to Fair. "Now I wanta know something. Who are you, anyway?"

"I'm a barkeep in the employ of the Honorable S. Jones of New York, Paris, Chicago, and points farther west. He'll tell you more about me."

"Why, you thundering fool! I've got half a mind to take you in!"

"Where?"

"To jail, you fool young puppy. That's where I got a mind to take you."

"What for?" asked Jess.

"For contempt of the law!" roared the deputy.

"Are you the law?" Fair wondered innocently.

The deputy gaped, grew still more purple, and actually gagged with his own fury, unable to speak.

"But I'll direct you to Jess Fair," continued the barkeep, "if you'll promise not to take me to jail."

That fool of a sheriff actually answered: "I'll make that a bargain. You ain't worth my while, only that I'm gonna teach you the right kind of manners."

"Yes, sir."

"Now tell me where this Jess Fair is."

"Standing in my boots."

"Hey?"

A wild burst of laughter filled in the pause. The deputy, looking wildly about him, suddenly realized how completely he had been made sport of, and he stuck out his under jaw like a bulldog.

"It's amusin', is it?" he asked defiantly. "You come with me. I hereby arrest you in the name . . ."

I hardly saw the gun flash into the hand of the bartender. I don't know whether he pulled it from within his neat white coat or snatched it from the shelf beneath the bar. But I heard the report, saw the muzzle of the gun jerked on high by the explosion, and saw the deputy go staggering backward, beating at the air like a man swimming. He fell flat on his back, twisted over on his face, kicked out his legs, and lay still. No one moved except Jess Fair. He jumped over the bar as light as a bird and leaned over the deputy.

When he straightened up after a moment of examination, he merely said: "It looks as though Skagway is short of a brand new deputy sheriff, and that's too bad. Here, boys. Lay hold of this and chuck it outside, will you?"

That was exactly what was done. The body of the dead man was lifted by two of the hangers-on of the place and thrown out into the street. Who removed it from the spot where it fell, I don't know. Perhaps another section of the gang did the work. What I do know is that no one inside of that saloon made any protest on account of the cold-blooded murder, not even Cobalt. In another few minutes, when the blood had been mopped up from the floor, men were walking about, talking and drinking, as cheerful as ever.

CHAPTER
TWENTY-SIX

The Yeggs

The body of the deputy sheriff had hardly been carried out of doors when Baird thrust back his chair from the table, exclaiming: "What's become of me, that I can sit still while outrages like this are carried through? What's happened to the rest of the men here? Are we all wild beasts?"

He stood up. He was very excited, quivering from head to foot with his emotion. He said directly to Cobalt: "If there's justice in heaven, I'll balk you in the thing you wish to do. I'll keep my girl from you if you are Satan himself, with wings and all!"

He turned on his heel and walked out from the saloon, while Cobalt looked after him without the slightest display of emotion. It was one of the upsetting features of Cobalt's behavior that you never could tell what would start the lion in him roaring. I preferred noise in him rather than silence.

I was anxious enough to get out of that saloon, and I'm ashamed to confess that the reason I did not get up was simply that for a moment I could not. I felt sick and weak about the knees after what I had seen. It was Cobalt who stood up first. Immediately after he had left, I pulled myself together and managed to get out into the street. It was a dismal day. There was a light, variable wind blowing, and the snow descended in thin, light flakes that whirled and danced like white leaves from a shrub whose branches filled the sky. But at least I did not find the limp, dead body of the sheriff lying there in the street. As I said before, he had been disposed of, no one knew where.

I turned toward the hotel, walking slowly at first, but with increasing speed as the freshness of the air and the cool touch of the snowflakes cleared my brain of the sense of faintness. Several men were walking in the same direction ahead of me and one of them, I saw, was Cobalt, sauntering along. I decided not to pass him, and it turned out a lucky thing for me that I made this decision. Lucky for Cobalt, too.

He came to a corner and paused a moment, looking up and down the narrow alley which bisected the main way. While he stood there, a man stepped up and accosted him. He spoke rapidly, making wide gesticulations, like someone arguing a point, and I saw Cobalt nod once or twice, apparently agreeing with what he heard.

I came up very close now, so that I could hear the murmur of the voices, and next I saw a man approach Cobalt from behind. The manner of his approach alarmed me. His step was the unmistakable glide of a stalking animal.

I hurried. I thought of shouting to Cobalt, but something stopped me from doing that until I saw the second man's hand come out from his coat pocket with

180

a revolver in it. He had the weapon by the barrel, and he swung the butt back over his head, straining arm and body so as to give full force to the blow he was about to deal. By the grace of luck I was just near enough. I grabbed the armed hand of the scoundrel with both of mine and shouted: "Cobalt! Cobalt! Look out!"

The fellow I had hindered turned around, cursing. He struck me on the side of the head with knuckles that felt like steel, heavily weighted. I was half stunned and could only stumble in blindly and grapple with him. Suddenly he dropped. I lurched dizzily over his limp body and almost dropped into the snow-flecked mud. Then I saw that another form lay loosely spilled in the street, and here was Cobalt holding me under the pit of one arm.

"Are you all right?" he asked me.

"Yes, I'm all right." My movements denied it, because I kept wavering back and forth like a gate in a wind, an old gate that dangles from one hinge.

"Stand back there against that wall," directed Cobalt.

He helped me to get to that comparatively sheltered position. In the meantime one of the thugs had scrambled to his feet and ran off up the street, staggering. The second one was beginning to stir also, and Cobalt picked him up by the nape of the neck as a laborer might pick up half a sack of oats. The fellow was still loose and limp, but he rapidly recovered his consciousness. It was the yegg who had attempted to brain Cobalt from behind. A smear of blood was on one side of his face, and the flesh was already swelling.

181

Plainly that was where the fist of Cobalt had delivered a hammer stroke. I noticed, as he got back his wits, that he showed less fear than sullen anger.

"Today ain't the last day," he said to Cobalt. "They's gonna be another turn, old son."

"Today may be the last day for you," said Cobalt. "I don't know. It depends on how well you talk."

"I don't talk," said the yegg.

"You're likely to be dead, then," said Cobalt. "Look at me, you!"

"Well," said the thug, "whatcha want? Gonna eat me?"

"I'll break you up small enough for eating, unless I find out who started you on my trail."

"You looked like you'd have a fat poke. That's all."

Cobalt with a jerk twisted the man's arm behind his back. "I'll tear that arm out at the shoulder, unless you tell me straight . . . who put you on my trail?"

"Leave go!" gasped the yegg. "You're gonna break my arm, you! Leave go, will you?"

"I want the name!"

"There ain't any name. I swear there wasn't anybody that put me on the job, but . . ."

"Take another minute to think," advised Cobalt, and gave the arm a fresh twist.

Once I was tormented like that by an older lad, when I was a youngster at school. I still can remember the blinding pain. Now, the face of the other wrinkled as though he felt flames.

"Soapy!" he breathed.

Cobalt released his arm. "You're number two from Soapy. Go back and tell your boss that I'm mighty flattered by getting so many messages from him. Tell him that the first chance I get, I'm going to call on him in person. I hope that he'll be ready to stage a good party."

The thug lingered a moment, held by the sheer excess of his misery. He was massaging the twisted, tortured shoulder as he said: "You'll have your party, you fool! You'll have a party. So will that other sick-faced rat that grabbed me from behind. If it hadn't been for that, you'd be having a fine long sleep right now, Cobalt!"

"That's pretty," said Cobalt. "Now run along, my friend. The next time we meet, I'll start, and I won't stop. You tell Soapy that I have all the information that I need. That's all!"

The thug went up the street, still bending forward and nursing his injured shoulder.

"He won't slug a blackjack with that arm for a few weeks," mused Cobalt with satisfaction, stepping up beside me. "How are you now?"

"I'm all right," I assured him. "He must have been an ex-pug. I never felt such a sock."

"He's tough," agreed Cobalt, "or his arm would have broken just now."

I saw that he was smiling a little, and that his eyes were bright. He kept watching me curiously. Plainly he had enjoyed the adventure.

"Chalmers, I don't quite understand you."

"Why not?"

"I thought you were against me."

"I never was against you," I told him.

"You never were?" he asked me, lifting his brows.

"I never was against you. I helped to keep Sylvia Baird away from you. That's true. But I never was against you."

"What would you call that? I mean, when a man carts a girl the most part of a thousand miles just to spite a friend of his . . . a funny kind of friendship, I'd call that."

"Maybe *you* would. You ought to see how it is, though, Cobalt. If I help a man to do a wrong thing, I'm not his friend from my way of seeing it. If I keep him from doing a wrong thing, that seems to me to be the real part of friendship."

"Oh, I see the point," he said, an ugly glint in his eye. "You're one of the old-fashioned moralists, eh?"

"I'm not a moralist. I'm just a common or garden kind of a fellow. That's all."

"Look here, you saved me from having my head split open today."

I felt rather modest about it, my part had been so small. "Not so much as that. You know, the rap would probably just have put you down and out for a minute."

"Not when Soapy sends his boys out to collect a scalp," declared Cobalt. He shook his head. "Are you cold?" he asked.

"No," I answered.

"Will you stay here and talk to me for a minute?"

"All right."

"I want to stay here," he explained, "because before long I hope to see one of Soapy's bright boys come back to pick up the trail."

"Well, I'll stay here with you."

"I want to know this. What made you grab the arm of that yegg? If he'd slugged me, everything would have been easy for you and for Baird. You could have got Sylvia out then, and nothing to bother you."

I nodded. "I don't know. The truth is, I like you, Cobalt. I couldn't help trying to bother the thug when he was about to hammer you over the head. It was just an impulse. Don't you go and make too much out of it."

He nodded, watching me, seeming to make a rapid mental calculation. "The trouble with you is that you don't add up right."

"What do you mean by that, Cobalt?"

"Well, I mean, knowing what I know about you, when I put you together, it doesn't make sense. There's something missing that I don't know."

"Perhaps, but don't make any mystery out of me. I'm as simple as they come."

"Maybe, but tell me another thing. What does Sylvia mean to you?"

"Nothing."

Cobalt raised a forefinger. "Don't lie!"

CHAPTER
TWENTY-SEVEN

Some Questions

It was not a pleasant subject. "I'm not lying, Cobalt. She means nothing to me."

He merely smiled and said: "I want to believe you. I want to like you, Chalmers. You know what Soapy Jones means in this town, and you've got yourself into his bad graces by helping me in a pinch. I want to like you. I want to trust you. But you ought to be straight with me."

"I am being straight. She means nothing to me."

"You think that she's ugly maybe, or just merely pretty?" he said, half sneering.

"She's the loveliest thing that I ever saw, with one exception."

"What's that exception?"

"A half-bred yearling filly that I saw at an Arizona horse fair."

Cobalt started. "Come, come! Are you comparing a woman to a horse?"

"Yes. The horse had her beat."

"All right. Go on and make a joke."

"I'm not joking, man. Just because I differ from you, it does not mean that I'm joking."

"Well, maybe not, but I find you mighty hard to understand."

"You've said that before, but you're making a mountain out of a molehill. There's nothing unusual about me."

"I'll try to take you at your word. But about Sylvia. You don't mind my talking to you about her, do you?"

"I'd rather that you didn't."

"Well, tell me why you'd rather not talk about her?"

"Because she has a right to be consulted," I suggested.

"Oh, come, now," he replied. "Let's not split hairs. You know that Sylvia's everything to me."

"I don't know that."

"You don't?"

"No. I know that she's a lovely picture to you. She's equal, say, to a fine emerald. Or have you changed your mind about that, perhaps?"

"No, I haven't changed my mind. I see what you mean . . . that everyone is apt to have a different view in looking at her."

"That's about it."

"And your point of view is that she doesn't mean anything to you. You think she's lovely, but she doesn't mean anything. Not to you. Is that it? You don't think that she's clever, perhaps?"

"She's as keen as a whip. She's a lot too clever for me to handle, I can tell you. She has brains enough, if you want that."

"You don't want brains in a woman. Is that it?"

He hung on like a bulldog, and I began to grow a little irritated. Besides, my feet were numbing rapidly as I stood still. "Brains or no brains, I don't want the woman, if that's what you mean. If you're going to be a jealous fool about her, I'll give you the answer straight off. I don't want your woman, Cobalt. I hope that you'll believe me."

He was not offended. He looked at me in rather a dazed way. "But everybody wants Sylvia. You must be half crazy, Tom. What's the matter with you? Why don't you care about her the way other people do?"

"I like to be with her. That's true. I like to be with her. She's good company. She's as good a sport as any man. She's tough. She does her share. She can walk like a man. She has a good nerve. She's clean, and she's gentle. She's amusing about everything that you could name. But I don't want her. You can have her, Cobalt, as far as I'm concerned. It's only her own preference that I'm considering."

"By the jumping thunder! I sort of believe that you mean what you say."

"I mean it. You can bet that I mean it."

"I want to believe you because there have been times when I wanted to tear your heart out. Do you know that?"

"I've guessed it. I'm glad that you passed us on the trail without seeing us."

"I'm glad, too. In the open country a man gets pretty hard. I was hard when I was marching down from Circle City. I wanted your blood, Tom. But that's over.

To put it in one word, you don't love Sylvia." He waited eagerly for the final confirmation.

I had to search my mind when I was on the verge of replying. "Of course, I love her," I stated.

"Hello! What are you doing? Trying to make a fool out of me?"

"No. Don't you see what I mean? Sylvia's a darling. But she's a child. I'm old enough to be her father."

"No, you're not."

"I am. Almost. You don't understand, Cobalt. Women don't mean anything to me any more. I'm done with all that."

"You have me beat," answered Cobalt. "I try to follow you, but you're too far away. I don't see what you mean. You haven't taken a vow or something, have you?"

"I've got a pair of children back home. All the woman part of life is finished for me. You ought to be able to see that."

"Well, I don't, quite."

"I'm sorry if you don't understand, but I don't want to talk any more about it."

"I'd think," said Cobalt, hanging on to the subject with his usual determination, "I'd really think that if you had a couple of kids down there . . . who's taking care of them?"

"An older sister of mine. She takes care of them for me."

"Well, I should think that you'd be looking for somebody to take their mother's place, you know, and who could be better than . . ."

"Oh, shut up, Cobalt! I don't want to talk about it any more. Are you trying to make me fall in love with Sylvia? Let me tell you all over again, I'm ten years too old for that."

He stopped there. He only added a final, rather startling thing to end our talk. "Well, partner, I hope that she doesn't decide to lift those ten years off your shoulders one of these days!"

I grinned a little. It was the sort of remark at which one has to smile. But I was glad the subject of Sylvia was out of the way, for the time being at least. How the man carried on about her.

He explained: "Maybe I'm a fool, but I was jealous. I don't see things the way you do. You have a different slant. You make me feel like a silly kid, Tom. But I hope we can shake on this."

I hesitated with good reason. "If I shake hands, it means a lot to me. It means I'm your friend. And how can I call you my friend when I'll still be trying to block you?"

"You're going to keep it up. You're going to try to stop me, even now?"

"Yes. I'll have to try to. I'm pledged to stop you, if I can."

"Oh, it's all a confusion and a mess. Tom, here's my hand, if you want to take it. Here's my hand. I'll be a friend to you in every way I can, except in one way."

You can imagine how glad I was to take that famous hand of Cobalt's and grip it with all my might. "We're friends. And this puts another ten years on my life, I think!"

190

"Do you? Have you been noticing the yegg on the far side of the street who's watching me?"

I saw the fellow now. He was standing with arms folded, wearing a big parka and puffing at a pipe. About all I could see of his face was a bristling mustache, sticking straight out. "D'you think he's watching us?"

"Nothing much else for him to see," replied Cobalt. "Let's move along. Believe me, Tom, what you've done today for me has tangled you up pretty badly. They'll all go out for you much as they're going for me."

I nodded. Speaking was not so easy for me just then. "What should we do about it?" I asked him.

"Are you packing a gun?"

"No."

"You're not! What sort of a fellow are you, Tom?"

"Not much with a gun for one thing."

"Here. Take this." He shoved a Colt into my hand.

"I can't take your gun."

"Don't worry. I have another. Don't worry a bit. But keep your eye sharp. I'm going to try to get at Soapy Jones, old-timer. I'm going to try to get at the tap root of his institution and cut it so that the tree will die."

Suddenly he began to laugh. I stared at him, bewildered, but as a matter of fact he seemed to think that this was a grand party he had embarked on, and he went up the street with that light, aspiring tread of his, head held high. I followed along with him.

A gust of wind struck us in the face. He merely laughed louder and started to whistle through the blast. I wished, with all my might, that I could have borrowed

191

certain qualities of nerve and mind from this master of men. At the door of the hotel, he said good bye.

"Hold on, old fellow," I said. "Why don't you room here?"

"They wouldn't want me. Sylvia wouldn't want me. Neither would her father, and neither would you, for that matter. Good bye again. Keep your eyes open and your gun ready. You may need it one of these days."

He simply had escorted me home, do you see, and now he was going off into a veritable sea of dangers. I began to wish for one thing only, and that was the arrival of the ship that would give us all a chance to escape from Skagway and travel toward the south, toward law and order. My mind was on this as I entered the hotel lobby.

CHAPTER
TWENTY-EIGHT

The Lion's Den

When I passed the desk, I spoke to the proprietor. He merely grunted and did not raise his head to return the greeting but pretended to be busy with the summing up of an account. I was not fooled. Something had turned him against me, and was it not the swift-winged rumor which must have gone forth, saying that I was opposed to Soapy Jones? I had not the slightest doubt that the fellow was really a member of the gang which was plundering and murdering in Skagway.

There was this new weight on my mind when I got upstairs. Sylvia smiled at me in her charming way when I entered after knocking on the door. I found that, while she was awake, she still looked sleepy, yawning from time to time. Even the wild tales which her father had been telling her were not enough to get the weariness out of her eyes. She was sitting at one end of the bed, with a blanket twisted around her, for the wretched room was a mere house of cards, and the wind was whistling through a thousand cracks.

"Father has been telling me everything," she said. "Don't you feel like a page out of the *Arabian Nights* or something? And what became of friend Cobalt?"

"He left me at the door of the hotel."

"Is he taking a room here?" asked her father in an ominous voice.

"He's not taking a room. He's gone on. He only brought me here to see that no one bumped me over the head while I was on the street."

"Come along, man," chided Baird. "You mean that he was really friendly?"

"Yes, he was friendly."

"He's changed," remarked Baird. "He's quieter, older, sourer."

"Sylvia's ripened him a good deal."

She gathered her ankle in one hand and looked seriously at me. "You're sympathizing with Cobalt, just now."

"A wee bit," I told both of them. "The gang is after him, hot and heavy. They tried to brain him! I managed to help him a little."

"What?" cried Sylvia. "Have you got mixed into a fight?"

I stared darkly at her, for I saw that she was stinging me again with her own peculiarly subtle malice.

"Be quiet, Sylvia. Stop this confounded wrangling, will you?" commanded her father. "Chalmers, will you tell me what's happened?"

"Cobalt and I have shaken hands. We're friends."

"Have you gone over to him?" queried Baird.

"No. I'm still free to help you."

"It sounds a little twisted," observed Sylvia.

"Well," I admitted, "no doubt it is twisted, but I've told you the facts. However, you don't have to worry about Cobalt. He won't interfere with you much longer. He'll be a dead man before another day comes around."

I watched Sylvia as I said this, to see if she would show any fear. She did not. Neither did she show any pleasure in hearing that the man's death was so imminent.

"You're guessing?" she suggested.

"It's no guess. It's about as clear truth as I've ever seen. No man can live in Skagway after Soapy Jones has decided that he must die."

"Decided that he must die?" cried Baird. "Is Soapy trying to have Cobalt murdered?"

"I saw the thing tried today," I told them. "It will be tried again." I could not help adding: "They've got me in their black book also."

Baird exclaimed again. He seemed very excited. "I'm going back to see Soapy," he declared. "You're coming with me."

"Thanks," I declined, "I'll stay here and rest a while. You can go. But I prefer to stay here."

"Sylvia," said her father, "persuade him to go, will you?"

"Of course I'll persuade him," replied Sylvia. "Tommy, you run along. There's a lot of drafts in this room, and you'll catch your death of cold, if you stay on here."

"There's not enough kindness in you, Sylvia," I said, "to warm the heart of a little fly-catching lizard. Come along, Baird. I'll go with you!"

At the door I looked back at her, scowling. She showed no emotion. She was merely thoughtful and detached, watching me as though I were a mere machine. The attitude became her, with her head canted over upon one side. It became her so much that my heart was still aching a good deal when we got downstairs.

There the proprietor gave us a corner of his eye and immediately lost himself in his accounts again. This made me so angry that I lost control of my temper entirely. Sylvia had irritated me too much just before. Now I stepped over and tapped the brute of a proprietor on the shoulder. He raised his head with a jerk, but he lifted his eyes slowly.

"Well?" he said.

"I'm watching you, my friend, I'm watching you all the time."

He looked me straight in the eye, sneering.

"You'll need the help of your patron demon," I told him, "if you interfere in my affairs, or in Baird's affairs. And if you go near the girl, I'll have your heart out. I'm holding you responsible for her safety. You hear?"

I thought he would jump over the desk to get at me, he was so swollen faced with fury, but he gradually settled back into the chair from which he had just risen. "Yeah, I hear," was all he said.

I went out into the street, Baird asking me if I were not mad to talk like this, making such a foolish scene. I told him that I was tired. I was tired of the crime and the treacherous suggestions that filled the whole air of

196

Skagway. He only answered, after a moment, that at least Sylvia was perfectly safe. Of course I agreed with him, but I was not so sure. Nothing that I can put down in words will give the true atmosphere of Skagway at that time. I really believe that it was a more dangerous cap than even those early murder nests, the Montana gold mines.

The wind had died down when we got into the street, and it was much colder. The snow that had fallen had collected, here and there, in ruts and depressions, crisp and grating under the heels.

I said to Baird: "Soapy is liable to have the pair of us knifed."

"I've got to take the chance," replied Baird. "That's twice in half an hour that they've tried their hands with Cobalt. They'll have the man dead before long. They'll never try only one man against him. Not after what he's done today."

I agreed with that. We went on, but there never was a more nervous and unhappy fellow than I was when we entered the saloon. Baird asked for Soapy from my friend, the barkeep, and he looked at us with his bright, unfriendly smile before he would answer.

"You'll find him back in the little room," he told Baird. "You know the way. Let your friend stay here and have a drink on the house. Soapy never sees more than one man at a time."

I only laughed. "Fair," I said to the bartender, "I'd rather put in my own strychnine. I'd rather pour it in my own coffee than let you in on the job."

The fellow was the coolest in the whole world. When I accused him of wanting to poison me, he merely laughed.

"I don't use strychnine," he said. "Matter of fact, I use something a lot swifter. You won't have a drink?"

"No. I'm with Baird."

We walked off but, as we turned away, I faced a small mirror at a side of the barroom. By chance it showed me the face of Jess Fair behind me, and I distinctly saw him make several movements with his head. At the same moment two or three fellows got up from a table in a corner of the room. One of them cursed loudly and swore that he would never try his luck at poker again. I was not surprised. I decided that Fair's signals must have been intended for this table. What a lot they were, the three of them. They did not look like the dregs of humanity. They were not even as near human as that.

A sapient thing is vice. In their wrinkled eyes, in their foreheads, and about their mouths was the stamp of worldly wisdom. They all seemed to have the same blood. They looked like brothers, but this was only because they descended from the same fatherhood of crime.

"We're followed, Baird," I said. "We're followed by fellows who would as soon brain us as take out a handkerchief."

"Shut up!" demanded Baird. "We're inside now, and we've got to try to fight it out."

"We've got to try to fight it out, but I'm scared almost stiff right now."

"So am I," confessed Baird, "but let's keep walking."

Our terror thawed a little by action of this sort, and so we came to the door of the small closet where Baird had been interviewed previously by the great Soapy Jones. First Baird rapped at the door.

"It's sound-proof," said one of the three, passing with a leering look of contempt.

"It ain't fool-proof, though," remarked another wag.

The three of them laughed, nodding their heads at one another. Then the door opened, and Soapy Jones was inside, looking out at us and smiling.

"Hello, Baird," he said. His smile went out as his glance fell on me. "I'm mighty glad to see you both. Come in, boys, come in."

Baird went in first, and I trailed after. The place was so odd. I never had seen anything like it.

"Not a sound goes through these walls, and not a sound enters," remarked Soapy Jones. "So you can explain the mystery, Chalmers, of your return to my place."

"No mystery at all," I said.

"Tut, tut, no mystery? You'll find it mysterious enough."

"Shall I?" I asked, getting more frightened every moment.

The door opened behind me. I dared not turn, but I got an impression of a dozen men entering the room.

CHAPTER
TWENTY-NINE

Soapy's Cabinet

My own eyes would not have served me as well at that moment as the eyes of my friend, Baird, for he was facing me, and in his face I saw mirrored the danger which was coming on me from behind. I still wonder that I did not cry out, or leap to the side, or attempt to pull out the revolver which Cobalt had given me, but I was paralyzed. Hands suddenly gripped me by each arm. There was enough power in their grasp to have mastered ten people like me.

Then Baird got his voice and shouted: "Soapy, is this the result of your promises to me?"

"What promises have I made to you?" he asked coldly. "You never mentioned this sneaking fellow." He pointed at me.

It was not pleasant to have Soapy scowl and sneer at me. His scowls and sneers were likely to possess a peculiar efficacy as all men knew. His gestures generally were quite as effective as axe or sword strokes.

"He's with me, he's my man," said Baird frantically, as the others drew me back toward the door. "I owe him more than I owe any other man in the world. He's been more a friend to me and to my daughter and . . ."

"What are your friends to me?" asked Soapy. He grew white. His face shone as if it were freshly covered with grease.

For my part I pitied poor Baird. The fury of the gangster was so intense that I felt that I was as good as dead. I was not even badly frightened. The horror which I felt of that black-bearded ogre was sufficient to make all other fears as nothing.

"My friends are nothing to you," insisted Baird, "but you owe me something. You're a man who pays his debts of gratitude. You won't let harm be done to poor Tom Chalmers?"

"Chalmers? Is that his name?" Soapy asked. "He looks like a cur to me. He has the hang-dog look. What use would he be to any man in the world? Why do you want him, Baird?"

"I want him . . . ," began Baird.

At this moment there came three knocks in quick succession on the door of the little cabinet.

"Who's there?" demanded Soapy. He did not wait for an answer but opened the door in person.

Framed in the opening appeared two men who supported a third man between them. The man was limp as a rag. His clothes were torn. His face looked as though it had been beaten with heavy clubs. I cannot describe the look of his features or the swollen, closed eyes. I thought he was dead, and so did Soapy apparently.

"Who is it?" he asked and added: "What do you fools mean by bringing a stiff here?"

"He's alive," said one of the two men. "We found him. It's Blacksnake Loren."

"Who jumped him? What gang did this?" demanded Soapy. "What in the hell is happening in Skagway?"

"No gang. Cobalt done it," said one of the men.

"You lie," insisted Soapy. "Blacksnake is a man-breaker. He's been in the ring. He's wrestled, too. No one man could do that to him unless he used a club!"

They said together: "We seen it!"

"What?" shouted Soapy. "You saw it, and you didn't give Blacksnake a hand?"

"It happened kind of fast," said one of the men sullenly. "I was taking him in front, and Buck here behind. Blacksnake, he jumped out of the doorway, and Cobalt sort of exploded. That's all I know what to say. He exploded. He seemed to hit us all at once. I went down hard. Through a haze I seen that Buck was down, too, and poor Blacksnake, he was in the hands of Cobalt all by himself. First he struggled. Then he was just hanging like a rag out of those hands, and Cobalt dropped him into the mud and . . ."

"Get out of my sight," breathed Soapy through his teeth.

They backed up. Soapy slammed the door again. If he had been angry before, he was almost hysterical now. Not that he shouted or pranced, but the fury showed in his rolling eyes and in the twitching of his lips, now and then, which gave him a most animal and frightful appearance.

Baird, I must say, was a fellow of a great courage. Even then he did not keep still, but went at Soapy vigorously. "There's the man you promised not be hurt," he stated, "and you've sent three of your best to murder him."

"Murder him?" asked Soapy, beginning to pace up and down. He laughed a little, excess of passion making the noise bubble over at his lips. He resumed: "Three of my men were to take him without more than giving him a crack over the head, but I wish now that I'd had them poison him. I will. I'll have them bump him off. There's room for him with the sharks of the Pacific, maybe. There's no room for him in Skagway!"

"I don't think you'll have him killed," counseled Baird, always surprising me with his equable manner.

"Don't you?" asked Soapy.

"No," Baird replied. "There's too much honor and decency in you. You're not a fellow to break your word of honor which you've given to me."

One of the men who was holding me broke into a loud, braying laughter. Soapy glanced at him, and the glance was enough. The fool cut off his laughter so suddenly that he almost choked. I heard him stifle and gag.

"I've made the promise, and I hope that I'll keep it," continued Soapy, "but I've never made a promise that has cost me more. You," he barked at the men who held me, "get that trash out of the room!"

"And do what with him?" asked the one who held me.

"What do I care?" Soapy shrugged. "Just get him out of here."

Baird exclaimed. He ran across the cabinet to get to me. He would have caught hold of me, I think, but they thrust him off, dragging me through the door, and hurried me almost at a run down a small corridor. My brain was whirling. I should not have been surprised if the final blow had fallen on me from behind at any moment. Then they took me up a short, narrow flight of steps, kicked open a door, and thrust me inside.

"Fan him," said one of them.

They fanned me. They went through my clothes and took from me nothing but my gun and a smaller pocket knife. When they had finished with that, one of them said: "Are we gonna waste time over him?"

"What do you think?"

"I'd tap him on the head and see how much salt water he can drink."

"I dunno. The chief didn't say."

"That's because he didn't care. He said that he didn't care."

There was this conversation about my life or death being carried on, and I was listening with the last hope gradually flickering out.

"If he don't care," said another, "suppose that we bleed him for what we can get."

"He's got nothing. He looks poor."

"He's from the inside. He must have something."

"Soapy don't like it when you bleed without orders."

"I'd like to get somebody's opinion."

"My opinion is what I said before. Soak him between the eyes and see how far he'll float on the tide."

I stared about me at the room and the faces. The only window was shuttered. The place was as dark as night. One lantern burned on a small deal table which stood in the center of the compartment. In a corner there was a cot with a thin straw mattress but no bedding on top of it. I knew that the stuffing was straw because it stuck out in a bristling handful from one torn corner. Worse than all else the miserable room was dripping with moisture. There was a dark, shallow pool in one corner, with a limp piece of paper half sunk in it. Altogether it was as depressing a cell as I ever have seen.

"I'm not gonna stay here forever," said one of the men.

"Let's do something."

"The gent that makes the wrong step for Soapy never gets a chance to make another."

I blessed that thug for his cool common sense.

"There's the door to Jess Fair's room," said one. "Jess, he'd know what to do with the bird."

"Go on, Kid. You find out."

"Yeah," said the Kid, "the rest of you ain't so keen to bother Jess, are you?" He sneered back over his shoulder at them as he went toward the door. What a face the Kid had! White, scowling, with puckered brows and ferociously flaring nostrils, there was still an element of debauched youth in him. He had big shoulders and a big, square jaw. He paused by the opposite door and knocked gently, almost reverently.

A quiet voice called out to enter, and the Kid opened the door. I looked straight into a room of about the

205

same size as the one we were in, but it was arranged more pleasantly. There was at least covering on the cot. Quantities of spare clothes hung from pegs along the walls. A small stove burned in the center of the room and near the stove, propped back in a chair with his heels on the edge of the table, was Jess Fair, reading a magazine. He held it with one hand, the read page turned back inside the hollow of his palm. He looked across at us with a quiet indifference, as cool and smiling as when he stood behind the bar. He showed no surprise at the sight of me.

"Hello, Chalmers," he said. "Poison might have been better at that, eh?"

"Yes," I said frankly. "I think that it might."

"Shut up, you," snapped the Kid at me. "Hey, Jess, what'll we do with this sap? Sock him or tie him?"

"What's the order?" asked Jess, not even giving me a second glance.

"There wasn't no particulars. Soapy said he didn't care," came the answer.

"Soaking him takes less time," said Fair.

"That older guy, that friend of his, has he got a real pull with the chief?" asked the Kid, rather anxiously.

Jess Fair looked at the ceiling and yawned. "Yeah," he said, "I guess he's got a pull, all right."

CHAPTER
THIRTY

The Kid

In this manner, by a casual speech, my life was undoubtedly saved. When I think back to it, I feel that this incident better illustrated the cruel callousness of Soapy's gang than all their murders. To kill me or not to kill me was a mere matter of convenience. It was only extraordinary that they wasted so much time in debate and, I am sure, if the remark of Jess Fair had not turned the situation in my favor, someone of my precious guards would have ended the dispute by braining me on the spot. Not that Jess took any personal part in the question. He merely delivered the one opinion and then, turning his eyes back to his magazine, he recommended his reading, saying in a drowsy murmur: "Shut the door, will you?"

They shut the door. I noticed that they closed it quietly, as if thus to show their respect, and this alone would have been enough to establish Jess as a person of importance.

When they had me again in the other room, the Kid said: "Tie his hands, and you birds slide. You find out something about him. Did he bring anything out of the inside? If he did, we'll get it. Go on!"

They thought this idea was a masterpiece. They tied up my hands as he had directed, and I was allowed to sit on the bed. The Kid took his place on the table, dangling his legs. His head sagged forward and thrust out like the head of a great bird. His back sagged and bent forward. He made a cigarette out of brown wheat-straw papers and some tobacco in a sack. He lighted it, tucked it in a corner of his mouth, and spoke, the cigarette flopping rapidly up and down while he talked. It never was shifted from this post until it was burned to a butt.

"That's likely to stick and take off some skin when you peel it away, isn't it?" I asked.

"Aw, maybe it sticks sometimes," said the Kid. "That don't make no difference. That's nothing. What was your lay before you come up North?"

"My lay? Oh, I was a common 'puncher."

"Was you? That's no kind of a lay, is it?"

"It's pretty hard work. It's all right if you like it. Cows and horses, I mean, and plenty of roof over your head."

"You mean sky? Eh?"

"Yes."

"No, I guess you never scrape off your hats ag'in' that roof." The Kid grinned a little at his own remark.

"I've had a mustang buck me up to the rafters of that same little old sky," I told him.

He lost interest in this conversation and yawned, exhaling a quantity of thin, blue-brown smoke. Just then we heard Jess Fair cough, a light, barking sound in the next room. The Kid listened, canting his head to one side, instantly intrigued.

"Listen to him," he said.

"It's not a very good-sounding cough."

"He's cooked," and the Kid nodded in confirmation of his words. "He's cooked, all right. You hear that?" He had lowered his voice, so that the sound of it might not reach the man on the farther side of the flimsy partition. "He just sets there. He can't sleep."

"The cough keep him awake?"

"The cough? Yeah. Maybe the cough, partly. He's got something on his mind."

"Nothing seems to bother him a great deal."

"No. Because he's cooked, and he knows it. That's why he gives you the glassy eye. He knows that he's cooked!" He laughed a little, inviting me to share in his amusement, but I could not laugh.

"He knows he's cooked. That's why even Soapy is afraid of him. When you know you're cooked, you don't care about nothing. That's the way with Jess Fair. That's why he could go and get anybody, because he don't care."

"I wonder if he could get Cobalt?"

"Cobalt? Oh, that's the strong boy from the inside. Sure, Jess could get him. Jess could get anybody. He always has."

"What's Jess done?"

The Kid jerked up his head and stared at me. "You think I'm a fool?" he snapped. "No, no, brother. I ain't as simple as that. I don't know nothing about him. Not a blooming thing. There was a bird up here from

Tucson. He said he knew a lot about Jess. He comes in and hunches up to the bar, shakes hands, and calls Jess by his first name and old hoss. But he lost his memory the next day."

"He shut up, did he?"

"Sure he shut up." The Kid silently demonstrated by placing a forefinger between his eyes and moving the thumb as if on a trigger. "Yeah, he lost his memory. He didn't have nothing left to remember with. But Jess is that way. He ain't no historian. He hates history, matter of fact."

I left the subject of Jess Fair. "What was your lay, Kid?"

"Me?" replied the Kid, puckering his white fleshy brows. "Aw, I dunno. I kind of floated around. I punched a cow or two myself," he concluded cautiously, eyeing me.

"Where was that?"

"Oh, around here and there," he said vaguely. Then he warmed up. "I'll tell you what, if I'd had a chance, I would've stuck to it. I liked it. I had everything from pretty near blizzards to pretty near sunstrokes. But I liked it all. Horses like me, if you know what I mean. They take to me, and I take to them. There was a little ornery no-'count filly on a ranch that I raised on a bottle till she could take to hay and stuff. I raised her myself. They used to laugh at me. She'd foller me around. They called me the 'old mare' on that outfit. That little beast, I tell you what, she used to come and steal lump sugar out of my pocket. She never thought I knew. She was a little witch, that filly." He laughed silently at the memory of that distant joy.

"What did you call her?"

"Her? I called her the Princess. That was what she was like. When spring came around, she lost her pot belly, and the way she stepped around, she looked like she could gallop on clouds. That was the kind of a look she had."

"What became of her?"

He scowled at his knuckles. "Well, I moved on. That's all." He stared earnestly at me. "You know the way it is. The way some people are, they never forget nothing. They never give you a chance." He sighed. "That little witch, she come into the bunkhouse after me one day. They was playing poker. She stood there and looked on, with the lantern reflected in both of her two eyes. She looked like she understood. I called her the Princess. That was what she was like!"

I thought that I could see the slender filly with her eyes like two stars. I wondered if she might not have been able to bring the Kid back into a clean life. But now she was only a symbol of all that was true and beautiful from which the cruelty of justice had parted him.

We fell silent, partly because the thoughts of the poor Kid were far away and, in part, because a strong wind had come up, battering and clattering away at the building, slamming doors, rattling shutters, and making conversation more or less difficult. So great was the force of the wind that the door to the room in which we sat oscillated violently back and forth, stopped, and slammed and shuddered noisily again.

"You've had a rough time of it, Kid."

"Me? Aw, I don't sob about it," he said hastily, defending his manly spirit. "I don't hang around and sob about it none."

The door opened. In the opening stood not one of the gangsters but Cobalt. He closed the door behind him, slamming it carelessly, as though the wind had accomplished the thing. The Kid was so thoroughly deceived that he did not even turn to look.

I tried to think of something to say to get the attention of the Kid and keep it. But he chose this moment for yawning. Well, I knew that was the end for him. Up came Cobalt, tiptoe. The floor creaked under him at the last moment, and the Kid jerked his head around to be caught in Cobalt's hands.

Have you seen a cat strike its claws into a bird and seen the poor thing flutter and turn limp? Or have you seen a mountain lion strike a young deer and watch the deer fall? I have seen those things, and I thought of them as the terrible grip of Cobalt paralyzed the Kid with the first pressure. As though his fingers were talons, they seemed to drive into the boy. There was no question of resistance. Cobalt lifted him from the table. The Kid vaguely struggled with his arms and kicked with his legs. Then he was still. He did not even cry out. With hypnotized eyes he watched the face of the other.

"What was it? Jujitsu?" he asked.

Cobalt placed him on the cot beside me. He stuffed a wadded bandanna into the mouth of the boy and lashed it securely in place with a cord. He cut the rope from my hands and, with an addition to it from the twine which he carried, he trussed the Kid hand and foot.

I leaned over the boy. "Can you breathe all right, Kid?"

He jerked his head to signify that he could. He shook his head again, looking at Cobalt, as much as to say that no ordinary but a supernatural agency had taken him in hand. I almost agreed with him.

Cobalt was already at the window shutter. He worked it open and told me to climb through. I told him to go first, but he took me under the pits of the arms and lowered me though the opening like a sack. My feet struck the ground, and the cold wind whistled about me. Cobalt jumped down at my side.

At the same time we heard a door open inside the building, and the voice of Jess Fair was saying: "Hey, Kid, what's the big idea of all the cold air?"

We waited to hear no more but went hastily down the street.

CHAPTER
THIRTY-ONE

A Little Smashing

When we had gone a short distance down the street and saw that there was no sudden pursuit, I asked Cobalt how he had managed the thing. He said that he had seen me enter the place, doubted my safety there, and made a tour around the outside. Luckily he heard voices, mine among them, so he spotted the room where I was kept and entered by forcing a nearby window. As he described the thing, he made it seem the most natural and normal act. A thing to be expected of anyone. But I know that the house of Soapy Jones was a tower of dread to everyone in Skagway. Not another soul in the world, I verily believe, would have dared what Cobalt dared that day.

It does not seem much compared with his final exploit in Skagway. It hardly seems to be a stepping stone to the tremendous achievement with which he staggered us all, and which I shall have to describe presently. Yet his present exploit of entering the Soapy Jones place was alone enough to shock the whole of Skagway into attention, you may be sure.

As we went down the street, the wind hurling us forward so that we had to lean back against it, we fairly stumbled into two other pedestrians who were going along with their heads down, bucking against the wind-driven sleet. It was the pair who, together with the Kid, had taken me in hand. I made a dive for one of them, shouting out to Cobalt. I think I should have had my hands full, for the fellow I tackled was a robust rascal but, when the two saw me, they were limp with astonishment. They did not even defend themselves. We got their guns from them without an effort.

They kept saying: "Did Soapy do it? Did Soapy turn you loose?"

"Cobalt pried me away from Soapy. That's all," I said. "And one day he'll go back, take an hour off, and kick that whole shack to pieces."

"I almost think he will!" rasped one of the thugs. "If he's got you away from Soapy, he can do anything."

We took them to the police. The thing was a perfect farce. The moment they found out that the two we had with us were accused of being employed by Soapy Jones, the police would have nothing to do with the case. I don't think they were originally honest fellows whom he had corrupted. They were thugs themselves, members of Soapy's gang wearing uniforms.

They asked me what I had to prove what had happened to me and anything that had been done against me by the men who worked for Soapy. I showed them my wrists, which the ropes had chafed, and Cobalt told how he had found me sitting with my hands tied together and under guard in the dingy room. They merely shrugged their shoulders. The two crooks we had taken in with us began to feel at home and to make a loud, violent defense of themselves.

I shall never forget the scene. The storm had covered Skagway with a twilight dimness. Two greasy lanterns flickered on the walls of the little room. By the stove sat one deputy, his feet wrapped in a quantity of sacking. At the desk was another, a desk spotted with many ink stains, though I don't think that it was much used for writing purposes. The fellow at the desk had a protruding chin and a protruding forehead. When he smiled, he seemed embarrassed.

When we saw that nothing could be done, Cobalt stood for a time with his eyes half closed, the old, familiar demon beginning to glisten in them. I knew that something was about to happen, as surely as when one sees the powder trail burning and the open powder cask to which the fired trail leads.

The thugs and the crooked deputies were beginning to grin at one another and enjoy themselves when Cobalt said: "The whole pack of you are a lot of thieves and crooks. You're all working for Soapy. I've known it for some minutes. But I'll tell you what, boys, I'm going to give him a message. I'm going to give him a letter, and you can tell him how I punctuated it, and where I made the underlinings. It won't be a long letter, but it will say something."

With that he leaned over and picked up the writing desk. The deputy behind it was knocked out of his chair and fell sprawling with a yell, while Cobalt poised that heavy mass above his head and hurled it at the stove. It knocked that stove to smithereens. It knocked over the second deputy as well, and it covered the floor of the shack with rolling coals and flaming brands of wood.

What a screeching and a yelling went up from that pair. The thugs tried to get out, but Cobalt threw them back into the place and bolted the door from the outside. What a yelling that started then! They were sure that they were going to be burned alive, and I suggested the same thing to Cobalt.

"Don't make much difference," he said, "but they won't burn alive. They'll be smoked meat before they get those embers out. They'll be singed meat, too."

That they were. We stood across the street and heard the four screeching for help and battering at the wall of the shack for ten minutes. No one came to their aid. Well, that was Skagway in the palmy days of its youth.

Finally they broke open, not the door, but a section of the wall of the shack. Three of them pitched out into the mud of the street and wallowed in it as if they loved the sty. Then one fellow got up and reeled into the thick white smoke that poured out of the shack. He came back dragging the fourth and last of the quartet, who had been overcome with the fumes.

"There's about half a man in that one," commented Cobalt.

I could agree with this, but a moment later the whole four spotted us, where we stood howling with laughter across the street. I thought they would go mad. They danced and raved and tore, and the two deputies started on the run to arrest us. The other thugs held them back. What they said to them did not take long, but it was enough. Those deputies stopped short, like dogs when they run out of a village to chase coyotes and find a wolf instead.

Cobalt and I went on together unharmed, and I was very thankful to heaven and to Cobalt for the dangers he had put behind me this day. We went to the hotel, and there he turned in with me.

"They've had time to think things over. It won't hurt if I go in and talk to them a little now?" he suggested.

I insisted that it was high time that he should do so, but I'm afraid that there was not much heartiness in my voice. When we walked in, the proprietor stared at us with open mouth. How much did he know? I never could tell. I could only guess that he was a complete scoundrel.

"Out again, you see," I said with mock cheerfulness to him.

He did not reply. He gaped only wider, and his face grew more pouchy, I thought, as we walked by him.

"He's one of them, all right," said Cobalt. "You're in a snake's den here."

I felt that we were, but how was it possible to get a better place in Skagway? I could hear the excited voice of Baird before we got to the room and, when we knocked on the door and he saw us standing there, it warmed my heart to hear the way he shouted out his pleasure and dragged me in, thumped me on the shoulder, and swore even then he had been mourning for me.

"That fiend of a Soapy Jones hates you. He's withdrawn all his promises. He swears that he'll start

218

with you and finish by making hash of Cobalt. Cobalt, why have you crossed him so often?"

"Because he's been in my way," said Cobalt, and it was a characteristic answer.

Sylvia was eating ham and hot cakes with plum jam, a frightful combination, but one gets peculiar hankerings after the diet on the inside. She had a great pot of steaming coffee beside her and a stack of pancakes a foot high. Now she stood up and told us to finish off for her.

So we sat down. Up there in the North it seems as though everyone is always hungry. Food is as welcome a sight as bank notes in milder climates. Sylvia stood by, simply passing things to us. It was her father who did the questioning.

"What happened?" he asked. "Where did they take you? Did Soapy change his mind at last?"

"Cobalt pried me loose from Soapy's gang," I answered. "He came into the house, and he got me loose from them. He says it was simple."

We all took a turn looking at Cobalt, but his face was hidden behind a tilted mug of coffee. "They've got a lot of chicory in this coffee," he commented. "Hand me another slab of those hot cakes, Sylvia."

He heaped his plate again. That furnace of his needed continual stoking.

"You can't pass it off like this, Cobalt," said Baird. "It was a grand thing. I think that I'd rather knock at Satan's gate than go near that place again. Soapy is a madman now. Some of his best men have been manhandled. You've done him a great deal of harm. His

219

gang takes it to heart that they haven't been sent on your trail from the first in numbers, not to take you but to murder you. That would be safer. They say that they might as well be sent to bait a grizzly bear. I think they're right. I was a witness of a half riot that started in Soapy's office, if that's what one can call it. They want your blood, Cobalt, and my solemn advice to you, son, is to clear out of Skagway and get as far inside as you can, as fast as you can. There's nothing but poison waiting for you here."

Cobalt nodded cheerfully at him. "Do you think I'll back down? Not I! Not for fifty like Soapy. The bartender, though, is a different matter. I think if there were only two like him, I'd give him plenty of room. It's good advice. It's kind advice, Baird, but I'll stay on here and try my hand with Soapy first."

When he had said this, he turned and looked deliberately at the girl. One could tell what he meant. It would be Soapy and the gang first. Afterward came Sylvia.

CHAPTER
THIRTY-TWO

The Right Club

I was sorry that Cobalt had to ring in his unfortunate attitude toward Sylvia at the very moment when we were all looking up to him as a sort of demigod. Silence fell upon us, but out of the silence came something of the old sharp hostility. I could see the eyes of Sylvia turn bright and cold, and the jaw of her father was set.

Sylvia went on serving until the edge of that vast appetite of his had been dulled. Then she said: "Make yourself a smoke, Cobalt?"

He had no makings. So she took mine and manufactured a cigarette for him. I wondered why she had learned the rather difficult and delicate little art of making cigarettes when she herself never smoked them. At any rate she made the cigarette, presented it to him for moistening, finished it off, gave it into his hand, then lighted and held the match for him. As the first big exhalations of smoke went upward, she stood there beside him and looked down at him through the smoke.

"Listen to me, Cobalt."

"Aye," said Cobalt. "Now that you've soothed me, you can use the club on the poor beast."

She brushed the smoke apart a little with her hand. "I'm only going to tell you the truth, Cobalt."

"Let me hear it then."

"It's this. It's the reason why you won't want me any longer."

"Go on," he urged. He actually smiled at her.

"It's because I care for another man."

This struck me, I know, with a great shock. It seemed to strike her father also, hard enough to bring him out of his chair, but Cobalt merely shrugged his shoulders.

"You remember the story I once told you, my dear?" he asked her. "About the thief and the emerald? Would the thief have cared where the emerald wanted to go or what the emerald felt about him?"

"You don't mean it," said Sylvia. "You're not as hard as you make out. You're a terribly great fighting man, Cobalt, but your heart is not so hard as you make out. It does make a difference to you. Particularly when you know that it's a friend of yours."

"Ah? And what do you mean by that?"

"A friend whose life you've saved, and who has saved yours. That's what I mean."

Cobalt stood up at last and gave me such a look as no man receives twice from another. "You mean Chalmers?"

"Yes," said Sylvia. "That's who I mean."

I could not speak. I wish to heaven that I could have spoken. It would have meant all the difference afterward. I could only stand there mute, like a fool, with a ringing in my ears that came from the thunderstrokes of my heart. I heard the voice of Cobalt speaking, and the sound of it was wooden and dead, saying: "Well, that's right, Sylvia. You've picked out the right club. It's the only club in the world that would have stopped me, I suppose. But you've stopped me now. I'll go out and get a little air."

He went past us, three standing clay figures, and the door closed gently behind him. Baird recovered himself before I did. He was greatly excited and, going up to Sylvia, he caught her by the hands and shook them, not in congratulation but with a vigorous impatience.

"Did you honestly mean it, Sylvia? Or was it only a ruse?"

She nodded her head. She had the look of a sleepwalker. "Yes, I mean it."

Baird seemed to feel that he could get no more out of her. He turned back to me, crying: "How long has this been going on? What's been between the two of you?"

I made a helpless gesture. My brain was still spinning. "I don't know anything about it. She's flirted with me a little. She'd flirt with a wooden Indian for lack of something better. But I never knew that she cared a rap. I still don't think she does."

"I do," stated Sylvia, "but I've been shameless. I haven't asked if you care a rap about me, Tommy."

"This is the most extraordinary thing I've ever heard of," said Baird. "You mean Tom Chalmers hasn't spoken to you, and yet you talk like that to Cobalt?"

"Do you want to call Cobalt back?" she asked him.

He threw up both his hands. "Great heavens, no! Let him stay away. I'd rather have you committed to the arms of an avalanche than to see you married to that man. But Chalmers . . . why, he's older, he's married, he has children."

"He's only thirty-two," said the girl. "He has a pair of darling youngsters. Don't you think that I'll be glad to have them for mine and mother them?"

"I'm beaten!" said Baird. "I don't know what to think or to say."

"Don't you think or say a thing," she commanded. "Let water run downhill. That's the best way. Tommy, you tell me, and let father hear. Do you think you can come to care about me?"

She came across the room toward me. I stepped behind a chair. At that she stopped. She let her head fall a little on one side. Her great blue eyes were soft with a sort of despair.

"You don't want me, Tommy. Is that it?"

"Look here, Sylvia, you know mighty well what I mean."

"I'm going to get out of here," said Baird.

"You stay right where you are," I called after him.

He turned at the door and looked back. "I don't want to interfere in your private affairs with Sylvia. I can't stay here."

"You can though," I insisted. "I want you to stay long enough to explain why you're in a sweat."

"I've heard and seen enough in the last five minutes to make an Egyptian statue break out in a sweat," he answered.

"Then I'll tell you why you're in a sweat. You're thinking that I'm nothing but a fellow on the make. A chap with a small bit of money, no great ambitions, and nothing but the hope of running cows on some range land ahead of him. Am I right?"

He came half way back across the room.

"Oh, talk to him, Daddy," pleaded the girl. "Try to persuade him for me. I know that you love Tom."

"I respect you, Tom," said Baird. "I have an affection for you. You've done a grand thing for me and for Sylvia, and I realize it. Don't think I don't. There's no other man in . . ."

"That's all right," I broke in. "Now let's have the other side."

"You've expressed the other side," replied Baird. "I mean, Sylvia is growing up toward another sort of life than what you offer to her."

"You mean, you don't want to picture her in the kitchen of a small ranch house, washing dishes and turning around to see that the boiling beans still have enough water on 'em. Is that it?"

"Well, that's about it."

"You see how it is, Sylvia," I said to her.

"All of this has nothing to do with it," argued the girl. "You have to tell me whether you care about me, or not."

"You're wrong again," I told her. "You know that every man in the world who has seen you cares about you, either as the thief cared for the emerald or as someone he wants for a real wife. I care for you in both ways somewhat. You know that I do. But I'm afraid of you. Besides, you'd always be in second place in my home."

"Is there someone else?" Sylvia asked.

"There's my dead wife."

Baird muttered: "This is too painful. I'm going out, Sylvia. Perhaps you'd better talk about this another time?"

"We'll talk it out now," insisted Sylvia, "if Tom doesn't mind."

"Go on," I said. "I'm glad to talk it out and have it done with."

"I swear," said Sylvia, "that I never would be jealous of her poor, kind ghost."

I shook my head. "But I would always be making comparisons. You're ten times cleverer than she was. And you're a thousand times more beautiful. But she was as clear as crystal. You take a mountain spring, Sylvia, . . . it may not be very big, and it may not be very important, but almost anybody could sit a day and look down at the water bubbling and listen to its song."

"You mean," she said, "I'm complicated? I'm really not. A little play-acting . . . I'll wipe that out, if you want."

"To change your mind would be to spoil you," I told her. I think that I was right. "Great Scott, Sylvia, to kiss the tips of your fingers would be joy enough to make me giddy. That's all very well. But I see the truth of this situation. You've only used me to shunt poor Cobalt away. You'd . . . by heaven, now I think that I see the truth!"

"What is it?" asked Sylvia.

"Stand away from me, then," I said. "When you're so close, Sylvia, I begin to forget everything. I can't think.

But isn't this true? There's another man you like a lot better than you like me."

"I? Nonsense!"

"There is. Confess it!"

"You're an odd man, Tommy." There was a shadow in her eyes. "But you know, I think if we lived together, we would each grow to love more and more. I've never met anyone so gentle and understanding as you are."

"Thank you," I said. "But now, look here! Suppose I name the other man for you, the man you like better but are afraid of."

"Stuff!" Sylvia went back a step from me and seemed alarmed.

"I saw it in your face a while ago," I declared. "I saw it when you stood yonder and parted the smoke and looked down into his face. You're afraid he's too great a force, that he'd dash you around the world, you don't know where. You'd rather dodge him and attach yourself to me, because I'm harmless, and because somehow Cobalt won't persecute you so long as you're with me. But Cobalt is the man you love. Stand there and honestly tell me whether I'm right or wrong?"

CHAPTER
THIRTY-THREE

Sylvia Goes Native

I cannot say exactly how the idea came popping into my brain. Perhaps it was the memory of a certain curious tenderness I had seen in her face as she stood before Cobalt. I was continually studying her expression. Her words mostly told you nothing. Sometimes they would be expressing only the shadow of the real truth about her and, when that thought came leaping into my mind, I threw it at her. The result was a shock to me and to Baird.

For Sylvia, the keen, clever, invincible Sylvia, who all her life had done exactly as she pleased, who was strong by nature and strong by habit of thought, no matter how delicately she disguised her power of brain, this Sylvia now looked rather wildly about her, and then she ran to her father and like any tiny child threw herself into his arms and began to sob and sway and tremble with a passionate grief. The Lightning Warrior came out of the corner in which he had denned himself all this time and crouched nearby, studying the situation, trying to make out whether or not the girl was being attacked and ready to cut the hand of the attacker.

That was a picture and a thing to hear as well, what with the wild sobbing of Sylvia, and the voice of the storm wind that was mourning outside. I started out of the room, tip-toeing. Baird stopped me.

"You'd better stay here and see this thing through with us. You're qualified, I'd say, as a sort of second father to her, Tom. You've seen through her as I never would have."

I stopped, of course. Sylvia left her father's arms, went over, and threw herself on the bed. There she lay, still shaken by her sobbing. Baird wanted to go to her, but I held onto him.

"Don't you go," I said in a whisper. "She's having it out with herself. There's a pack of wildcats screeching and clawing in her just about now."

He mopped his wet face and grunted, but he took my advice. The storm in her ended. The sobbing ceased. She lay still for a moment, and then she got up and went to the washstand. I poured some water into the bowl. While she washed her face, lifting the icy water in her cupped hands and holding it a long moment in place, I picked a towel off the rack and gave it to her so she could dry with it. Then I got a cup of coffee for her.

She sat down at the table and reached blindly for me, giving my hand a squeeze. Baird stood by as one who looks from a distance on a strange happening. At last the tremors left her, and the cup of coffee was finished.

"I wish that I smoked," said Sylvia. "I wish that I smoked! That would be comfortable now. I'm going to learn."

She never would, I knew. She never would foul her hands with yellow or stain her lips with tar and nicotine.

"You talk, father," she proposed. "You suggest what we should do."

Poor Baird had remained standing stock-still. Now he shook his head. "You know, Sylvia, that there's not much in me that can be useful for you in the way of advice. I've never really understood you."

"Oh, that's why I've always loved you so," said Sylvia. "You try, Tommy."

"I think Cobalt ought to be in on this," I said.

"No!" she cried out hoarsely.

I was astonished and shocked by her vehemence.

She went on: "You're tired, Tommy, or you wouldn't suggest that, since you've seen so much. You know I've been hypnotized by Cobalt from the first. But I feel that it's merely hypnosis and, if ever I belonged to him, some terrible thing would happen. I think of him as one might think of murder."

I stood up and said I was going to bed. My poor brain was not worth a rap, it was so befogged. So I went to the door and got to the room which Baird and I occupied. He followed me in just as I covered up as warmly as I could. Both in brain and body, all the strength was out of me.

"She wants to be alone," said Baird. "I don't know why. I wish to heaven I could see a way out of this. But I can't. There are too many threads. While we struggle with our own little problems, we forget that we're all caught in the spider's web, Soapy and his Skagway

230

gang. That would be enough by itself, but with this other added ... I don't know, not unless Cobalt himself breaks the web."

I shook my head. Sleep was coming over my mind like dark clouds in the sky. "He can't do that. Not even Cobalt can do that. One man, two men, even half a dozen. Yes, he could handle them. But this is different. Here you have something extra. Here you have Soapy and his cohorts. And there is that smiling young demon, that Jess Fair."

"The bartender with the buck teeth?" asked Baird. "What of him?"

"Oh, you'll hear of him before the wind-up," I remember muttering. Then blessed sleep came over me, as rain comes over a dry land.

CHAPTER
THIRTY-FOUR

Bucking the Thugs

I should have been there, though I have heard accounts from so many eyewitnesses that my absence hardly matters. After all, I could not have been inside the brains of those who were in action. Each word, look, gesture, intonation has been mentioned to me, I'm sure, at one time or another. For what did Skagway have to think about afterward? What else was there to talk about? At any rate there is no use crying over spilled milk. I was asleep when the crash came. I was up there in my room, sound asleep, and poor Baird was in the same room also, softly cursing my snoring but too sympathetic to awaken me.

I slept and dreamed of Sylvia, of course. Her delicate grace, as I remember, I found turned into a beautiful painting — all the life of her transformed into a brilliant shadow by the grace of the powers of this world who wanted to preserve her as she was forever, never aging, undying. While I dreamed, Cobalt was in the street.

When he got to the entrance of the hotel, he paused for a moment in the doorway and looked over the men who were lounging there. They were chattering, laughing, joking. When they saw him, they became silent. Skagway knew Cobalt by this time, you may be sure! The latest comers and the oldest dwellers knew all about him. He had split open the mind of the town and put a new picture inside of it, so that the murders and the robberies of Soapy's gang were no longer the only important themes of current news about which to gossip.

One of the men by the stove said: "I beg your pardon, Mister Cobalt, but is it true . . . ?"

"Not 'mister,'" said Cobalt. "I never wear a title, man. This is a little too far north for titles."

He went out into the street without waiting for the other man to complete his remark. I suppose it would have been a question about one of Cobalt's famous feats on the inside.

There in the street, where the wind howled and beat, Cobalt was seen to stride up and down for some time. What was going through his wild brain at that time? Well, I suppose that it was the same theme that filled my poor brain as I slept — beautiful Sylvia. Perhaps he had a few thoughts for me also. I dare say, he must have wondered how she could give herself to an unimportant chap like me, a comparative weakling. It must have been the bitterest gall to him. A sense of vast defeat too must have been in his mind. He had never failed before, when he bent all his will to the work, but now he had failed miserably.

I don't know what he would have done, if chance had not given a direction to his misery. As he walked through the cold, driving mist of the storm, he heard a

233

groaning, cursing voice ahead, and a big man came stalking through the dimness, walking with uneven strides. Cobalt listened, drinking in the sound of another's sorrow. Then he took the other by the arm.

"What's the matter?" he asked.

The big man cursed him and tried to shake him off. Of course, he merely shook himself, not Cobalt.

"What's the matter?" persisted Cobalt.

"Get your hand off me," shouted the big man, all his grief turning into rage, and he raised a big fist to strike.

Cobalt picked the fist out of the air and pulled it down. "Now tell me, what's the matter?"

The other grunted. "It's Cobalt," he said. "I didn't know you in the whip of the wind. Aw, it's nothing, Cobalt. They've trimmed me. That's all. Not much. I had a hundred ounces. It ain't a fortune. But it was all that I brought out with me."

"Soapy?" asked Cobalt.

"Yeah. Who but him?"

"One of the crooked machines? You gambled on 'em?"

"I started. I wasn't losing fast enough. They rolled me. They soaked me and rolled me for my wad. That's all. It happens every day."

"It's too bad," said Cobalt.

"It ain't the money," said the stranger. "It's me being such a fool. That's what grinds on me. Look at me! Forty-eight. Born with nacheral good sense. Now, see what's happened to me. I'll have to go back inside. I'd rather walk into fire and brimstone."

"Why not go another place for your money?"

"Hey? What?"

"Why not make a shorter trip to get your dust?"

"I dunno what you mean."

"Go to those who have it now. That's a shorter trip than Dawson or Circle City."

The stranger laughed. "I'm to go in and ask them for it, eh?"

"Why not?"

"Nothing wrong with that, except that I'd just get rolled again."

"Everybody gets rolled a few times in his life. Let's go back and see what happens."

"In Soapy's place?" gasped the other.

"Why, where else? Come along. We'll both ask for it. Two hands are better than one."

"By thunder, I see what you mean. But I'll tell you what. You have nerve to do anything, but I haven't. I've had enough of Soapy Jones and his gang. I like life pretty well. That's all. I won't go in there again."

"You don't know yourself," persuaded Cobalt. "The fact is that you're aching to get back in there and hand 'em some talk. Tell 'em that they don't play fair. Tell 'em anything surprising and new."

The other laughed. "You're a card, Cobalt. There's nobody like you."

"Come on, then. You come back with me, and I'll get your money for you."

"What!"

"I mean it."

"Get my money away from those men?"

"I'll get your money for you, or I'll die trying."

235

That was enough. That old-timer thought of his hundred ounces, he told me afterward, and he thought of nothing else. He turned right around, and down the storm-swept street he went with Cobalt. They came to the door of Soapy's place, pushed it open, and entered.

Of course it was packed. Weather like that would have sent people to any hole, for the sake of the warmth alone. Besides, as I have said before, the people of Skagway never got tired of gratifying their curiosity and showing their courage by going into Soapy's den. I said it was packed. As a matter of fact the majority of the people were in the gaming rooms. The bar was not at all crowded. Jess Fair was not attending it. He was enjoying a rest, a thing he allowed himself for only a few hours every day. Men said that he loved nothing in life except to stand there behind the long bar, peddle the drinks, and look into the faces of the customers with his pale, expressionless eyes. It was another matter, after the new pair entered — the big fellow and Cobalt. They got at a corner table with a couple of chairs, and there they sat.

"We'll warm up a little before we start talking," said Cobalt. "What's your name?"

"Joe Porter."

"All right, Joe. We'll warm up a little, and then we'll begin to argue with them."

"If there's any talk to be done," said Joe Porter, "why shouldn't we do it now, before the place gets crowded?"

"It's crowded now." Cobalt was cool as you please. "That fellow with the yellow face in the corner . . . that half-breed, or whatever he is . . . he's one of the

236

bouncers. He's a crowd in himself, if I'm any judge of some of the bulges under his clothes. There's another bouncer at the bar and two more beside the door. They're all full of guns. Do you pack a gun yourself, brother?"

"I've got an old bull-nosed Forty-Four, but I ain't much with it, and I don't aim to use it unless I have to. Self-defense or something like that."

"Well, seventeen hundred dollars is part of yourself. You'd be defending that."

Joe Porter rubbed his knuckles through his beard. "Are you gonna make a fight out of this, Cobalt?"

"There may be a little fighting."

"Then I dive for the floor," said Porter. "I ain't no hero. I'm for the safest place, and the floor's the safest."

Cobalt laughed. "You're all right, Joe. I like a man who speaks his mind."

"The crowd's thickening up a good deal." Poor Porter was not relishing his position a bit.

The word had gone instantly through the place that Cobalt was there and, of course, that was enough to bring people with a rush. They came swarming in from the gaming rooms. They thronged before the bar, and every one of them had his eye upon Cobalt and Cobalt's rough-looking companion. I suppose that crowd was as hard a looking lot as ever gathered into one room.

"Do you see the fellow who rolled you?" asked Cobalt of his companion.

Porter took off his hat and rubbed his head. There was a great lump on the top of it, where he had been slugged. "Over there," he said. "That fellow with the Stetson hat on, the pale-gray hat and the skinny face. He's the one, I guess, that done it."

"Are you only guessing?"

"Well, I had a drink or two on board."

"We'll try to find out," stated Cobalt. "Hello, friend!" He signaled to the man in the Stetson, and the latter turned slowly toward the table.

He was a man of middle height with a wizened, evil face. I have seen him myself, and his hands, his mouth, the very whites of his eyes were tobacco-stained.

"Yes?" he said to Cobalt.

"Partner," said Cobalt pleasantly, "sit down with us and have a drink, will you?"

The yellow-stained man hesitated a moment. I have often wondered whether fear or courage made him accept the invitation, since he must have seen Porter sitting there as big as life, ready to accuse him. But up he came and down he sat, signaling to a boy to bring on the drinks. They had a round of them. Cobalt turned his drink around and around. He did not taste it. The other turned down his glass in a moment.

He coughed. "The stuff's wildfire!" he said.

"Yes. It gets into the brain, all right," said Cobalt. "What's your name, partner?"

"Name of Louis Trainor," said the thug.

"Let me introduce a friend of mine. This is Joe Porter. Porter, Mister Louis Trainor."

The two looked at one another without shaking hands.

"I guess we've met," said Porter.

"I guess I've seen you somewhere," said the thug.

"It wasn't my hand you shook," said Porter.

"No?"

"No, it was my head that you knocked on and my poke you entered," said Porter.

Cobalt laughed. The thug followed his lead and laughed in turn. "I don't know what he's talking about," he explained to Cobalt.

"That's a pity," said Cobalt. "Maybe your pockets will remember, though."

"What?" asked Louis Trainor.

"Maybe your pockets will remember," said Cobalt again. "Turn them out and let's see what's in them."

Louis Trainor was not a fool, and he was not a coward. His hands twitched once, and then they remained still on the edge of the table. His eye shrank from the steady gaze of Cobalt and wandered, first to the right and then to the left with significant glances.

"You help him," Cobalt said to Porter. "You see that he is feeling pretty tired and doesn't want to budge his hands from the edge of the table. One would think that he even felt it was dangerous to move those hands. So you just dip into his pockets for him, will you?"

Porter, grinning, half frightened, surveyed the crowd around them. Everyone was interested, but no one seemed inclined to interfere. The whole thing had been so soft-voiced that no one of the spectators could be actually sure of what was taking place. But they began to suspect when they saw Porter go through the pockets and up the sleeves of Trainor. He pulled out of them a queer heap of things.

From a breast pocket of the coat he took a handkerchief with a moistened corner and a red-and-blue chemical crayon for marking cards. From a side coat pocket he took a sling-shot with an elastic wristband. From the belt of Louis Trainor he removed two knives, one a regular Bowie, the other a slender sailor's dirk. He also got from Trainor a deck of cards, probably already prepared to be slipped in the place of an honest deck. He took out a good revolver, .32 caliber. Trainor, in his shooting, apparently did not wish to strike heavy blows but deadly ones. Porter found, finally, a gold belt strapped about the waist of the thug. In it there was a considerable quantity of dust. Cobalt weighed it with his hand.

"About forty ounces in this," he said. "Where's the other sixty, Trainor? Did the house take all that for a commission, or did you split a part of it with your pals?"

"I don't know what you're talking about," said Trainor.

He looked wildly about him and savagely. The crowd was half laughing and half growling. The pile of crooked implements on the table was a sufficient comment upon the character of Trainor, and even a complete thug has some scruples of conscience about seeing himself exposed.

"You go up and invite me to sit down here," said Trainor, "and you order up drinks, and then . . ."

"And then I take a look at you," said Cobalt, "and I think your lining will be more interesting than your exterior. I seem to be right."

"I'll get your . . ."

"If you stir those hands," said Cobalt, almost under breath, "I'll take you and break you in two. Now listen to me. I want to learn what you did with the other sixty ounces. You got those forty from this fellow, didn't you? You're one who rapped him over the head and rolled him for wad, aren't you?"

He was so quiet that Trainor looked at him twice before he understood that there was a tiger, and not a man, sitting there before him at the table.

He moistened his stained lips, and then he said: "I rapped him. I wish I'd smashed his skull in for him. I slugged the fool, and I rolled him. And . . ." He hesitated, and then he went on, seeing the danger in Cobalt's face: "I got twenty ounces. Twenty went to my side-kicker. Sixty went to the house. It's a hog."

CHAPTER
THIRTY-FIVE

A Showdown in Sight

"We'll take the forty ounces for security," said Cobalt, after he had heard the confession of the yegg. "We'll back the house for the rest. That sounds fair, doesn't it?"

Trainor said nothing for the good reason that there was nothing to say. He got up suddenly and walked off into the crowd, leaving his crooked implements behind him on the table. Men sneered at him and shouldered him as he passed, for his villainy had been too clearly exposed. He would never again be a useful member of any gaming house in the Northland.

He pressed through, regardless of the looks and hard words that he got from all sides. In the farthest corner he found a bouncer and said to him: "What's your job? To stand around and watch holdups in the shop?"

"You dirty crook," said the bouncer pleasantly, "I wish that I'd had the picking of your pockets myself. What do I care what happens to you in this shop? It's happening to you and not to the shop. It's just another act to keep the show running good and smooth. Don't stick out your jaw at me, or I'll bust it for you."

242

"You know that chief wants us to pull together," Trainor reminded him.

"The best thing that the chief could do," replied the bouncer, "would be to slam you out into the street. You're no good. You're a spoiled egg in this house from now on."

Trainor regarded him wickedly but seemed to see that there was something of truth in what he had heard. Therefore he walked on. He tried another bouncer with the same results.

Finally he saw that there was nothing to be gained directly from others. He said to a third of these fighting men: "Bill, lemme have the loan of a gun, will you?"

"So you can use it, or so you can hock it?" queried Bill.

"So I can use it."

"Well, all right," agreed Bill. "It ain't natural for me to keep a man out of a fight if I see a good way of getting him into it. Here's a gat. Go and use it, but use it good. That gun has told the truth to four men in its day."

"I'll use it like an angel, and no mistake," swore Trainor, and he turned to make good his promise.

He was the cornered rat now ready to show his teeth but, as he turned toward the table at which big Joe Porter and Cobalt had been sitting, other things were happening in the room. I have often wondered and often asked how it was that Cobalt was able to sit in that room so long before an attack was made upon him? I have often asked, but the answer was always a mere conjecture. Probably, in a case of such

243

importance, the bouncers wanted an order directly from Soapy or from his lieutenant, Jess Fair.

As soon as Trainor left the table, Cobalt singled out a lanky fellow with a sour, dignified look. You could not tell whether his pride was mostly his nature or simply a stiff neck. Cobalt called him over, and the fellow came suspiciously. He was not one to let himself be trapped, as Trainor had been trapped, by getting within the reach of those famous and terrible hands of Cobalt.

Instead, he paused at a little distance. The crowd gave back suddenly to a good distance. For this looked like a gun play. They got so completely out of the way that Cobalt could talk to this ruffian without much danger of being overheard.

"You're Booze Gabriel, aren't you?" asked Cobalt.

"Yeah. There's some that call me that."

"You're the finest fighting man that Soapy has, they tell me. The finest fighting man in Skagway. Is that right?"

"Are you aiming to kid me? D'you think that I rate myself along with Jess Fair?"

"Oh, Jess is in a class all by himself," conceded Cobalt with a wave of his hand, indicating the exception. "I was meaning among the regular run. They tell me that you're one of the best."

"I ain't here to brag," said Booze Gabriel. "What are you driving at, Cobalt? Is it me that you want to break up next?"

What a curious thing it must have been to see Cobalt there in that saloon surrounded by enough guns to blow him off the earth and out of all recognition. Yet he could pick a man out of the crowd and make even the hired ruffians come to his call.

"Will you sit down and liquor with us?" invited Cobalt.

"No. This is my day for standing," countered Gabriel with a grand, stretching grin that suddenly made him look like a wolf. "I ain't sitting down today."

"All right," nodded Cobalt, "maybe you can make a better speech standing up. A lot of the greatest orators like to be standing, I suppose."

"What kind of a speech am I going to make?"

"You're going to tell me what's what about Soapy Jones."

"Oh, I am, am I?" drawled Gabriel.

"You are," went on Cobalt. "I've heard a lot of rot about him, since I came to Skagway. A lot of people say that you boys throw in with him partly because you're afraid to stay out and partly because of the money that you make working for him."

"And what's your idea about that?" asked Booze, cautiously trying out his man.

"My idea is that you all know down in your boots that Soapy is one man in a million."

"You're right. He's one man in ten million," agreed Booze Gabriel emphatically.

"That's why you stay on with him. Thuggery isn't all the truth about him. What is the truth, Booze?"

"Why, this here talk is takin' a kind of a strange turn, where I would like to say that Soapy Jones ain't wearin' his right moniker. I ain't tellin' nothing. I'm only saying

245

that Soapy ain't wearin' the true moniker that belongs to him."

"Of course, he's not," agreed Cobalt. "He wouldn't hurt his family. He wouldn't drag them down by letting the weight of his reputation fall on their necks."

"No, he wouldn't." Booze Gabriel straightened a little. "The fact is that Soapy's a gentleman and don't you make no mistake."

"That's not the mistake that I'm making." Suddenly Cobalt laughed. The whole crowd could hear him say: "Great Scott, Booze, would I be here if I didn't know that Soapy's a gentleman?"

That was a poser for them. They looked at Cobalt then at one another. Soapy Jones, a gentleman? That was a new conception, to be sure. Cobalt went on developing his theme: "The fact is, Booze, that a gentleman once is a gentleman always. That's the point, isn't it?"

"You bet it's the point," said Booze Gabriel. "And I've known Soapy . . ." He stopped himself.

"All right," said Cobalt, "you've known him for years, haven't you? And you've always known what he is at heart. That's why you're with him. Am I right?"

"Of course, you're right!"

"And that's why I'm sitting here in his saloon," Cobalt asserted. "Because I trust him."

That was about as odd a speech as ever was heard in Skagway. It stunned the crowd that listened. A stir and a murmur passed though the listeners, hearing, as they thought, that Cobalt was making overtures to the master criminal of the town. For I think that most of the law-abiding men had begun to hope that Cobalt, out of the greatness of his strength, might provide the rock on which Soapy was at last to split.

"You're here because you trust him," echoed Booze Gabriel, not comprehending at all.

"Of course, I am. It's because I know a gentleman's reactions. He may tap a few fools on the head, here and there . . . not referring to you, Porter . . . and he may slip a knife into somebody's gizzard from time to time. He may mark a card, and he may put a brake on a roulette wheel. But his instincts are right when it comes to a pinch. So I came in here with my friend, Porter. I want to talk to Mister Jones. I know he will realize that the time has come for him to step out in person. Another day he might send one of his agents, to speak to another man. But the time has come when I have to see him face to face, and he has to see me. We both know it."

He pointed. People suddenly turned their heads toward the farther doorway, expecting something to appear at once. "I know," Cobalt resumed, "that he won't even come into the room behind me. He'll come through that doorway, so that we can face one another as gentlemen should."

Booze Gabriel straightened even more, and his color brightened as well. I believe it was a fact that he had long been devoted to Soapy. He was the same as others of the gang like Jess Fair who had followed Soapy for years with a strange fascination. "I'll tell you what," Gabriel assured Cobalt, "my boss will meet anyone, any time, on his own level. Are you asking to meet Soapy now?"

"That's what I'm asking," Cobalt stated.

"All right," said Gabriel. "I'm gonna go and tell him so." He turned on his heel briskly, smartly like a soldier, and marched out of the room, the crowd making way for him.

Joe Porter said softly: "You ain't gonna do it, Cobalt?"

"No? Why not?"

"If you do, you're a dead man."

"How's that?"

"You're dead on two counts. One is that Soapy himself is a regular wizard with guns. They say that he's as slick, almost, as Jess Fair when it comes to pulling a Colt and using it, front end or back. And the second count is, even if you drop Soapy, his boys will load you full of lead afterward. You can't get past those two counts."

"Perhaps I can't, but I'm going to try."

"You ain't. You're going to get out of here, and you're going to get quick!"

Cobalt merely smiled at him.

"You're a dead man otherwise." Porter repeated. "I'll have you on my conscience all the rest of my days."

"I'm nothing to have on your conscience. If I live, or if I die, there's nothing much to have on your conscience, Porter. Life's not a song to me. The taste has gone from it."

Porter argued no longer. He sank back in his chair and sat there, rigidly waiting. When he looked around the room, he saw that everybody else in the place was waiting in the same manner and that all realized, like him, that the showdown between Cobalt and Soapy Jones was about to follow.

CHAPTER
THIRTY-SIX

A Necktie Party

What did occur at this particular point was a blank for many years. It was never filled in until a party of Wyoming cowpunchers got on the trail of a man suspected of being a horse thief. Wyoming men ride hard. They don't fear dim trails, and they don't spare their mounts. So they caught that fellow on the second day of the ride, up near the state border, and they examined him under the shade of a spruce. The examination did not last long, for he was riding on a good gray mare which belonged to one of the members of the party. He was a horse thief and, when he was pressed, admitted that he had "borrowed" the mare. Horse thieves are not popular anywhere in the West but, it is said, they are least of all popular in Wyoming. At any rate the thief in this case was told to commend his soul to the infinite mercy of a better world, for he was about to be started toward it within the next few seconds.

At this it is said that he merely blinked once or twice and then admitted the justice of the sentence. He even said that he had once helped at the execution of a horse thief himself. Having thus opened the conversation,

250

while they were preparing the rope and going through other formalities, such as the selection of a limb, the posse talked with their condemned man and asked his name. He said that his name was Gabriel, and that most people called him Booze. At this, one of those present cried out that he had seen this fellow before on a certain day in the saloon of Soapy Jones in Skagway, and that he had always wondered how Soapy had been worked on to come out to the fight that followed instead of simply sending a few of his henchmen to murder Cobalt.

"I'll tell you about that," said Booze Gabriel. "I'll tell it to you short, and I'll tell it to you true."

The leader of the posse sat down on a rock and laid the noosed rope aside.

"Go on, Booze," he said. "The better you tell it, the higher we'll hoist you, and the quicker you'll finish. We'll snuff you out just like a shot."

"That's good," said Booze, "because it's not the dying but the choking that kind of bothers me." Then he proceeded with his story as follows:

When he left the barroom, he went straight back to the office of his chief, but there was no answer to the code rap which he gave upon the door. This did not trouble him, since Soapy was often out of the place. Then he went upstairs and tried Soapy's bedroom door. After he had knocked twice here, using the same code tap, he heard the creak of a bed, and Soapy presently unbarred the door to him. His face was puffed, and his eyes were wrinkled with sleep, which he

251

began to rub out of them as he asked Booze, with several oaths, what the matter was.

"Soapy," answered Gabriel, "there's a gentleman downstairs asking for Mister Jones."

Soapy laughed in his face. "For 'Mister' Jones he's asking, is he?"

"Yes, that's the word."

"And who is he?"

"Cobalt."

Soapy got him by the arm and jerked him into the room. Gabriel said that the face of his chief was twisted into knots. "You're lying to me. No man and no demon would dare to come back into my place after what he's done to me, not even Cobalt!"

"Cobalt's not a fool, and yet Cobalt's down there," insisted Gabriel.

"If Cobalt's down there, then he's a fool."

"Not a fool," objected Gabriel, "because he knows that he's as safe there as he would be in his own house."

Soapy only stared at him. Then, retreating to a table in the corner of his room, he lighted the lamp and held it above his head so that, in a brighter light, he could look at Booze.

"No, I'm not drunk," said Gabriel. "I'm cold sober. Thank goodness for it! I can tell you that the time's come, and you'll have to believe me."

"The time has come for what? If the cur is down there, the time has come to rouse up some of the boys and send Jess along with them. It's Cobalt's last day." Soapy ended up this speech by roundly cursing Cobalt,

252

but he found that Booze Gabriel was only smiling. "What's the matter with you? I think that you're half out of your wits today."

"No, I'm not out of my wits, but you've got to go down there and face him man to man, single-handed, like one gentleman faces another."

"Hold on! As one gentleman faces another? Is that what you said?" Then he began to laugh.

At this moment Booze simply quoted a better man than himself — Cobalt. "Once a gentleman, always a gentleman."

"What?" cried Soapy. "What do you mean by that?"

"You know right well what I mean. And I know, too, that nothin' that a man does can rub out his blood. There's right blood in you, Soapy, and you know it."

Soapy Jones actually smoothed his long curling beard and stared at the floor, silenced.

Booze went on: "I'll tell you, Soapy, that what you're thinkin' of right now is the Negroes singing in the cotton field, the hounds baying the 'possum of a night, and the look of the bayou with the swans slidin' across it, their white shadows beside them. That's what you're thinkin' of, and of pictures hung along a wall in a big white house with columns in front of it."

"Ah!" said Soapy Jones through his teeth. "What if I am?"

"Only I was recollecting you. Cobalt, down there, he knows mighty well what kind of a man you are under the skin. He's guessed what there is that makes me and Jess love you, Soapy. And that's why he's as safe as if he

253

was in his own house, until you come down there and face him yourself."

Soapy looked at his follower patiently, thoughtfully. Then he said: "I think you're right, Gabriel. The day's come. I'm going down to do as he asks. Only I feel that my luck has run out, and I'm as dry as a squeezed lemon. Here, man, you give me a hand with my clothes, will you?"

Booze Gabriel stayed there and helped his chief to dress. He felt no shame in this menial employment. Instead he spoke with pleasure and with pride about the clean linen of his chief, the silken socks which he drew on, and the fine quality of the suit with its long-tailed coat. He spoke of how Soapy shrugged his heavy shoulders until the coat sat on him in exactly the way he chose to have it and how critically Soapy regarded himself from every angle in his mirror, and then got Booze Gabriel to give his boots another rub.

"What boots they were!" said Gabriel, "as soft as velvet and as bright as moonlight in water." Then Soapy drew on gloves of a fabric so light and thin and soft that they did not in the least impede the freedom of the fingers. He pulled both of them on but on second thought, just as he was about to leave the room, he drew off the one from the right hand and carried it in his left.

Next, he took from a doorway a short-bodied revolver of a make which Booze Gabriel did not know, although he knew that it was his master's favorite weapon. This gun he unloaded and loaded again, after he was sure that it was in perfect order. Finally, he fixed a spring holster under the pit of his left arm and placed the gun in this. Having done so, he made two or three turns through his room, drawing the gun like a flash and then returning it to its hiding place.

He washed his hands. He gloved his left hand again and carried the other glove in the same hand. Then he took down from a bureau drawer a handkerchief of the finest linen, folded it precisely, and thrust it into his outer breast coat pocket. He allowed just a trim corner of it to appear above the lip of the pocket.

"Look at me, Booze, and tell me how I seem." He stood up for inspection.

"There ain't a breath of dust on you," said Gabriel, "and you look like the walkin' image of the old major himself."

At this Soapy turned on him, cursed him, and called him a rotten fool.

"But he did look like the major," Booze Gabriel told his listeners in the posse as they sat that day under the shade of the spruce tree. "He looked as like him as two peas out of the same pod, except that the major had a pile more stomach on him and not quite so muscular in the shoulders, if you foller me. But that was the way that Soapy was dressed when he left his room and marched down toward the saloon with me behind him."

"What happened then?" asked one of the posse.

Booze grew suddenly dark of brow. "You know what happened. And it ain't for me to tell you what happened. Get your rope ready."

After his talk some of the men found their blood cooler, and they would have left the rope behind them and taken Booze into town for a regular trial and legal punishment. But the leader of the posse declared that he was sure Booze didn't much care what happened to him, and that it would cost the county a lot of useless extra expense.

With both of these points Booze at once agreed and made no protest whatever. So they asked him for his last wishes, his last message, and his last prayer.

"I got one message for Satan, and one prayer to him, and one wish. The message and the prayer and the wish is for one of the shady spots in Hades. Good bye, boys!"

He stood up on the back of his stolen mare. They led it out from under him. He dropped heavily until his toes actually touched the dust. Mercifully, the shock snapped the spinal column, and poor Booze Gabriel died as quickly as though a bullet had passed through his brain. Thus the posse redeemed its promise, having heard the strange story of how Booze persuaded Soapy Jones to descend from his room and meet Cobalt on equal terms in a duel.

CHAPTER
THIRTY-SEVEN

They Meet

When I think of what happened in that room, I groan, remembering that I was not present. But, again, I assure you that I have heard the story so many times, from so many points of view, that sometimes I forget that I was not actually inside the doors. The whole scene is so vividly spread before my eyes.

Red Loftus, Champ Evens, and Harry Gay were tending bar at this time, and they had to work like fury to keep the drinkers supplied with the red-eye. The clash of the glasses and the dull, bumping sound as a spun bottle went whirring down the bar and rocked into place mixed with the murmurs of the drinkers. The mirror behind the bar was spotted and blurred with the many faces that it reflected. It was a great business stroke, when that ingenious Soapy decided to place a mirror along the back of the bar. For it gave his place an air of elegance that almost amounted to decency.

The suspense by this time had grown nerve-wracking. Joe Porter said afterward that every man in the place from time to time would mop his forehead or loosen his shirt collar a trifle. Joe's own big, hairy hands were sweating profusely, but he said that Cobalt's were cool enough apparently, and the face of Cobalt was perfectly calm also.

The crowd understood this thing that was to come as perfectly as though it were a rehearsed performance. They left a long lane from one door leading directly toward the table at which Cobalt was sitting. That lane was astonishingly narrow as though everyone took it for granted that, when such men as Cobalt and the great Soapy Jones met, no bullets were likely to fly astray from the mark.

Just then there came a strange interruption, a most unexpected thing. Trainor, who had been so thoroughly subdued before with his borrowed gun ready in his hand, now rushed to the front of the crowd and screamed hysterically at Cobalt: "You don't have to wait for Soapy Jones. I'll meet you now! I'll take you down!"

Cobalt did not stir a hand to reach his gun. He merely said: "Some of you take the fool away."

Imagine that in the saloon of Soapy Jones where the other fellow was a trusted crook. More amazing than the order was the fact that it was obeyed, not by mere members of the crowd but by a pair of Soapy's own bouncers. They actually mastered Trainor, jerked the gun out of his hand and, taking him to the door of the saloon, hurled him into the mud and told him they would break his neck if he ever came back again.

This brought loud applause, hand clapping, feet stamping, and yells of laughter from the crowd. There was a hasty round of drinks, and the atmosphere seemed to lighten at once. The incident could not be explained by Joe Porter, but I think that I understand it. Everyone was so bent on seeing the meeting between Cobalt and Soapy that practically no attention was paid to Trainor. He was not even exciting — he was a mere nuisance.

The remarkable thing to me is that Cobalt was able, so accurately, to see into the minds of the crowd. That drink was hardly down, and the bustle subdued into its former murmuring, when even that murmur died out. Through the doorway came, not Soapy Jones but the lofty, emaciated form of Booze Gabriel. He was dead white, his eyes glittering like the eyes of a drug fiend. He halted near the table of Cobalt.

"Mister Jones is about to join you, sir," he said.

It sounds silly, but it was not silly, according to Joe Porter who said that he could feel an electrical prickling running up and down his scalp at this moment. Then Soapy himself stepped into the doorway and sauntered slowly toward Cobalt.

Cobalt stood up. "Mister Jones, I believe."

"The same, sir," replied Soapy. "Mister Cobalt, sir?"

"Carney is my name, sir," said Cobalt. It was the first time anyone in the North had heard the true name of the strong man. "James Carney," repeated Cobalt.

"Mister Carney," Soapy said and bowed a little.

"I have come in here, Mister Jones," explained Cobalt, "to represent a friend of mine who has lost a little money in your gaming rooms."

"Is that why you have come?" asked Soapy. "But you must realize that games of chance are games of chance."

"Yes, even when there are brakes on the wheel. Of course, there's always a chance, but as a matter of fact the game of chance that beat him was simply coming into your saloon. He was thumped over the head and thrown into the street. They took a hundred ounces from him."

"Are you a lawyer, Mister Carney?"

"No."

"Then may I ask you what brings you to the support of Mister . . . your friend, yonder?"

"A sense of decency and a liking for fair play."

"And just what can you do for him?"

"I can persuade you to return him sixty ounces. I took forty away from one of the thieves."

"Persuasion," philosophized Soapy Jones, "is a gentle art."

"It depends upon the kind that's needed. I'll tell you what, Mister Jones. It occurs to me that here I am, occupying a seat at one of your best tables and not spending much money. So perhaps you'll see your way clear to paying down sixty ounces to Mister Porter, my friend here. Then I'll promise you that I'll walk out and leave you to better company."

"What could be better company?" asked Jones. "No, no, my dear sir, I wouldn't dream of buying you out. You're welcome to sit in that chair forever. A man so well known will draw trade for me. I would be glad to give you a bonus on the amount that you bring in for me above my average, if you'll appear there every day."

I have always thought that this was a fairly clever way of turning the thing off. Joe Porter said that he began to

260

yearn for something to happen, for this stiff verbal duel excited him almost to a madness of suspense.

"I see that you're a true Southerner," observed Cobalt, "for you perfectly understand all forms of hospitality."

"Thank you, but really all that people complain about is that I am apt to entertain them a little too much."

"There is only one good way to entertain my friend, Porter, here."

"And what is that?" The chief appeared as pleased as he could be.

"By giving him sixty ounces."

"I saw no theft," replied that smooth fellow. I suppose that he got his nickname from some such source.

"Do you see this?" asked Cobalt. He lifted the hat off Porter and showed the rising bump.

"If you feel that there's a cause for complaint, there is always the law."

It appeared that Soapy Jones felt this last point with a peculiar force, for he actually bowed to Cobalt and then smiled at him. With his gloved left hand he parted his black beard and still smiled at him. Porter told me that this smiling of the archvillain made a great impression on him. Suddenly he realized that even a scoundrel may be flattered and, if not flattered, he may be amused sufficiently to have his mind turned from his purpose.

"A great many things are above the law," continued Soapy Jones. "The law is made for those who go along the road, not for those who cut across country where there's no need for traffic regulations. As for your friend, you ought to remember that even the fly has no right to complain to the spider, and yet the fly loses a good deal more than money."

"We claim sixty ounces, duly paid over," said Cobalt. "If the money is not paid, we will appeal to the court."

"To what court?" asked Soapy with an evil grin.

"The court of arms," said Cobalt, as ceremonious as ever.

Then, Porter said, Soapy gave one swift, malignant glance around him, as though he were regretting his fine first display. Now he would be neither civil nor courtly but simply put his heel on the stranger's neck. However, that moment did not last very long. He was still half infuriated and half amused by the attitude of Cobalt.

"A good fight," he said, "will end almost any argument, so long as the fight lasts long enough and comes to a complete end."

"I agree with you," said Cobalt. "That's the sort of a fight I suggest."

"But, even if you win, you're not out of the web."

"I take my chance."

"I'll give you something better than a chance." Soapy raised his gloved hand to draw attention. "Friends, Mister Carney and I have a few little differences of opinion, mostly it appears, about a big bohunk who claims he was rolled in my place. Perhaps there are some other things into the bargain, but let that go. We are going to have the matter out between ourselves, as

262

gentlemen ought to do. We won't crowd the law courts, and we won't fatten the lawyers. I think it's a good example that we're setting.

"If I go down and I'm flattened . . . even if I'm on the floor wriggling but beaten, I put a curse on any man who steps in to help me. Let Mister Carney go safely out of this place. And you there behind the bar, if I'm beaten, before he goes, see that Porter gets his sixty ounces. No, make it a hundred and sixty . . . for luck!" He laughed as he said this.

Porter said that his excitement was so intense that he simply forgot to think of what the wager meant to him. He could only stare and gape from one of these men to the other, wondering at the polite, circuitous way in which they expressed themselves and wondering still more at the fierce emotion which was in both of them. This miracle already had been accomplished. Cobalt had come into the spider's den, and the spider had consented to fight without using the advantages of his web. And here Jess Fair came for the first time into the picture.

CHAPTER
THIRTY-EIGHT

Terminus Ad Quem

When Fair came in, he walked right up to the shoulder of his master and was heard to say: "Leave it, Soapy. This is my job."

"It's my job," replied Soapy. "Your job is only after the finish, to see that the pair of them get safely out of here after you've paid them what I've promised. There'll be no crawfishing today, Jess. This is my day. I feel it in my bones. Old Lady Luck is smiling at me. Don't worry about me, because you'll see me turning up on top."

Jess Fair in reply murmured — so at least one of the nearest bystanders said: "Look at his heart, not at his face. Let his eyes alone, and shoot for the heart."

The man who heard this looked across the room to where Cobalt was standing, and he said that he could understand the warning for the eyes of Cobalt were blue lightning.

"What rules do you want?" asked the gambler, turning back to Cobalt.

"We're in your own house," replied Cobalt.

"Nevertheless, we won't use the rules of the house," said Soapy Jones. "We'll try a new set, like a new pack.

We stand, back to back, in the middle of the room. We step off ten paces which are counted by anyone . . . say by Jess Fair. At the tenth step, we turn and start shooting. If we can't finish with shooting, we take the knives. If the knives won't do, we end with our hands. Is that agreeable?"

"That's agreeable," said Cobalt.

"And if hands are not good enough, then anything we can get hands on will serve as a weapon."

"Anything from poison to dynamite. Why, we agree so well it's a pity that we haven't worked as partners, Mister Jones."

At this, Soapy's face grew as black as his beard. "You've been the one man to thwart me and beat me. You've smashed up my men. You've walked alive through Skagway as if Satan were giving a charm to you. I'm going to have your heart for it, Cobalt!"

"All right," agreed Cobalt. "There's a heart in me to get, if you can win. It's free for you to have. You've been liar, murderer, thief, and sneak all your days. You're a greasy scoundrel, Jones, and we'll see the end of you. Commence when you're ready. Fair, will you give the signal?"

"Yes," said Jess Fair.

For an instant the two glared at one another. Then they came together, making the last few steps slowly, their eyes glaring straight at one another. For the gambler disdained to accept the advice of Jess Fair.

They turned their backs on one another, and Jess Fair said in the most casual way: "All right, friends. One! Two! Three!"

265

He counted out the paces, and they took them, Cobalt stepping short, and the gambler stepping long. A grim thing it was, Porter said, to see those two men, hardly matched in the whole world, walking so stiffly away from one another, while the only man who could have made a third to them stood by and quietly gave the measure of that dance.

"Ten!" came from the lips of Jess Fair as quietly as any other number in the count, and the two turned.

Porter said that he expected them to side-step — or that one of them would throw himself to the floor, but he was amazed to see that neither of them did such a thing. They whirled and stood as straight and tall as fencers, their guns whipping into their hands and their arms flying straight out. It was marvelous, the speed with which each turned, and still more marvelous that they seemed to do it in a single beat, like trained dancing partners. Their revolvers exploded to punctuate the measure. Neither man fell at the first shot, but the Colt dropped from Cobalt's hand. A sound like a weird, high-pitched moan came from the crowd.

Cobalt leaned for his fallen weapon, but he was beaten, it seemed, by the bad start. Perhaps by one millionth of a second, the bullet of the gambler had been fired first and leaped across the room in time to strike the very gun that was in the hand of the enemy. For there was Cobalt, leaning, the red blood running from the shattered hand with which he reached after the weapon on the floor. The second bullet fired by Soapy slashed the shirt of the other across the shoulder, but the sudden stoop forward of Cobalt saved his life

266

for another instant. He scooped up the fallen Colt and, without straightening his body, he flung the heavy gun straight at Soapy. The whirling revolver struck not the head or arm, but merely the powerful body of Jones. Yet, even so, a full-weight Colt .45 is not a toy when it is hurled from the hand of a fellow like Cobalt. It banged into the body of Soapy and staggered him just as he was firing his third shot.

Thus there came about the miracle of that battle: of the first four shots fired only one reached a mark and that mark was only the hand of the enemy. The hurled revolver was followed by the tigerish leap of Cobalt. Porter swore to me that it was not a run across the room but a single, terrible bound that brought him upon Soapy Jones. The impact knocked them both from their feet, and thus entangled they rolled over and over and struck with a crash against the wall. The dust puffed up about them.

Then it was seen that they lay, each on his side, facing one another. The revolvers had been dropped, but Soapy, with a great, bent-bladed Bowie knife, was striving to cut the throat of Cobalt, and Cobalt had caught the moving knife hand in his left, not in his right. The crimson, fast bleeding right was merely good to control the other hand of the gambler.

The moan of the excited, frightened crowd rose to a higher key. Porter said that it was like the keen wind on an autumn day, the last day of the whirling leaves and the first of the black winter. But the knife was not traveling toward the goal at which Soapy had aimed it. Instead, it wavered for a moment in between, its point a scant inch from the throat of Cobalt. Then it was seen that the knife was turning. It wavered and shuddered, but turn it did, while those two mighty men struggled for its possession. The point crooked back toward the breast of Soapy Jones, and it was Cobalt's hand which turned it. He was the master now.

Then, Porter told me, he could not look, so unnerved was he by the hideous slowness of the thing. He glanced away across the room and saw Jess Fair standing nonchalantly against the bar, his legs crossed, the buck-toothed smile flashing about as usual. Then, in a rush, the color left the face of Jess. Porter knew what it meant. At the same moment, he said, there came from the crowd of watchers a faint sigh in unison, as though drawn by a single throat, and the sound froze him to the very marrow of his soul. It lifted him out of his chair and, looking back toward the corner, he saw Cobalt rising to his feet, while big Soapy Jones remained motionless on the floor, looking at the ceiling, a high light gleaming on his forehead. Porter knew very well that the upturned eyes saw nothing, and that the tremor was in the light and not in the flesh. Soapy Jones had breathed his last.

The next thing that Porter knew he was being led to the bar by Cobalt, as if for a drink, while every man in the room remained rooted to his place by the terror and horror of what had been seen. Only one man moved, a big, husky miner who slumped to the floor in a dead faint. It was not a drink that Porter got at the bar. Behind it stood Jess Fair, marble-white but with his buck-toothed smile still flashing. He laid a ten-pound gold belt before Porter, and the latter took it. He said that Jess Fair did not look at him at all but only at the face of Cobalt. His eyes wandered curiously from feature to feature, as if he were an artist and strove to remember that face, that he might sketch it later on, though Porter very well knew that it was not as an artist, with brush or pen, that the barkeeper stared at Cobalt.

They turned toward the door together, Cobalt and Porter. As they did so, pandemonium broke loose in the saloon. The bouncers, the strong-arm men, all had quietly vanished, and the crowd which had been like sheep under the eye of Soapy Jones alive, now roared like lions when they knew that he was dead. They paid no attention to Cobalt and his red-dripping hand. They were only intent upon smashing and looting the saloon, and they did a good job of it. Chairs were used as clubs. Glasses were smashed. Men pulled open the cash drawers behind the bar and looted them. They rushed in swarms to do the same thing at the gaming tables.

No one opposed them. The organization of Soapy Jones was just as strong as it had been before his death. There were just as many bloodthirsty and expert criminals, but the head had been struck from the body. At one blow Soapy's gang was dispensed.

At the door, Porter said, he looked back and the swirl of the crowd, like the dashing of water in a cataract, parted before his glance for an instant and gave him a view of Jess Fair, on his knees beside the body of his dead master with one hand upon his face. It was a gesture of infinite gentleness and grief, and Porter

269

never could speak of it without amazement and a shake of his head.

When they got into the street, he did a foolish thing. He told Cobalt that he had received two for one, two ounces for every ounce of dust that had been stolen from him. He offered half of the loot to Cobalt and even remarked, like a tactless fool, that it might be some time before his right hand was in working shape again. Some time, indeed!

Cobalt made no answer. I don't suppose that he ever had been in the least interested in Porter and Porter's loss or gain. It was merely the small entering wedge which he had used to topple over the huge structure of Soapy's organization.

CHAPTER
THIRTY-NINE

The Monarch Beaten

All this happened while I had been sleeping. What could I have done, had I been awake and on the spot? Well, nothing, perhaps, but it was a time when a man would wish to be on the ground where the action took place. What wakened me was Baird's shaking me by the shoulder.

"The town is on the loose!" he said. "And hell's to pay! Listen! Look out the window!"

I sat up in the bed. The noise from the street instantly cleared the fog of sleep from my brain and left me perfectly alert. I heard the dull roar of many voices. I looked through the window as I jumped up from the bed, and there I saw a tall red flame leaping into the sky.

"What is it?" I asked. "Have the fools set the town on fire?"

"It looks like Soapy's place," said Baird. "I can't quite make it out, but it looks about the location of Soapy's place. Let's find out what's happening. I'll get Sylvia."

Sylvia did not need to be fetched. She was tapping on the door of our room as her father spoke, and he let her in. We went down together. There was no one in the lobby except a small, greasy-looking boy who was rummaging through the desk of the proprietor. He had half the drawers out and their contents scattered over the floor. When we spoke to him, he jumped up and looked at us like the guilty little rat that he was. Then he gathered courage. The boss was gone, and he would not come back.

"Not even come back for the rent that's owing to him?" I asked the youngster.

"Naw! He'll never come back. He's started overland. All that he wants is fast mushing and a good dog team. He'd rather have a good dog team than all of the rent in the world."

"What in the world has happened?" Baird asked him. "What buildings are burning down there?"

"Soapy's gone up in smoke," replied the boy and deliberately turned his back on us, starting to rummage once more through the ravished drawers of that desk.

We went out into the street. There was a crowd running about, breaking into buildings, shouting and screeching with an insane pleasure. We managed to find one man who was an onlooker, like ourselves. He told us the story in brief. It was not until a long time afterward that I gathered the full details from Porter and many others. It was far more impressive, when one heard it from that stranger briefly, for he made the thing more of a miracle. With the details stripped away, it seemed Herculean, inhuman, the courage and the power that a single man had shown in advancing into the house of the gambler and killing him there in the presence of all his followers.

"Did Jess Fair do nothing?" I remember asking.

"Jess Fair? Sure. He buried his boss!" He laughed in a strange way.

"Buried already?" I asked.

"Yeah. In fire."

"Did Jess set fire to the gambling house?" I asked.

"Yeah. That's what they say," replied the other. He was indifferent, but he chuckled every now and then, looking up and down the street at the smashing going on and the crowd dashing about.

"Tell me something," I said to him.

"Well?"

"You're a newspaper reporter, aren't you?"

"The hell! How did you guess that?"

Then we asked where the hero was to be found. Certainly, the best that Skagway could offer would not be too good for him now. But our reporter friend of the detached manner and the chuckle had not been able to find Cobalt.

"I'd rather listen to him for five minutes now than to have a five-column head!" he said.

We went on, pursuing our inquiries, and the story grew and grew with every step that we made. We went down to the gaming house, and there we saw a number who, like ourselves, were gazing with wonder and a little awe upon the crimson and black, fast-dissolving remnants of the famous house of crime. I asked one of them who stood nearby if it was really true that Jess Fair had kindled the fire to cremate the body of his master. He said that it was true and that he had started the fire in order to drive out the crowd which was getting rough and looting the place. In other words, he preferred to let the flames take the gold of his crooked master.

"What's made Jess Fair so devoted to Soapy Jones?" asked Baird of another man.

"Well, Soapy got him young," said the other. "That's all. If you start early enough, you can make any pup into a one-man dog."

That was the only explanation I ever heard of the singular attachment which the gunman showed for the master criminal. We were to learn more later on.

We were standing there, watching the crumbling of the last of the ruin, out of which there came small explosions from time to time, and leaping columns of sparks, fire, and smoke. The heat was welcome and bathed us in a blood-red glow.

"You see?" said Sylvia aside to me. "That's the reason. You see what he's done?"

"You mean Cobalt?" I asked.

"Yes. That's what I mean. You see how he's smashed that place?"

"I see that he's removed a curse from Skagway," I told her. "I see that he's done what the whole mob of the so-called law abiding, including your father and myself, never had the courage to attempt. I see that he's given Skagway a chance to draw a breath and make of itself a decent place. That's what I see, Sylvia."

"Don't be so indignant," she replied. "I hoped you'd see what I mean."

"I think you're only blind, Sylvia. You won't open your eyes to the truth about him."

"I won't give myself into the hands of a hypnotist," she replied. "That's all. If I'd let myself go, I could be mad about him. But there's no check on him. There's no rein that would hold him in. He'd run away. He'd be apt in a crisis to smash things right and left. A man who wronged him would be apt to lead him into a murder. There's no holding him."

"You could hold him," I told her.

"I? Why, he saw through me at the first glance. He wasn't fooled by my little airs. Not a bit! He saw there was trouble in me. I was the first woman that looked strong enough to amuse him, strong enough to give him a little occupation in mastering her. That's the whole trouble. He'd have me mastered soon enough, and then he'd lose interest."

I wondered if she were right. She had a keen way of looking into things, I must say, even from the first. She could be a doctor who prescribed for the physician. She had prescribed me as an antidote for the great Cobalt, simply because I was the reverse of him in every way.

A pair of men came up and stood beside us and talked about the fire and the cause of it. They mentioned Cobalt, of course. Both of them had been in the gambling den when the fight took place. It was from one of them that I first heard of how the knife had been turned in Soapy's hand and used to take his life. It was a neat and horrible detail, and I looked askance to see how Sylvia was taking it. Her lips curled.

"Like a dog fight?" I heard her faintly whisper.

275

That enraged me suddenly.

Then one of the two strangers said something about its being the end of Cobalt, too. You can imagine how that interested all of us.

"What do you mean?" asked Baird sharply. "What do you mean by its being the end of Cobalt?"

"Well," said the other, "he had two hands, didn't he?"

"Of course, of course!" snapped Baird impatiently.

"Well," said the stranger, "now that he has only one hand, wouldn't you say he's divided in two?"

"Only one hand?" asked Sylvia in a quiet voice but one that set my teeth on edge. "Has he lost a hand?"

"Yes, it's practically ruined. Where the bullet tore the gun out of his hand. They say the cords are cut inside the palm. I saw it dripping red. It was bleeding pretty fast, and he went right out into the cold with it. I reckon he'll never use that hand again."

Sylvia took her father and me, each by an arm, and drew us together.

"We've got to find him!" she said. "He's gone somewhere. We've got to find out where he's gone. I'm going to find him if I have to crawl on my knees around the world!"

We started making inquiries. It was a long, hard job. At the name of Cobalt everyone was willing to break out into exclamations and encomiums, but no one could give us any practical hints about where we could find him. That is, no one could for a long time. Then we came across the man who kept the rooming place where Cobalt had stayed, and he told us Cobalt had come straight home from the scene of the fight and had dressed his hand — the proprietor holding two lanterns close to it in order to give him light for the work.

"And the hand?" asked Sylvia in a breaking voice. "What had happened to it?"

He looked down at her. "If you're a friend of his," he said, "well, I'll leave a doctor or himself to do the telling of it. It ain't a job I want."

I felt sick. Cobalt was ruined. Was the destruction of Soapy Jones worth it? No, not the destruction or the salvation of all of Skagway!

"Where is Cobalt now?" asked Baird in a husky voice.

"Oh, he's gone," said the man. "He hitched up his dogs quite a while ago, five big Huskies, and he hit for the inland trail. I asked him if he was going inside."

"What did he say?" cried Sylvia.

"He said he was going inside and would never come out," answered the man.

CHAPTER
FORTY

Inland

Baird expressed what I'm ashamed to say was in my own mind. "He's gone back to his own kind. That's the place for him. He doesn't belong out here! He'll be happier inside."

I remember that the girl looked fixedly at me and said: "What do you think, Tommy?"

What did I think? Well, it barely mattered, with her glance telling me I had better start thinking all over again, and at last I managed to say miserably: "I don't know. It doesn't seem right. They say his hand is gone."

"This is the point," she said. "Why did he start inland again?"

"Because he's hankering after his kind," said Baird. "That's it, of course."

"What do you think?" Sylvia addressed me.

The Lightning Warrior, who had been following her like a ghost, stepped forward, and she rested her head absently on his head. He glared at me with an undying hatred.

"I don't know," I replied. "I suppose, perhaps, you had something to do with it, Sylvia."

"Then there's only one thing for us," she answered. "We've got to go after him. Do you agree?"

"To go after him?" exclaimed Baird. "My dear, do you think we could ever catch up? Do you remember how he came up with us and passed like the wind when we were trying to beat him out with a huge head start and couldn't manage it? What could we do now *he* has the start?"

"You're speaking of a time when he had two hands," said Sylvia coldly. "Besides, his heart was up then. It's down now, I imagine."

"You're not serious, dear," said her father. "You don't mean we'll actually chuck everything and go after him?"

"Chuck everything? Chuck what?" asked Sylvia. "What are you? What's Tommy? What am I, compared with Cobalt? We're going after him. I'm going after him, at least, if I have to go to the North Pole!"

That settled the thing on the spur of the moment. There was no argument, no discussion. Baird simply looked at me, and I looked back at him. Each of us gave up. I had a keen picture of her trekking alone through the wilderness. I knew she would do it, too, and so did her father.

From that point on, we simply spoke of getting ready as soon as possible. Then there was the question about the trail he might have taken. It was Sylvia, again, who suggested that he might have gone around the point and started in from Dyea. While Baird was getting the dogs ready, along with the sleds and packs, I hurried down to the waterfront and there, after a time, I found a pair of Indians who had seen Cobalt. They had helped him paddle around the point. He had gone to Dyea, to shift the pursuit, in case anyone decided to go after him.

I asked one of the Indians in broken English if the white man helped with the paddling. He said that he had, but he had used his left hand only as the oarlock, driving from the heel of his right hand. He never shifted the paddle.

"This hand no good!" said the Indian, and he grasped his right hand with his left.

I went back to Sylvia and her father with the news, and we went down to the waterfront. There we got two good-size boats and made the trip around the point, though the water was kicking up a good deal, and we got pretty wet before we ever managed to make the other landing.

We camped in Dyea. Plenty of people there knew about the smashing of Soapy Jones and his gang, and we were bombarded with questions, but no one seemed to have seen Cobalt go through. I wondered if he had dodged like a fox, merely landing in order to take fresh boating and double back to the point from which he had started? I would not have put it past him, and I wondered at his state of mind. Who could have wished to pursue him? He would not have dodged the vengeance of the Soapy Jones gang, not even with his right hand useless. Then what pursuit could he fear, except from Sylvia and us? And why should he fear that?

The three of us never talked of Cobalt. We kept his name for the questions that must be asked of strangers, but I could guess that all of us felt and thought about the same way. In that time Sylvia never smiled, never laughed. She did not seem depressed, either; she was simply set like iron.

After that one rest in Dyea, we started the march inland. The climb seemed worse than ever. We had to relay the packs to the top of course and, after that labor was completed, we skidded down the steep of the farther side. There we sorted and repacked the sleds, and we began to forge ahead.

We had seven good dogs — rather, we had seven not counting the white King. He stayed with Sylvia. Sometimes she went up to the lead and harnessed him as the first dog of the string, and then it seemed to me that we doubled our rate of travel. Sometimes she trailed behind with him, his great head always just under her hand and his pale, strange eyes fixed ahead like a thing that hungered to be farther north, as I suppose in all his blood he hungered.

That was the worst march I had ever made. There was something depressing about turning back from the outside after we were safely there. My heart sank in my boots. There was something also about the quest which we were following. What would happen, what could happen, when we overtook Cobalt — if we did?

I think it was three days from the crest when we came upon the first outfit on the trail, a pair of partners who'd already quarreled and decided to split. Poor fellows, they walked about with the expression of sulky

281

dogs and didn't speak to each other. They were dividing their supplies. They had only one rifle, one axe, and one tent cloth. One took the handle of the axe. They smashed the rifle and threw it away. They cut the tent cloth exactly in two, and each took a part. They had two sleds and five dogs. Each of them took a sled and two dogs. They offered to sell us the extra dog, but we didn't want it, so they butchered it instead of turning it loose. Each of them tried to prove that it was only the villainy of the other that was responsible for their break-up.

We asked if they had seen an outfit that might have been Cobalt's. They were very polite. One of them, a big Swede with a mouth large enough to swallow a veal pie at a gulp, said he thought he'd seen an outfit go by, just as they were getting ready for their start the day before — five dogs, one man, and two sleds. The man walked with an easy rise in his step. It might have been Cobalt.

That cinched the matter for all three of us. That springing step we all remembered keenly enough, and from that moment we pushed ahead, assured we were traveling in the right direction. An odd group we made. Baird and I agonized throughout that march, but Sylvia scorned delays, and we pushed ahead with speed for her sake. Or was it so much for her sake as because her stronger spirit had mastered ours and forced us on?

At the end of the next march, when we were making camp, a chill, misty, unseasonable rain began to fall. I was out at a little distance from the camp foraging for wood of a size that would make decent cutting. As I came to the edge of the heavy brush, with a clear swale of shining snow before me, I saw a four-dog outfit go by. It was pulling one sled, and the man with it was out ahead breaking trail.

He was a smallish figure, hardly larger than a boy. He walked like a snowshoe expert, however, with short, rapid, tireless steps. And he made exceedingly good time. I did not step out to greet him, I hardly know why. Perhaps it was because I'd gathered my firewood and was about to turn back to the camp. At any rate there I stood, almost entirely screened by the brush. As I waited, the driver drew nearer and nearer, never altering his pace, never changing his quick, untiring step. I admired him. I was about to shout out a greeting and a congratulation to him, when he turned his face a little and I recognized him. It was the buck-toothed smile of Jess Fair.

The moment I spotted him, you can be sure I choked back my greeting. I only wished for a thicker screen of shrubbery between me and the other fellow. There I stood, forgetting the freezing of my feet, while he tracked on and on and gradually the misty rain closed in and shut his retreating figure from view. A welcome riddance!

But, on my way back to camp, my thoughts were not pleasant, I can assure you. I knew that Jess Fair had loved Soapy Jones. It seemed to me that I could follow the train of his thoughts. First, he had delayed long enough to see the cremation of his strange master. Then he had gone on the trail of his destroyer.

Well, he was ahead of us, and what would happen if he came up with Cobalt first — Cobalt with only one hand and that hand his left? It was not the mere matter of strength. If Cobalt ever got to grips with him, that terrible left hand alone would be enough to settle the business in a few seconds, but he would never get to grips with Jess Fair. The fight would be from a distance, where guns would settle it. What chance would Cobalt have, great as he was, great even with a single hand? No, he would have no chance at all.

I trudged back to camp in low spirits, I can tell you, and Baird said to me: "Well, I thought you'd likely bring in some venison as well as the wood. You've been gone long enough to stalk a deer."

I threw down the wood and said: "Baird, we'll have to break camp. I've seen something more than a deer, and it's on our trail, heading us."

"What have you seen?" asked Sylvia, coming toward me slowly, staring.

"I've seen Jess Fair with four dogs, traveling fast. And he's headed us already."

Baird exclaimed and struck a hand against his forehead. "Fate itself is against us," he said.

"There's no fate," said Sylvia, in a strange, rapid monotone. "It's too far north for fate to bother. We've got to break camp, Daddy. Hurry, hurry! We've got to make a double march this time!"

CHAPTER
FORTY-ONE

Fatigue

There are two kinds of weariness. There is that which the body feels and which the mind submits to willingly, the kind a man feels grateful for when he's in bed and knows he will not have to wait for sleep. The second kind is a different matter. It's the fatigue which the body feels and the brain denies. The body begins to call out from all its members. All of its muscles, nerves, limbs, its very bones begin to groan and ask for rest, and the brain has to scorn this appeal and declare it is nothing.

It is not so hard, at first. The will wells up in you. The heart swells, as it were, and becomes greater. The body is a pitiful, contemptible, complaining crew that mans a great vessel, incapable of halting. After a while the matter is altered, greatly altered. You can force the legs ahead. You can think of old songs and sing them. Then, finally, the words of the tune change and begin to sing silently in the innermost ear: *You've done enough. You can't do more. You have to stop. You have to give up. All things must die, and death is no sweeter at the end of the longest trail.*

The mind resists. Once the vast labor is ended, it says, life will be sweet again, sweeter than ever. Someday there will again be a soft bed, and the body will stretch its weary bones in such a sleep as gold cannot buy for the kings of the earth. But the promises of the brain grow dimmer and dimmer. And the outcry of the tormented muscles begins to predominate. At last, the traveler knows that he cannot go any farther. Still he goes.

He picks out the crest of the next hill and vows that there he will pause. From that hill he sees a bush in the valley and declares that this will be the outermost edge of his voyage. There he will sink down, let come what may. When he reaches the bush, however, there is still another object before him, and he fastens his mind on its nearness, scorns his conquered body, and marches on with a staggering step.

All of this we went through on that forced march which was killing us, but we dared not pause. I speak of Baird and of myself, for we had a spur in our sides — the girl. She never faltered. Once in fact I heard her moan, and I turned sharply toward her, about to say: "Sylvia, we have to camp! This is madness! We can't win. They have too long a lead over us!" But as I turned to her, she lifted her dauntless head and smiled at me in such a way that the weariness left my body, and for a moment I was strong and fresh again.

What a spirit was in her, fresh and free and noble as the spirit of some matchless Thoroughbred, some queen of the desert, for which tribes fight because of herself as well as her flawless lineage. Who would think

286

of mere goodness, gentleness, when looking at her? For she was more. She was something in which one could see only the great heart, the great soul, the matchless strength of will, all locked up as priceless jewels are in a casket of a still greater price.

So she was to us on that grisly march which was to bring us to the end of it all. She was a light shining, pouring out not radiance but infinite beauty. She talked to us, when there was no breath left in her to sustain her own body. She laughed joyously, when all her soul was wrapped in pain. She walked with a light step, when her knees were leaden and her heart was bowed.

All during that march, I said to myself: *She has fought against it. She has denied it. She has struggled to keep herself from him, but she is overcome by a greater love than any woman ever felt for a man. It is out of that love that she is able to pour forth for us these drafts of strong wine, buoying our courage.*

I had no jealousy of Cobalt. I felt toward him and toward the girl, as men in the street feel when they look at the shining, obscured windows of the palace and hear inside the music of the dancers, for I knew that both of these were spirits from a realm above mine. And so we slogged on, Baird and I, setting our teeth, shifting our glances from the trail only to let them rest on the girl.

Once I thought she was about to fail — actually to fall on the trail. She was walking behind the sled at that moment with both her hands on a line which the Lightning Warrior pulled against, and she leaned heavily back, and finally her head fell limply and dangled back on her shoulders, her face turned up to the sky.

"Sylvia," I cried to her. "How is it with you?"

"Oh, I was star-gazing. I forgot for a moment," she said. "I'm as fit as a fiddle. I'm going to break trail for a while."

And she did it! I tried to stop her, but my poor spirit was too weak for her. She went on ahead, and she broke trail, stepping gallantly with the Lightning Warrior as gaunt and great and powerful as a polar bear. When I think back to it, I see it with the same whirling of the senses that I felt then, half overcome, half stupefied with deadening fatigue. There was an unearthly something about it. I used to look at the slender body of that girl and tell myself how little her strength was compared with mine. Then I could only say this was a miracle which I was seeing.

It was about the latter quarter of that march when we found the first significant thing on the trail, a moccasin. The thing was picked up by Baird. It was small enough almost for Sylvia to have worn it. Had some poor child come across this trail then? Or was there another woman before us? It had not fallen in the snow very long before. It was not even thoroughly frozen and bent in the hand without cracking.

"Do you know what it is?" said Baird to me.

"No," I replied.

"Sylvia seems to know, however," he said.

She was acting very oddly. She called the Lightning Warrior to her and showed him the thing. Then she threw it down into the snow and stamped on it. The beast began to growl. When she picked it up, he tried to snatch it from her hand with his needle-sharp teeth, but she kept it and, holding it high, she spoke angrily, turned and twisted it, and seemed trying to tear it. Then she struck it with her hands until the Lightning Warrior went into a frenzy. He would leap up high, whining in his frantic eagerness. He bounded all about her and seemed ready to knock her down with a blow of his massive shoulder and so get the thing from her.

Finally she gave him a half of it, which she tore from the rest, and that wolf slashed it to bits as though it were a living thing. She rewarded him for this show of foolish ferocity until I had to ask her: "Sylvia, what under heaven are you about?"

"Who owns the moccasin, Tommy?" she asked.

"How in the world should I know?"

"There aren't many men with feet as small as that, are there?"

"No, there aren't, of course, and it must be . . . say, a child."

She showed me the remnant remaining to her. "See the way it's worn under the toes. No woman or child has so much strength in the toes, such a foot grip. That's a man's moccasin, Tommy, and haven't I heard that the great Jess Fair is a very small man?"

The thing clapped together like two parts of the same apple and made a whole again. I could understand her well enough. We all were enemies of Jess, and it might be as well to have the Lightning Warrior as an extra foe to him. Baird saw and heard all this, but he was too sick from fatigue to make any comment.

So we slogged on again in the remorseless march, the memory of which is etched with all the acid of pain in my mind so that the latter part of it I can recall almost step by step. It was two or three hours after the episode of the moccasin that we heard the first shot of the battle. The sound came clanging to our ears from a distance, and we all three looked at one another. Sylvia nodded.

"We'd better go that way," she said. "You never can tell . . ."

So we headed to the left and immediately heard another rifle shot to guide us more accurately. Baird got out the small field glasses, which he carried, and Sylvia herself unlimbered the rifle. I went ahead, being more fit than Baird, and started to break trail.

There was a new fall of snow, light, dry, flying like dust under the broad web of the shoes, and this sort of snow always makes heavy pulling for a sled. In addition we had a gradual slope to surmount, and the dogs made hard work of it until the girl fastened the Lightning Warrior in the lead. Then we hummed along with me staggering in advance, and the fangs of the wolf inches from my tired legs.

In mounting that slope, I poured out the last of my strength as utterly as one pours out the last drop from a cup of water. I knew somehow that over the brim of it we would come on something of importance, and I gave myself in a last frantic outburst. The blood came surging into my head. My eyes thrust out until they

290

ached. But we made good time right up to the brow of the hill.

There the team stopped, for I had pitched into the snow ahead of them and sat there, bowed far forward, supporting some of my weight on shaking arms, nauseated and done for. I heard Sylvia say: "This is the place!"

I looked rather vaguely about me, for there was a quiet emphasis in her voice. A treasure hunter might have spoken with just these words and in just this manner, arriving at the destined spot. This was the place?

The white ground sloped from the brow of one hill into a wide hollow which was empty of all growth in the center, but to right and left low trees and shrubbery went away like rolling smoke across the hills and hummocks. The sky was comparatively clear, but it seemed to me a narrow horizon, a sky without an arch, flat as a floor and low above our heads.

What Sylvia was pointing toward was a pair of sleds in the center of the hollow with five dogs attached to it. Three of them were standing and two seemed to be stretched in the snow, resting. As I watched, another dog dropped down and, immediately after, I heard the sharp ring of the rifle report, like a hand clap at my ear.

CHAPTER
FORTY-TWO

The Last Battle

Baird spoke first. "It's Cobalt!"

He had the glasses fixed against his eyes. When I heard him say this, I reached over, and he handed me the glasses. The picture drew closer. It *was* Cobalt. He had dragged from the pack on his sled a rifle which he held to his shoulder with his left hand alone, and at this moment he was firing into some brush to the right of the sled.

There was no answering shot at Cobalt, but another of Cobalt's dogs went down. Then I understood. It was Jess Fair of course who had overtaken his man, and now from the secure shelter of the bushes he was playing with his victim. He would let Cobalt have a foretaste of death before death itself arrived. The dogs would go down first, and then the master would follow them at the leisure of Jess Fair.

I dropped the glasses and tried to struggle to my feet, but my knees were unstrung. I could only kick feebly with my legs. "Give me a hand up!" I called. "He's murdering Cobalt!"

There was no answer. I turned my head and saw that Baird had taken the rifle and was aiming at something

292

he saw in the brush — the hidden assassin. The girl in the meantime was running off to the left, along the brow of the hill. She ran with all the strength she could muster. The Lightning Warrior was beside her.

I heard the heavy, hollow click of the hammer of the rifle falling, but no report followed that sound. I heard a moan from Baird. Another report rang in the hollow, and the fifth and last of Cobalt's dogs went down. Cobalt himself would be the next to follow.

Baird was sobbing like a desperate child as he fought and struggled with the jammed cartridge. Then he took the weapon like a club, by the barrel, and ran down the slope with staggering steps. Somehow, I got strength enough to heave myself to one knee then to the next. I caught hold of the shoulders of the nearest dog. The Husky showed me his murderous teeth but endured enough of my weight so that I found myself presently standing erect but wavering. I began to move cautiously forward, down the slope. I was like a man drunk, with a mist before his eyes. Through that mist cut a streak of white.

It was the wolf, running with nose down, hot on a scent that wavered a little from a straight line, and heading toward the shrubbery from which the hidden marksman was firing. Baird, overstepping on his exhausted legs, tumbled headlong into the snow before me. I overtook him and got the rifle away from him, and then I went on, stumbling, floundering, gasping for breath but always struggling with the infernal jam. I could do nothing with it, however.

I saw a smaller form come up beside me. It was Sylvia, running desperately, and she went by me as though I were standing still. The last of Cobalt's dogs was down. His turn would be next. Perhaps he might have sheltered himself behind the sled and fired his rifle, left handed, across the top of the pack, but I think Cobalt was tired of life. For now he stood up from the snow in which he had sunk upon one knee, shooting from the left shoulder, the bandaged right hand supporting the weapon. He cast the useless gun from him and charged at the patch of shrubbery which held the murderer.

That, I think, is the way I shall always think of him when I ride the range alone — of Cobalt's running with all his might, leaning forward, throwing out his hands before him. Only one of them was useful, but that one would be enough, if ever he could come to grips. But how could he come to grips with that remorseless gunman?

The rifle rang again, and Cobalt pitched on his face. Dead? No, he turned over in the snow, regained his feet, and went forward, hobbling. There was no use in his charging now, but he would not give up. He preferred to take his death while in action, his face to the foe. It was a noble thing to see.

I saw Sylvia before me throw up her hands at the moment when Cobalt dropped. An instant later as he rose, the savage voice of the Lightning Warrior, baying on the trail, came back to my ears. There followed another rifle shot. I looked to see Cobalt fall again and

294

lie still forever, since he was near the edge of the shrubbery, but Cobalt did not fall.

Another gunshot followed and then silence. That silence held during the mortal seconds which elapsed before we got into the shrubbery together, Baird and I. For his greater strength at the moment had permitted him to overtake me. We went crashing through, regardless of what happened to our snowshoes, and so we came on the picture of the end. Jess Fair lay on his back with the Lightning Warrior on top of him. Both were dead, and each had slain the other.

We turned our backs on them for there was something else to see. It was Cobalt, who sat in the snow with his back against a bush, his head hanging on his breast, his hands dangling into the snow, while Sylvia kneeled before him, cutting away the furs, trying to get at a wound between knee and hip.

When we came up and spoke, Cobalt lifted his head. He gave us a blank look. His face was ghastly, and there seemed no recognition in his eyes. Then down rolled his head again, and the chin rested on his breast.

Sylvia began to give us orders in a quiet, metallic voice. She never spoke to Cobalt or asked him how he felt. She didn't comfort or question him in any way. She never expressed a regret for her past treatment of him or confessed her true feeling, but she went on with the work steadily and got a shelter prepared, a bed of boughs constructed, and a good fire roaring.

It was a slow business. We wanted to second her in every way we could, but exhaustion had almost the best of us. I took three axe strokes to a branch which ordinarily I would easily have slashed in two with one. But the camping drew to an end. We had the wood in, the fire going, and the shelter tent up, and Baird was proceeding with the cookery, while I trimmed up odds and ends and drove in pegs to make the tent more secure in case a heavy wind should blow up.

We heaped one mound of snow to make a temporary grave over Jess Fair and the dead wolf. That might seem strange, since they had slain one another, but there was a similarity in their faces — for each had died for the love of a master.

At this point the girl announced that the wound in Cobalt's leg was dressed and that it would do very well, since it was only a clean, clipping hole through the thigh. Now she asked for hot water and more light, because she was going to dress the wounded hand. I was standing by, having brought the water, when I saw her begin to untie the bandage which Cobalt himself had clumsily wound around the hand. He seemed to start back, and suddenly he caught her arm with his left hand.

"No!"

"Why not?" she asked.

"I won't have it touched," he said by way of answer. "It's doing very well. The air will be bad for it."

"Will you let go your hold on me, Cobalt?" she asked.

"I will not, till you let me be."

"You're breaking my arm," said Sylvia.

He continued to stare at her for a moment, then he relaxed his grip and surrendered. As he lay there, he closed his eyes and said a thing I shall never forget.

"I've been cut down to your size, Sylvia," he said.

Ah, the bitterness in that quiet voice of his. He kept his eyes closed while she unwound the crooked, heavy, clumsy bandage which he had made. When it was off, she hesitated for a moment, holding the wounded hand back up, and I knew that she was gathering courage to turn it palm upward. She did at last, and she did it without flinching, though the red, horrible, puckering thing that I saw made my brain spin and my stomach turn.

I managed to stand by while she washed and prepared the hand. Then she made five small pairs of splints, a pair for each finger, stretched the hand on them. It must have been a painful thing for Cobalt, but what was pain to him? He remained there on the bed of boughs, looking up into space with a faintly puckered brow, as though he were not aware we were doing anything at all to him.

Afterward she went away, giving me a look that made me stay beside him, though I was groggy for the lack of sleep. We heard poor Baird begin to snore. Then there came a small, thin, wailing sound.

"What's that?" asked Cobalt sharply.

"It's the wind coming up."

I lied as cheerfully as I could, but I knew well enough what it was. It was the whining, high-pitched sobbing of the girl. Poor Sylvia! Poor Cobalt! The sound ended. It began again and was stifled.

297

"Call her, will you?" said Cobalt.

I went and called Sylvia. She said she would not come, but I urged her, and at last she came.

"Are you here?" asked Cobalt.

"Yes," she said.

"Now, listen to me," said Cobalt. "I hoped this would be the last day for me. Fair would have finished me off quietly enough, and there would have been an end. But you had to come in between and smash things. Very well! But let me tell you, though there's only a third of me left, I won't have your pity. I won't have your whining."

I looked at Sylvia and wondered what she would say to this cruel speech, but she said nothing. She only stood there with a white face and big eyes and the look of a beaten child. I cannot say that I regarded her altogether with sympathy, since I could look back rather clearly through the events of this history which I have been writing, and all the sins were hers, I felt. There never would have been any trouble except for her. Yet my heart ached for her.

She saw that his eyes were closed, after he had spoken, and she took advantage of being unseen by him to hold out her hands to him. I hardly knew what to do, but I tried the simplest thing. I got her by a hand and drew her down close beside Cobalt. I took Cobalt's sound hand also and put Sylvia's small one beside it.

"I'm going to tell you the truth, Cobalt," I said. "She's about half wildcat but, if you don't hold onto the hand that you've got hold of now, you're missing what no other man ever can have."

"Say what you mean, Tom," he said quietly.

"Why, Cobalt, you blind fool! If you'd had your eyes open there in Circle City, you wouldn't have fought with her. You wouldn't have tried to crush her. You would not have talked rot about thieves and emeralds. You would simply have told her you loved her, and she would have answered that she loved you. For she's honest, Cobalt. But she has her pride. Would you want her without pride as big as your own?"

"Chalmers," said Cobalt gravely, "I love you and I trust you, and no one else. You wouldn't lie to me. Not now, I think. But say this again."

I got a look from Sylvia, however, that was enough for me. I did not repeat myself, but I got out of the shelter as fast as I could and stood outside. The sky was dark, without a star. The vague outlines of the trees were all around me; and out of the distance came a moaning, weeping voice. It was not Sylvia this time but, in fact, the wind.

CHAPTER
FORTY-THREE

Reminiscent

How we trekked back to Dyea is no matter, or how we took shipping south, or how we parted. I would like to begin again with Talking Mountain, the land I bought, and the look of the children when I saw them again. How we built the shack and how we put a wing on it the next spring. I would like to talk about the cattle, too, and the way they fattened on the highlands, just as I had known they would. For I've a theory that never has played me false, that the higher the land, the better the grass. It grew sparsely in bunches on my range land, but it seemed sweet to a cow. They fed on it greedily, and they were never tired of rooting the snow away to get at the cured, dead-looking grass in the winter. It may be a false theory of mine. It may only be true of Talking Mountain, but I know that the cattle throve wonderfully well on those clean uplands.

I would like to talk about my life with the children too and the school work of an evening. How they rode range with me, growing sturdily but never hard minded. For there again is the beauty of the highlands, that the pure air touches the spirit in some mysterious way I never have understood.

However, I know that in such a history as this, one must cling to the main events of the narrative. One event is surely part of the main course. I had gone to town to buy bacon and flour and other necessaries in the pinch of the early autumn, when a man looks to his winter larder. As I jogged my span of buckskins down the street, I saw a fight whirl out of the door of a saloon, and three men came tumbling in the dust, two fighting one. One of them was too much for the other two. He left them writhing in the street and stood up, a pale-faced youngster with a great hulking jaw and heavy, square shoulders and long arms.

I stopped the team. "Hello, Kid," I said. "You'd better jump in here with me before they slam you in jail."

He gave me one look, and then he came with a leap and sat in the seat with me. I drove on without pausing for provisions this trip, for I understood that trouble might be coming in the rear of the Kid. He had not changed much since Skagway.

After we got clear of town, he turned and gave it a look. "Where are we going?" he asked.

"Up high where the air's better," I told him.

He looked at me, but he said nothing. On the whole journey he asked only one question, I think.

"Him, he got married. Cobalt, I mean. He got married, didn't he?"

"Yes, he got married."

"And where is he now?"

"I don't know," I answered. "You know how it is. Out on a ranch, your fingers get too stiff to handle a pen."

I thought the Kid might stay a week. I was wrong. He told me he had been looking for me and Talking Mountain all his life, only he hadn't known our names. So he refused to budge and settled down and became a man I can trust my life to, this day or any other day hereafter. The good, sharp mountain winds blew him clean, as they have a way of doing.

There is one more thing to add, the most important of all, I suppose. On a bright spring day, a May day, with all that May brings to the mountains, my girl spied two riders coming up the valley trail. She called to me. We have few strangers on Talking Mountain, and some of those who come our way need watching. So I put the rifle just inside the kitchen door and stepped outside into the bright sunshine.

I watched them for a moment. The wind was running in brilliant waves along the flowers of the mountainside, and then I saw they were a man and a woman.

"It's all right, my dear," I said. "It's a man and woman. Go put on the coffee pot and slice some bacon and clean a couple of the trout your brother brought in."

She went to do as she was told, while I stood there, shading my eyes until they rode straight up to me, and still I did not know them. It was so unexpected, and our foolish eyes will only see what they are taught to expect.

In fact, they had both dismounted, and he had cried out: "Tom, by thunder, you've forgotten!"

Then I saw the black, thick glove on his right hand.

"Cobalt!" I said.

He took me with his left arm alone. It was enough. He sprained every rib in my body with a bear's hug. While I was still staggering and gasping, Sylvia kissed me and cried out about seeing me again.

Before they would talk, they wanted to see everything. I showed them the haystacks, the new barn, the chickens, the corrals, and the pasture with the saddle stock in it — enough to warm a man's heart to see the beauties. The Kid was in there, gentling a four-year-old, but he drifted away from us.

"He's a little shy with strangers," I explained. "We won't bother him."

I showed them the spring, and the new stone steps we had made from it to the house, and I showed them where I was going to build the windmill that would pump water to the corrals and to the house also.

Then we went into the house, and they saw the children, as brown as squirrels and as shy. Only once they saw Sylvia, they would not leave. They were always standing in the corner, in the shadow, worshipping her beauty.

So we had a meal together, but my guests did most of the eating, for my heart was a little too full for that. "And everything goes on pretty well?" I asked at last.

I looked at the gloved hand, and Cobalt stretched it out.

"Everything's going beautifully!" he said. "Look at this." He wriggled his fingers a very little, stiffly. "It will be as good as ever, one of these days."

"I always knew it would." I managed to steal a glance at Sylvia. She tried to turn her eyes down in time, but I saw the tears in them.

Well, everything was very well with them in one sense. Cobalt was in business and prospering. He was smashing stocks instead of men. He insisted one day they were coming West to join me. He would buy all the rest of the range. We'd live together always. I listened and pretended to believe.

They could not stay long. I rode back with them part way to show the shortcut into the valley. There we said good bye, and Sylvia kissed me again. I held her in my arms for a moment and whispered: "Is everything well, my dear?"

"Oh, Tommy," she said, "I try and try, and maybe one day he will be what he was when he first met me."

"Trust yourself," I said, "You can make wild things love you. And everything will end well. Heaven bless you both!"

They went on. I watched them riding over the rimrock, the rim of my world, brilliant with light, and then they passed into the shadows of the quieter valley and were dimmed a little, as memory is dimmed by time.

Max Brand® is the best-known pen name of Frederick Faust, creator of Dr Kildare^{TM}, Destry, and many other fictional characters popular with readers and viewers worldwide. Faust wrote for a variety of audiences in many genres. His enormous output totalling approximately thirty million words or the equivalent of 530 ordinary books, covered nearly every field: crime, fantasy, historical romance, espionage, Westerns, science fiction, adventure, animal stories, love, war, and fashionable society, big business and big medicine. Eighty motion pictures have been based on his work along with many radio and television programs. For good measure he also published four volumes of poetry. Perhaps no other author has reached more people in more different ways.

Born in Seattle in 1892, orphaned early, Faust grew up in the rural San Joaquin Valley of California. At Berkeley he became a student rebel and one-man literary movement, contributing prodigiously to all campus publications. Denied a degree because of unconventional conduct, he embarked on a series of adventures culminating in New York City where, after a period of near starvation, he received simultaneous recognition as a serious poet and successful popular-prose writer. Later, he traveled widely, making his home in New York, then in Florence, and finally in Los Angeles.

Once the United States entered the Second World War, Faust abandoned his lucrative writing career and his work as a screenwriter to serve as a war correspondent with the infantry in Italy, despite his fifty-one years and a bad heart. He was killed during a night attack on a hilltop village held by the German army. New books based on magazine serials or unpublished manuscripts continue to appear. Alive and dead he has averaged a new one every four months for seventy-five years. In the U.S. alone nine publishers issue his work, plus many more in foreign countries. Yet, only recently have the full dimensions of this extraordinarily versatile and prolific writer come to be recognized and his stature as a protean literary figure in the 20th century acknowledged. His popularity continues to grow throughout the world.

ISIS publish a wide range of books in large print, from fiction to biography. Any suggestions for books you would like to see in large print or audio are always welcome. Please send to the Editorial Department at:

ISIS Publishing Limited
7 Centremead
Osney Mead
Oxford OX2 0ES

A full list of titles is available free of charge from:

Ulverscroft Large Print Books Limited

(UK)
The Green
Bradgate Road, Anstey
Leicester LE7 7FU
Tel: (0116) 236 4325

(Australia)
P.O. Box 314
St Leonards
NSW 1590
Tel: (02) 9436 2622

(USA)
P.O. Box 1230
West Seneca
N.Y. 14224-1230
Tel: (716) 674 4270

(Canada)
P.O. Box 80038
Burlington
Ontario L7L 6B1
Tel: (905) 637 8734

(New Zealand)
P.O. Box 456
Feilding
Tel: (06) 323 6828

Details of ISIS complete and unabridged audio books are also available from these offices. Alternatively, contact your local library for details of their collection of ISIS large print and unabridged audio books.